HOW A REALIST HERO REBUILT THE KINGDOM

HOW A REALIST HERO REBUILT THE KINGDOM:
VOLUME 16

© 2021 Dojyomaru
Illustrations by Fuyuyuki

First published in Japan in 2021 by
OVERLAP Inc., Ltd., Tokyo.
English translation rights arranged with
OVERLAP Inc., Ltd., Tokyo.

Follow Seven Seas Entertainment online at
sevenseasentertainment.com.
Experience J-Novel Club books online at j-novel.club.

TRANSLATION: Sean McCann
J-NOVEL CLUB EDITOR: Meiru
COVER DESIGN: Kris Aubin
INTERIOR DESIGN: Clay Gardner
INTERIOR LAYOUT: Jennifer Elgabrowny
PROOFREADER: Dayna Abel
LIGHT NOVEL EDITOR: T. Anne
PREPRESS TECHNICIAN: Melanie Ujimori, Jules Valera
PRODUCTION MANAGER: Lissa Pattillo
EDITOR-IN-CHIEF: Julie Davis
ASSOCIATE PUBLISHER: Adam Arnold
PUBLISHER: Jason DeAngelis

ISBN: 978-1-63858-763-7
Printed in Canada
First Printing: May 2023
10 9 8 7 6 5 4 3 2 1

"EVEN IF I FAILED... I DID MY PART..."

IN A FEW MORE MOMENTS, HER BODY WOULD SLAM INTO THE GROUND BELOW, SPLATTERING IT WITH HER RED BLOOD.

AND YET, MARIA WAS THINKING ABOUT IT LIKE SHE WAS WATCHING SOMEONE ELSE EXPERIENCE IT.

Maria Euphoria

Shabon

Kishun

Leporina

Taru

Kuu

Jeanne

Maria

SPIRIT KINGDOM
OF GARLAN

GRAN CHAOS EMPIRE
(WHITE LINE INCLUDES VASSAL STATES)

Hakuya

Julius

Poncho

Tomoe

Ichiha

Yuriga

REPUBLIC OF TURGIS

MERCENARY
STATE ZEM

LUNARIAN
ORTHODOX
PAPAL STATE

STAR DRAGON
MOUNTAIN RANGE

NOTHUNG DRAGON
KNIGHT KINGDOM

GREAT TIGER KINGDOM OF HAAN
(DIAGONAL LINES INDICATE
SPHERE OF INFLUENCE)

DEMON LORD'S
DOMAIN

Fuuga

Mutsumi

Hashim

Shuukin

KINGDOM OF
FRIEDONIA

NINE-HEADED DRAGON
ARCHIPELAGO KINGDOM

Naden

Roroa

Juna

Aisha

Liscia

Souma

HOW A REALIST HERO REBUILT THE KINGDOM

XVI

WRITTEN BY

DOJYOMARU

ILLUSTRATED BY

FUYUYUKI

Contents

XVI

Two Years After

IT HAD BEEN TWO YEARS since the members of the Mankind Declaration, the Maritime Alliance, and the Fuuga Faction joined together to stop the spread of the Spirit King's Curse—an illness known as the Blood-Borne Magic-Eating Bug Disease, or Magic Bug Disease for short.

Although the three great powers competed on the continent of Landia, their combined effort resulted in peace throughout the continent. The Demon Lord's Domain still remained to the north, but during this time, there was no great outpouring of monsters. No countries were ravaged, nor were any annexed. It was a harmonious era—however fleeting it seemed to be.

Despite the silence within the Demon Lord's Domain, however, its threat to mankind was ever-present. And held steadfast alongside this was Fuuga with his great ambitions. While there was a premonition of great waves to come, until that came to pass, each country spent this peacetime developing itself for the future.

First, there was Fuuga's Great Tiger Kingdom, which was bound to be at the eye of the storm. For these two years, Fuuga had been actively expanding his territory into the Demon Lord's Domain. He gained land, increased his population by calling for those who'd initially fled south, and steadily increased his power. This resulted in a state that rivaled the Empire in landmass.

Their liberation of the Demon Lord's Domain also steadily built their fame. It solidified Fuuga's position as the "great man" of the era.

In foreign affairs, Fuuga had strengthened his relationship with the Orthodox Papal State and the Spirit Kingdom and—together with them—surpassed the Empire in power. With internal affairs, he'd learned medical techniques from the Kingdom and the Empire, and he was hiring a wide variety of personnel to fix his shortage of bureaucrats. Using Fuuga's fame to recruit, the Great Tiger Kingdom was able to take in those who were upset with the status quo, those who wanted to make a name for themselves up north, and those who were inspired by his heroic tale. The adventurers spread around the continent were especially likely to heed the call and join Fuuga's country.

"Thanks to him liberating so much territory, there's a lot of work. Adventurers drift from country to country, having no real attachment to any of them. But the expansion up north really appeals to our sense of romanticism. I hear adventurers in other countries have all been heading there," Juno the adventurer explained at a late-night tea party with the queens present.

When adventurers weren't exploring dungeons, they were basically jacks-of-all-trades around the towns they stayed in. So the north being a frontier abundant with opportunity really appealed to them.

"You're not going north yourselves?" I asked.

Juno smiled and shook her head. "No, adventurers can make a decent enough living in this country. And if we ever want to quit, we can go to school and train for another line of work. All of the policies to improve the lives of slaves have also worked to support people like us, who tend to be at the bottom of society. Any adventurer working in the Kingdom who wants to go through the inconvenience of heading north is either ambitious or an idiot."

Having said that, Juno drained the rest of her tea, then put on a slightly more serious expression.

"But on the other hand... Those who can't stand this sort of treatment—who don't want to be looked down upon—will be drawn to the north, right? They're looking for an upset to turn things around in their miserable existence. With nothing to lose, it's easy for them to gamble it all."

I shuddered at those words. It meant more ambitious people were gathering around a man who already had great ambitions. It might be difficult for Fuuga to completely fix his shortage of bureaucrats with the kind of people he attracted, but it was creating a group that would be even harder to deal with.

Next, there was Maria's Gran Chaos Empire. The size of the Mankind Declaration had shrunk, and Fuuga had stolen the attention of the world, but Maria was still able to remain the Saint of the Empire. In contrast to Fuuga's expansion of his territory, Maria had her eyes focused on internal matters.

She'd hired capable personnel, gradually reforming the old systems. And if there was new science and technologies her country lacked, she wasn't above looking to other nations to teach her. She'd learned medicine from us and other technologies from the Republic and the Archipelago Union. She also had matched pace with us in abolishing slavery in all but name— even before the Republic and Archipelago Union did the same. Now they had a social safety net that was at the same level as the Kingdom's. That made the people support her even more, and there was no sign that she'd stop being the Saint of the Empire anytime soon.

Meanwhile, there were those among their nobility and knightly class who couldn't accept that Fuuga had stolen the world's attention from them. They regularly pressured Maria to send a force into the Demon Lord's Domain. Maria, however, refused to stop focusing on domestic matters, so they were getting more and more discontent.

In regards to this, Maria had told me over a broadcast conference...

"I've said this before, but if our country grows any larger, it will only result in more places that we can't adequately look after. If we obsess over appearances, we'll lose sight of what's really important."

Her exhaustion was almost palpable.

Now let's talk about our allies in the Maritime Alliance. First, Kuu and his Republic of Turgis.

Not long after returning home, Kuu took his father's place as head of the Republic and set to work reforming their technology with the help of his fiancée, Taru the blacksmith. With the revolving mechanism that they'd developed alongside the Kingdom and Empire, the Republic was hard at work using drills to dig tunnels through the mountains. This would support their transport network when it was shut down by snow. Plus, it meant that travel between cities in winter, which normally required a numoth—a beast that resembled a wooly mammoth—would be possible without one. These tunnels would also allow them to trade with other nations, resolving their perpetual shortage of supplies.

He'd also taken my advice—or careless slip of the tongue, rather—and created a lift near the hot springs in Noblebeppu for a ski resort. It looked like he was seriously trying to use that to bring in some foreign currency. We were even sent invitations. Kuu was a man of eccentric tastes, so he'd asked his genius technician Taru to make a variety of "improvements," turning his country into something stranger than it already was.

Speaking of Kuu, he was supposed to marry Taru and his former servant Leporina soon. Knowing him, I thought they'd tie the knot the moment they got home, but he got so busy with reforms that it apparently went on the back burner. *That invitation to the ski resort came with a wedding invitation too. Does that mean he wants us to try skiing while we're there?*

I was arranging things so we could go as a family.

And we have our other ally, the Nine-Headed Dragon Archipelago Union.

Over the past two years, Shabon centralized power within the islands and renamed the country to the Nine-Headed Dragon Archipelago Kingdom. (Shortened to "Archipelago Kingdom" for simplicity's sake.)

With the assistance of her father Shana, the previous king, and Kishun, the royal advisor, she solidified her position as the Nine-Headed Dragon Queen, ruler of the archipelago.

Shabon had formed a skills and technological exchange treaty with the Kingdom and Republic, and she was strengthening her country with knowledge from the continent's mainland. In particular, she'd unified the maritime forces of the individual islands into one force known as the Queen's Fleet. Even if another massive creature like Ooyamizuchi appeared, they wouldn't run into the problem of not being able to coordinate a response. The fleet also made travel between the islands easier than ever, and they cooperated with us and the Republic to bring in foreign currency.

During this time, Shabon had also married Kishun and given birth to a boy and a girl. Perhaps because islander names tended to be said all as one word, neither of them had changed their family names when they'd married.

According to our earlier promise, her first child, Princess Sharan, would be my eldest son Cian's fiancée. Shabon and Kishun had visited one time to let them meet each other, but the easygoing Cian just sort of vaguely looked at her. It was actually Kazuha who seemed more interested in Princess Sharan. *Maybe she'll get along with her sister-in-law.*

Next, let's talk about the Nothung Dragon Knight Kingdom, which didn't belong to the Maritime Alliance but did have relations with us.

After becoming the Dragon Knight Queen and inheriting the throne from her father, Queen Sill Munto was running the dragon knights as a courier service—initially beginning two years ago. With their lands surrounded by the Fuuga Faction, the Dragon Knight Kingdom was engaged in trade with them for now. Rather, Fuuga hadn't decided to blockade them yet. But they'd received permission from the Star Dragon Mountain Range to pass through their airspace when making deliveries, and they were flying all over the nations of the south.

Their pact with the dragons made it so that other countries could trust them with transporting supplies and VIPs. This resulted in the nations of the Maritime Alliance and the Mankind Declaration using their services. In our case, our ambassador to the Empire, Piltory, used them for short trips back home. And the Empire's ambassador to us, Trill, used them when Jeanne demanded she come back home (to be lectured).

Their treasury was apparently more flush with lucre now than when they were operating solely as knights.

Lastly, let's talk about my country, the Kingdom of Friedonia.

In these two years, we made steady progress in trade, technological development, and military preparations. The overscientist team, composed of Genia, Merula, and Trill, was focusing its efforts on the theory that magicium were nanomachines—which we'd discovered while studying the Magic Bug Disease.

This led to the theory that curse ore, which was the power source for the drill, was made up of nanomachines that had lost all of their functions other than the ability to recharge. Using this idea as a basis, we deepened our understanding of curse ore as a storage tank for magical power, and we were able to utilize that in a variety of different applications.

Incidentally, among the first implementations was a lighter that didn't need gas or oil. Fire mages could create sparks with ease, but this lighter could store the magical power of any type of mage in its curse ore. By using the formula carved inside, it could then turn the stored power into fire magic power and create a spark.

Frankly, this lighter had no practical application. It'd cost as much as a small destroyer to build one, and it was no more useful than a standard oil lighter. And anyone who could use fire magic didn't even need it. While impractical, the ability to store magic power and convert it had a wide range of applications, and we were looking forward to seeing what came of them.

On the topic of military preparations, our island carrier, the *Hiryuu,* had been joined by two more, the *Souryuu* and *Unryuu,* giving us a three-carrier fleet.

Using Tomoe's ability, we'd set up an environment the wyverns could be trained in and expanded our air force at the same time. This meant we could now deploy aerial forces overseas in multiple theaters at the same time. In other words, we could launch bombing runs from three locations at sea simultaneously. That was a pretty major threat to other nations. Just about all our allies understood this, though. Fuuga's faction was focused on the land, so it was hard for them to grasp the importance of sea power and recognize the threat of it.

Now, moving on to personal matters—during these two years, another member joined our family.

Juna gave birth to her second child, a boy we named Kaito. We chose it because "kai" means "sea," which Juna had a deep connection to. Not much else had changed. Me and my wives were all over twenty—although some of their ages were still undisclosed—so a couple years barely changed how any of us looked.

But there were some people whose appearance had changed a lot in two years.

In the 4th month, 1552nd year, Continental Calendar— Tomoe, Ichiha, and Yuriga graduated from the Royal Academy.

On a spring day, when the sun felt warm on my back as it shone in through the windows...

Recent graduates Tomoe, Ichiha, and Yuriga were standing in front of me at my desk in the governmental affairs office. They were all going through puberty and had grown to the point where I couldn't treat them like kids anymore—though they still looked young.

Standing on either side of me, Liscia and Hakuya were both smiling at the trio too.

"Ahem... Tomoe, Ichiha, Yuriga. Congratulations on your graduation."

"Thank you, Big Brother," Tomoe replied with a smile.

Tomoe was fifteen, going on sixteen this year. Now at the same age Roroa was when I'd first met her, Tomoe had gotten taller, and her figure was getting more womanly. She was growing her hair a little longer too.

Aside from her studies, Tomoe had also been taking lessons from Juna in etiquette and how to make herself look beautiful. Thanks to that, even just standing there, she had a beauty that could overwhelm people.

I probably shouldn't say this, but she looks a lot more like a princess than her big sister Liscia.

"I guess we can't go calling you 'little' Tomoe anymore..."

"Hee hee. Call me whatever you like, Big Brother."

"That laugh... It's just like Juna's. Seductive...I guess you could say," Liscia said with a sigh.

At some point, Tomoe had evolved from a cute little girl into a pretty girl.

She could have men dancing in the palm of her hand, should she want that... If we don't find her a partner and announce their engagement soon, she'll end up making men go mad. As her big brother, I had complicated feelings about that.

"You're going to keep working in the castle, right?"

"Yes. I'd like to keep using my ability to help arrange environments where we can breed all sorts of different animals," Tomoe said, nodding. Clapping her hands, she added, "Ah, I've also been learning about royal ceremonies from the royal chamberlain, Marx. I love living in the castle with you and all my big sisters, so I'd like to take over for Marx and run things inside the castle at some point."

"A successor for Marx... That sounds good."

"O-oh, I see."

I welcomed this, but Liscia seemed a little conflicted.

"Hm? Is there a problem?" I asked.

"No, but in Marx's position, he had to worry about producing heirs, right? I'm not sure how I feel about Tomoe being the one to pester us about that from now on..."

"I see where you're coming from..."

With that in mind, I felt awkward about it too. Marx was a man, so while he'd been fussing about an heir, it was the court ladies who kept track of the queens' health and scheduled our nights together. But with Tomoe in his role, she would be making the decisions herself.

While Liscia and I were exchanging awkward glances, Tomoe grinned.

"Big Brother, Big Sister, isn't it about time you had your third?"

"S-sure..."

"W-well, give us time... Okay?"

The king and queen were powerless before this little devil.

I cleared my throat loudly, trying to get past this awkwardness, and looked over at Ichiha. He was fourteen, turning fifteen this year. Of the three of them, he had grown the most. He was taller than both the girls now, and was rapidly catching up to my own height of 174 centimeters. His face was still youthful, but he had grown into a handsome, literate young man.

If we put him on the broadcast, housewives'll love him. When he stood next to Hakuya before, it looked like something off the cover of a fetishized manga magazine targeted at women.

"I assume you're going to keep serving with us, so do you want to be assigned to Hakuya's place?"

"Yes. Please let me work for Hakuya as I continue to learn."

"I'd like that as well, sire," Hakuya said, bowing his head too.

While Ichiha had become recognized as an expert in the field of monsterology during his time at school, he'd also been learning about politics and strategy from Hakuya. When he saw his elder sister Sami—who fled here after being caught in the political struggles of their homeland—he'd been motivated to study those sorts of things to protect the people he cared about.

Hakuya had taken a shine to him and was raising the boy to be his successor. I was considering him as a candidate to be the next prime minister too.

"Hee hee. Do your best, Ichiha," Tomoe cheered.

"Okay! I will."

Tomoe and Ichiha smiled at each other.

For a foreigner like Ichiha to attain an important position, he needs powerful backers... Like a marriage to an adopted daughter of the royal family of Elfrieden... Is it time I had a talk with the two of them?

As I was thinking that, I looked at Yuriga. "And Yuriga..."

"Yes..."

Yuriga was older than the other two, and would be turning eighteen this year. She was about as tall as Liscia now, and also had a more womanly figure. Her hair was the same length as before, but now she wore it half up and half down. According to her, "Wearing twintails at my age would be pretty cringey!"

She had a brave, dignified appearance that reminded me of how Liscia was when I'd first met her. While she didn't have a unique skill like Tomoe or Ichiha, she'd developed into an all-rounder who could handle military matters, academics, and administrative tasks better than average. But...compared to the others, she was in a much more delicate position.

"Has Fuuga given you any instructions? Like about what to do after graduation?"

"No."

"He hasn't called you back to the Great Tiger Kingdom or anything?"

"Nope."

"Seriously, nothing?"

"I told you, there's nothing! Augh!" Yuriga crossed her arms and peevishly looked off to the side. "I've asked him for a long time what I should do after graduation, but all he'd say was to 'stay in the Kingdom.' Seriously, what does he want me to do?! I'm just stuck here in the dark otherwise!"

"Whoa, Yuriga," Tomoe said. "Please calm down."

"Shove off!"

Yuriga pinched Tomoe's cheeks. Their relationship hadn't changed much even as they got older.

Still...what's Fuuga planning? Back when Malmkhitan, the precursor to the Great Tiger Kingdom of Haan, was part of the Union of Eastern Nations, Fuuga had sent Yuriga to study in our country. He'd done so in order to protect her from the chaos during their war of unification, and also to have her learn. I never would've expected that she'd have no instructions for what to do post-graduation.

Things had settled down in the Great Tiger Kingdom, so there shouldn't have been any problem with her returning home.

"Is he intending to leave Madam Yuriga in our country as a hostage?" Hakuya suggested.

Yuriga let go of Tomoe's cheeks and snorted. "Hmph! If that's what he wants, I wish he'd just say so. I wouldn't mind being a hostage for his sake. As long as Tomoe and Sir Souma are around, I won't be mistreated, and I can lay back and relax. The worst thing is being left hanging with no instructions."

That was an incredible way to look at it. *Yuriga's pretty gutsy.*

She turned and looked at me. "Hey, Sir Souma. Is there any work I can do while I'm waiting to hear from my brother?"

A job for Yuriga, huh? We could always use another pair of hands, but... Thinking about it, I said, "Well...your abilities make you an appealing candidate, but until we know what position you're in, I don't know how we can utilize you. The way things stand, you're still a guest, which makes it hard to give you a job in the military, administration, or academia."

Hearing my response, she slumped her shoulders. "I don't want to just sit around... Velza and Lucy are working too."

Their friends Velza and Lucy had also graduated. Velza had joined the land forces through her connections with the House of Magna. Apparently, she was acting as a secretary for Halbert now. Lucy had taken over her family's parlor, and I occasionally spotted her at the castle, planning events with Roroa. Yuriga felt impatient, seeing all four of her friends doing their own things while she had nothing.

Ah! Come to think of it... That was when I remembered something and pulled a document out of my desk.

"It just occurred to me, there was a request from someone who wants your help."

"There was?"

"Yeah. A mage soccer team, the Parnam Black Dragons," I said, handing her the document.

Mage soccer started as a club in the Royal Academy. It was soccer, but you were allowed to use magic. So, people went around doing things like kicking literal balls of fire. We'd tried broadcasting a game, and the people really liked it, so we'd ended up forming several pro teams to make it work as a broadcast program. The Parnam Black Dragons, based out of the royal capital, was one such team. Their mascot was actually inspired by Naden in her ryuu form.

"You played a lot of mage soccer while you were at school, right? They were saying—if it's possible—they want you on the team. I just assumed you'd be going home after graduation, so I never brought it up before."

"This could be good..." Yuriga said as she looked through the document. "It looks like some of my seniors are on the team, and it might be nice to keep on playing. Not like I have anything else to do."

It sounded like Yuriga was on board for it. She wasn't going to run into any classified information as a mage soccer player, and she'd make the broadcasts more fun, so it suited her well.

"Good for you, Yuriga," Tomoe said. "You don't have to be an unemployed bum."

"Don't call me a bum!"

I smiled as I watched the two of them go at it.

HOW A REALIST HERO REBUILT THE KINGDOM

CHAPTER 1

A Wedding and a Family Vacation

END OF THE 4TH MONTH, 1552nd year, Continental Calendar. On this day, in the capital of the Republic, Sapeur, there was a major celebration.

Sapeur had many white-walled buildings. And in this season, the snow in the streets had yet to fully melt, so it was blindingly bright with reflected sunlight on a clear day. There wasn't a cloud in the sky. Under the open blue expanse, a large crowd of people had gathered at a temple-like building that'd been built in a slightly elevated position. We were but a few of the people in that crowd.

"Come to think of it, I've never been to the capital of the Republic before, huh?" I said quietly to myself, as it had just occurred to me.

Liscia tilted her head to the side. She was standing next to me wearing a dress with a thick shawl to protect her otherwise exposed shoulders from the cold.

"You haven't?" she asked. "You came to the Republic while I was pregnant, didn't you?"

"Sure did, but we only ended up goin' to Noblebeppu near the border then. The meetin' with their former leader, Sir Gouran, ended up happenin' in secret there too," explained Roroa, who was dressed the same as Liscia.

I nodded. "It's my first time coming. The architecture in a place like this sure is interesting."

This building was the center of the Council of Chiefs that ran the Republic's government, and also where ceremonies were held. It had large, thick pillars that reminded me of historical Roman or Greek architecture. It was seemingly called Sapeur Temple. And today was the marriage of Kuu, Taru, and Leporina.

Invited as a foreign guest of honor, I had come with my wives and children—Tomoe, Yuriga, and Ichiha. Carla had also come, doubling as both maid and bodyguard. We were seated in a section reserved for guests of honor. In attendance were Liscia of the Royal House of Elfrieden, Roroa of the Princely House of Amidonia, and our bodyguard Aisha. Yuriga was attending as a representative of the Great Tiger Kingdom. She wasn't here strictly as Fuuga's representative, but at the request of Kuu, who wanted to make himself look more impressive by having more foreign attendees.

Juna, Naden, Carla, and Ichiha were with the children in a room a little further away. There, they could watch the ceremony anonymously. Being a ryuu and a dragonewt, Naden and Carla found this country's weather too cold even in April. They were all bundled up to keep warm, so they were probably happier watching from indoors.

Incidentally, Nine-Headed Dragon Queen Shabon had also been invited to this ceremony, but unfortunately, she was unable to fit it into her schedule. In her stead, I'd been given a congratulatory message to pass along.

"Aren't you two cold?" I asked Liscia and Roroa.

"A li'l bit... I wouldn't be able to keep sittin' here long if it weren't for this shawl."

"The wood furnace behind us helps keep it bearable."

In this cold land, human women needed spirit and guts if they wanted to dress fashionably.

Kuu's subordinate Nike Chima came out to announce, "His Excellency Kuu Taisei, Head of the Republic, and his wives Lady Taru and Lady Leporina have arrived!"

Kuu and his wives emerged, having finished a traditional marriage ceremony inside Sapeur Temple. Instantly, there was roaring applause. We rose to our feet as well, applauding the three of them.

Today, instead of dressing like a kabuki actor, Kuu was wearing a dashing white tuxedo. Meanwhile, Taru and Leporina were both in pure white wedding dresses. Taru's dress was long-sleeved, while Leporina had short sleeves. Their shoulders were fully exposed, but as members of the Five Races of the Snowy Plains, they were used to the cold.

The crowd was so large, it felt like every person in the Republic was in attendance. Turning to face them, Kuu raised his hands.

"This kind of reminds me of our own wedding ceremony," Aisha said, and Roroa and Liscia both nodded as they continued to clap.

"Me too. The people were cheerin' for us the same way back then, right, Big Sis Cia?"

"Hee hee, you're right. It was the biggest day of my life. Not just as a public figure, but as a woman too."

"Hey, Yuriga. Is this the kind of thing you want for yourself?" Tomoe asked, whispering in Yuriga's ear.

"Yeah, I guess." Yuriga shrugged. "It seems like the kind of thing you'd like."

"Mm-hmm. I only wish I could have a nice ceremony like this someday..."

"Well, try asking for it. I mean, you've already got someone lined up to be your husband."

"Heh heh, if I push him too soon, he'll probably run away on me, so I'll have to take my time."

"Yeah, yeah..."

T-Tomoe?! I didn't know what to think. Both of them had started to have some rather mature conversations these days.

Suddenly, Yuriga's smile faded and she stared off into the distance. "I wonder...what's going to happen to me. Ultimately, it's all up to my brother, I guess."

"Yuriga?"

"It's nothing..."

I saw Kuu whisper something to his brides. Taru nodded, and Leporina started walking over to us. She then offered the bouquet to Tomoe and Yuriga.

"Master Kuu says it's for the future brides," Leporina explained.

"We hope you'll both find happy marriages. We received a bouquet ourselves in the Kingdom of Friedonia, so consider this repaying the favor."

"Wow! Thank you so much!"

"Y-yeah? Uh... You have my thanks."

Tomoe seemed delighted, while Yuriga was not entirely displeased with the gift.

Some days later...

"Yahoooo!"

"Please wait, Master Kuu!"

Kuu effortlessly slid down the powdered slope on a snowboard as Leporina chased after him on skis. Athletic as he was, Kuu had mastered the snowboard not long after being told they existed.

We were at a ski slope near Noblebeppu, the city where Taru had her workshop. Having taken an interest in the idea of recreational skiing, Kuu got to work setting up this place shortly after returning to the Republic. The location was ideal since Noblebeppu was in proximity to snowy mountains, hot springs, and fresh seafood from the port of Moran.

The ski lift utilized the revolving mechanism of the drill, and Noblebeppu had turned into a serious ski resort town in the time since I'd last visited. We'd been invited to come here after the wedding. Kuu had said it would do us good to take some time off, soak in the hot springs, and enjoy skiing as a family. Obviously, the offer wasn't purely out of the goodness of his heart; he had his own motives, but, well... For now, we decided to enjoy the slopes.

"Whoa, Ichiha. Easy. Take it easy."

"R-right. I can handle it."

"Unsteady as you are, it's only a matter of time before—"

"Ahhh!"

"Told you so..."

Glancing over, I saw Yuriga, who had been the first of the trio to master skiing, teaching Ichiha and Tomoe. Those two were bookish by nature, and they seemed to be struggling to learn. Now Yuriga was watching with exasperation as they took a tumble together.

Tomoe was bowing her head and apologizing profusely for landing on top of Ichiha. *Well, I guess that's one way to experience the joys of youth on a ski hill...*

"Doesn't this seem...wrong somehow?"

"Hee hee! It's nice, me being the one to ride you once in a while... It's still cold, though."

Currently, I was skiing with Naden on my back. She'd curled up into a ball due to the cold, but I wanted her to experience skiing at least once, and this was the only way she'd do it. Granted, Naden being on my back all bundled up in warm clothes made maneuvering kind of hard. I had to take it slow doing snowplow turns, but she was still enjoying herself.

"You're sure you don't want to do it yourself?"

"Not a chance! I'd freeze to death if I didn't have you acting as a windshield and warmer."

"Come on, you're exaggerating."

Right now, we look like Onbu-Obake, or Konaki-jiji, or Obariyon... Wait, now that I think about it, there're a lot of youkai carrying someone on their backs, huh?

Naden tightened her arms around my neck, pressing her chilly forehead against its nape. I shuddered at the sudden cold touch.

"Whoa! Cut it out!"

"Hmph! That's what you get for saying I'm exaggerating. I feel like hot springs are more my style."

"Ah ha ha... You figure?"

By now, we'd reached the bottom of the slope. Cian and Kazuha; Juna's daughter, Enju; and Roroa's son, Leon, were all bundled up in warm clothes at the base of the hill. They were playing in the snow with Liscia and Carla. Kaito couldn't stand very well yet, so Juna was carrying him.

Looks like they've rolled a bunch of snowballs too. Looking at Liscia, I asked, "What are you doing? Making snowmen?"

Liscia groaned in confusion. "What *are* we doing?"

"Huh?"

"Ah ha ha... The kids just got really into making snowballs," Carla explained with a wry smile.

Rolling balls of snow around was apparently the only thing they were interested in doing. Once the snowballs got to the same size as them, they'd start rolling another one... *Oh, so they aren't making snowmen or an igloo.* Now that she'd explained, I counted about ten knee-high snowballs scattered around.

"And that's supposed to be fun?"

"I guess? They're doing it, after all."

This looked to be true. Cian, Kazuha, Enju, and Leon were all having a good time rolling snowballs around. Kazuha and Leon competed on size, and Cian was just doing his own thing—with Enju following behind Cian.

As an adult, it's hard to understand what kids are thinking, huh? Looks like they're all enjoying themselves, though. As I was thinking that, Roroa and Aisha slid down to us at high speed.

"Aw, yeah! I win!"

"Y-you sure are fast, Roroa."

They seemed to have been racing.

Grinning, Roroa said, "Whew, never thought I'd be able to beat Big Sis Aisha at anythin' athletic like this."

"Maybe because I walk normally so often it's hard to get the knack of it..."

"Big Sis Cia, Big Sis Juna, we'll be watchin' the little tykes, so why don't you go ski now?"

Hearing this from Roroa, Liscia and Juna looked at one another and smiled.

"There's an idea. Okay. We'll take you up on that. Right, Juna?"

"Yes, let's. Aisha, would you hold Kaito?"

"Yes! Leave him to me!"

Juna handed Kaito over to Aisha. Meanwhile, Roroa rushed over to join Cian and the other kids, making stacks of three with all the snowballs they'd rolled. The kids watched her excitedly.

"It's so cold! I'm going to go hit the hot springs," Naden said as she got down from my back, and she hurriedly left.

Everyone's really enjoying themselves in their own way. I muttered, "I would never have thought we'd be able to take a family vacation like this..."

"Souma?"

"Darling?"

Liscia and Juna looked at me dubiously, but I just smiled.

"Nah, I was just thinking how grateful I am to Kuu for giving us this opportunity."

"Hee hee, yeah."

"Yes. We're having the loveliest time here."

They each took one of my hands.

"That's why it'd be a shame not to enjoy it more."

"You join us too, darling."

"Oh, yeah... Of course I will," I replied. *Honestly, I was thinking of going to warm myself up too...*

The two of them dragged me off, and we boarded the ski lift up to the summit again.

"Cian, Daddy's back feels cold right now."

"No! I want to do it!"

We'd moved to the bath at the hot springs inn that we'd reserved for our exclusive usage. Half of the bathing area was an open-air bath, while the other half was an indoor bathing area with an area for washing off.

Currently, I was at the baths with Cian, Kazuha, and

Leon—along with Aisha and Roroa. Enju and Kaito had already been in here with Juna and Carla. All of the children except Kaito, who was still breastfeeding, could do a lot more now. And they had begun to show their individual personalities in the things they chose to do.

Cian's favorite thing to do right now was scrub people's backs for them in the bath.

"Ngh... Ngh..."

Ah ha ha... That's cold! He was trying his hardest, but he lacked the power to really scrub off any grime. It was adorable how earnestly he tried, but...the Republic's winters were pretty cold. I was itching to get in the tub already.

"Whee!"

"Ah! Lady Kazuha! I told you, you mustn't run like that!"

While Cian scrubbed away, Kazuha ran around buck naked with the equally nude Aisha chasing after her.

Kazuha seemed excited to be in an open-air bath for the first time. She'd done the crocodile walk—placing her hands on the bottom of the bath, stretching her legs out and letting them float behind her—in a shallow part of the bath. Now that she was out, she was racing around and making Aisha worry.

"Hah! Caught you!" Aisha declared, grabbing Kazuha and lifting her up.

"No, you caught me!"

"Jeez... You need to warm up properly or you'll catch a cold."

"Okay, Momma Ai..." Kazuha said, resting her head on Aisha's ample chest.

Kazuha was always an energetic little tomboy, but when she was held against someone's breast like that, she always settled down and fell asleep. Carla was the one who'd discovered that, apparently.

Aisha came to soak in the tub, holding Kazuha in her arms. Meanwhile, Roroa, who was holding Leon the same way, shrugged.

"Here we all are, at the hot springs, and she's makin' it hard to relax."

"Momma..."

"Hm? What is it, Leon?"

"Potty."

"What?! Keep holdin' it for just a little longer!"

Roroa jumped up out of the tub, hurrying off in the direction of the changing room. It was tough enjoying a leisurely soak in the hot springs with young children around. *Go figure.*

"Thanks, Cian. Okay, we're getting in the bath now."

"Mmm."

I picked him up and joined Aisha and Kazuha in the open-air bath. *Whew... I feel the warmth bringing my body back to life.* Aisha, Kazuha, and Cian all had these goofy, relaxed looks on their faces too.

Once before, when I got in the hot springs with Juna, I'd gotten all worked up. But with the kids around, I wasn't going to lose my cool just because I saw Aisha's sexy naked body. *Paternal instincts, I guess...* I just couldn't take my eyes off the kids.

"It feels like we've become a real family," Aisha said, and despite feeling a little embarrassed, I nodded.

A little while after we got out of the bath, there was a banquet in the reception hall. Kuu and I called for a toast.

"Okay, let's have a toast to Kuu, Taru, and Leporina's wedding."

"And to a long friendship between the Kingdom and the Republic!"

"Cheers!"

And everyone from the Kingdom and the Republic knocked their glasses together.

There were many large plates laden with dishes from both the Kingdom and the Republic in the middle of the room's luxurious carpet. We each sat on cushions, taking and eating whatever we liked. We chatted, looked after the children, and generally did as we pleased.

I was seated at the head of the table with Kuu. We were each pouring the other's drinks.

Downing his fermented snow yak milk all in one go, Kuu then asked, "Whew! How was it, bro? Were you able to enjoy skiing?"

"Yeah. I had a great time," I replied as I sipped my own fermented milk. "Snowy mountains that are well-suited for skiing, open-air baths, and fresh seafood from Moran... Even the Kingdom doesn't have a place like this. I'm sure it'll be popular."

"Ookyakya! Glad to hear it!" Kuu said cheerfully.

"But are you sure this is okay, Kuu?"

"Hm? What do you mean?"

"I mean, leaving your wives alone when you just got married."

I could see Taru and Leporina drinking and chatting with Liscia and the others.

Kuu waved his hand dismissively. "It's no problem. I told them ahead of time I've got stuff to talk about."

"You do?"

"Yeah. It's about Noblebeppu." Kuu's expression was serious now. "I want to make Noblebeppu into a tourist destination to bring in some foreign currency. We export medical equipment to the Kingdom and the Empire, but we import medicine from the Empire. And we pay to send our people to study in the Kingdom too. We're essentially breaking even. Now, I don't have a problem with that, but..."

Kuu held his cup with one hand as he scratched his head.

"We're in the Maritime Alliance with the Nine-Headed Dragon Archipelago Kingdom, and they have a high level of technology too, right? They want medical knowledge, and I'll bet they also have the technical expertise to make the equipment. We can't just rely on one thing. We need to be able to compete with them on all sorts of industrial products."

"Yeah...I guess that's true, huh?"

If they could make scalpels with the techniques they used to make those sharp nine-headed dragon katanas, surgeons like Brad would be thrilled. I was also hoping that the competition between two nations with a high level of technical development would make both of them keep improving.

"I have no intention of letting them beat us on a technical level, but it'll be a problem if they cut into our profits. That's why

I was thinking of using Noblebeppu as one way of bringing in foreign currency. Adventurers, merchants, and others will all visit here and hopefully drop some money. If we're looking for someone to really profit off of...it's the rich. And there have to be rich people in other countries."

"I get you... So that's how it is." I could envision Kuu's plan for this. "You want us to find tourists for you, right? We'd have our nobles, knights, and wealthy merchants visit this town and drop some money for you."

"This is why I like you, bro. You pick up on things quick. You go, Hero King!"

"What a smooth talker..."

Still, he was on the right track. The Republic's only hope for the future had been its unrealistic and fruitless policy of northward expansion. But Kuu's proposal to turn it into a tourist destination was offering them a new set of values. A fun town like this might become the hope for them. *Man, you really are something.* Similar to Fuuga in a way, Kuu was the kind of ruler who drew the people to him.

Thinking through all this, I then nodded and said, "Fair enough. If I were to subtly talk up the merits of this place to the merchants and reward my retainers who do well with family trips to the hot springs and skiing here...they might enjoy that. And maybe the people who enjoy themselves will pass the word on to the nobles and knights."

"Oh! Nice!"

"But I doubt it'll happen in winter. It's pretty cold even now in the fourth month of the year. I doubt many races can take the midwinter cold in this country."

"Yeah...that makes sense," Kuu agreed, nodding. "Ookeekee! Well, it doesn't have to be winter for them to ski, so we should still be fine. I can open the ski hills to my own people for free in the winter, and that should make them happy."

"That sounds like a good idea."

Kuu had sounded like he was complaining, but I thought it was a smart way to spread the word about how fun skiing was. I'd heard the people here tended to stay cooped up in their houses because of the snow and ice, so maybe this would help them build a new relationship with the snow.

If he came up with ideas this easily, that was more evidence he was going to be a good ruler.

Some days later, in Mercenary State Zem...

In the Colosseum in Zem City, a crowd of over ten thousand people had fallen completely silent. Their eyes were focused on two big men. The taller and more muscular of the two lurched to one side. Then, with a thud, he fell to the stone floor of the Colosseum.

The fallen man was Gimbal, their king. Looking down at him was the Great Tiger King, Fuuga Haan. The judges were speechless for a time, but coming to their senses, they shouted at the last man standing.

"We have a victor! The winner of the martial arts tournament is the challenger, Fuuga Haan!"

That was the moment Mercenary State Zem passed into Fuuga's hands.

CHAPTER 2
Ambitions Resumed

MIDDLE OF THE 5TH MONTH, 1552nd year, Continental Calendar. On this day, I was holding a broadcast meeting with Nine-Headed Dragon Queen Shabon. Kishun stood behind her, holding a newborn child in his arms: their second child and eldest son, Sharon.

Now, to me, that felt like a girl's name. But in their country, it was the custom to tie a short name to their short surname and use both at the same time, so his name was actually Ron—or Sha Ron—which wasn't unusual at all.

Shabon had inherited the heavy responsibility of ruling from her predecessor, Sir Shana. She had struggled at first, but with Kishun as her husband and prime minister, she'd definitely gained her footing by the time she gave birth to her two infants. With the love and respect of her islanders, she was now a female sovereign who was every bit as capable as Maria.

On the other side of the broadcast, Shabon said, "In regards to the items you placed an order for the other day, we have already secured half of the requested amount. However, as we will need to wait for the remaining half to be produced, we must ask that you tolerate a slight delay."

"I know. It was an unreasonable request on my part," I replied.

"No, not at all." Shabon shook her head. "It was a large order. It will be profitable for us, so we intend to handle the matter with all due sincerity."

"That helps. I'd like to ask you to send the half that you already have by means of the bases we've exchanged."

"Understood. Um...Sir Souma." Switching into a more relaxed tone, Shabon asked, "Why are we receiving such a large order?"

"Well, I've got a little something in mind..." I replied, changing over from negotiation mode to friendly conversation mode.

"Have you heard that Fuuga has brought Mercenary State Zem under his control?"

"Yes. I received reports."

Shabon nodded with a serious expression. I looked down at the map on my desk.

"In total, this means that the Great Tiger Kingdom is now larger than the Gran Chaos Empire. They're not as powerful overall, but in terms of just their land forces, it's an even match. And he probably can't expand any further into the Demon Lord's Domain."

"Why would that be? Does the acclaim for Sir Fuuga not come from his liberation of the Demon Lord's Domain?"

"Fuuga's theory is that what we call the Demon Lord and the demons only exist deep inside there. Maria and I happen to agree on that. And Fuuga's expansion has been careful to avoid contact with those demons. They were the ones who trounced the united forces of mankind led by the Empire, after all. So if he tries to go any further north..."

"I see what you mean. He wishes to avoid the risk of coming into contact then?"

"Precisely. That's why the Great Tiger Kingdom is unlikely to expand any further to the north. Fuuga gathers fanatical support by making his country bigger and stronger. I don't think he can stop that. Which brings us to the question of what he does next... In Hakuya's view, he'll have to attack either us or the Empire."

"Huh?! So suddenly?" Shabon's eyes widened in surprise. "You are the heads of the Mankind Declaration and Maritime Alliance. It would lead to a great war."

"Yeah...and there's something Fuuga wants from us and the Empire that makes him prepared to accept that."

"And what is that?"

"Bureaucrats and lords for the territories he controls."

Clearing my throat, I then explained it exactly as Hakuya had told it to me. "Fuuga's retainers consist of commanders who served him well during the unification of the Union of Eastern Nations and people who flocked to him in the hopes of changing the current situation. That latter group is made up of refugees and others who are being treated badly under the status quo. Essentially, the vast majority of his people know nothing about how to manage a state. That's why the Great Tiger Kingdom has lacked adequate personnel to handle its domestic affairs and to be entrusted with lands to rule as their personal domains."

Shabon furrowed her brow. "Normally, I would think he'd have to stop expanding and focus on developing members of his administration."

"Right, but the Great Tiger Kingdom's expansion has been too rapid for him to be able to do that. There's also the problem that the moment Fuuga stops walking the path to total conquest, there may be those who lose faith in him and try to break away. He doesn't have room to focus on internal politics."

"Which is why he would force either the Kingdom or the Empire to submit? In order to gain a new group of retainers?"

"That is how Hakuya thinks it will go, yes. We've been recruiting far and wide, and the Empire has a large population. If he can get his hands on either, his shortage of administrators will be resolved. If he can't stop advancing, then he might as well move in the direction of something he wants... I'm sure Hashim will advise him as such."

The Republic was locked in snow and ice during the winter, so they couldn't act, and the Nine-Headed Dragon Archipelago Kingdom was surrounded by the sea, making them hard to rule and unrewarding to conquer. The same went for the Spirit Kingdom now that they were a smaller power. That left only us or the Empire.

"If Fuuga decides we're easier to conquer than the Empire... we'll need to be prepared for war with the Great Tiger Kingdom. We have to do what we can now to prepare for the worst."

"I see. And that is why you made such a large order from us."

"You got it."

The air in the room grew heavy.

After some time, Shabon said, "I do hope that your fears prove to be unfounded."

"Tell me about it..." I agreed with her from the bottom of my heart.

The day of Zem's martial arts tournament, Fuuga was looking down at Gimbal, the fallen King of Zem.

Gimbal's right hand and upper arm lay by his side, still clutching his greatsword. The light mages who had been on standby rushed in. They removed the sword from his hand, then rolled Gimbal onto his back and pressed the limb against its stump to begin healing him. Light magic worked on external wounds, so there was little doubt they could reattach the severed arm.

However, while he might retain his hand, it was unlikely to ever be as usable as before.

As they were treating him, Gimbal sensed he was finished as a fighter. "Never in all my life did I expect anyone would want to be king of this country... Challengers always desired wealth, armaments, and other superficial prizes. Although, there was one strange individual who wanted to know the truth about their father, who had been branded a rebel..." Gimbal said to Fuuga. "Not one person desired to become king of a country with so many restrictions."

"Sounds to me like they were satisfied with your rule then, wouldn't you say?"

Gimbal chuckled. "King Souma said something like that too."

Fuuga narrowed his eyes slightly as if to respond, but he remained silent.

"So, Sir Fuuga... Now that you've bested me, what will you do with the country you've won?"

"Build a new world. That's what I need this country's mercenaries for," Fuuga said, returning Zanganto, his rock-rending blade, to its sheath. "But what will *you* do? Your reign as the Mercenary King is over."

"Nothing... I started from nothing and won until I rose to where I was. Now that I've lost, I'm back to where I started."

"Doesn't that feel kind of...empty?"

"Not really, no. I'm free from the weight of being king—the responsibility to stay the strongest. It's not a bad feeling."

Gimbal must have felt like a champion who'd failed to defend the title he'd held for many long years. The greater the honor, the heavier the responsibility of defending it. And for a title with national consequences, the weight must have been great indeed. This defeat let him finally set down that burden.

The frustration of losing, the humiliation of falling to the ground, the sadness of knowing he was finished as a warrior, and the elation at being set free from his heavy responsibility... All these emotions came over Gimbal one after another.

"If you ever have the chance to live without the burdens of ambition...you'll understand how I feel too."

"Heh. Maybe," Fuuga said with a laugh, seeing Gimbal's satisfaction.

Gimbal had lived by the might of his sword arm, and now he lay defeated. He had lived the ideal Fuuga aspired to. The only difference between the two was whether they were satisfied to rule only one country or had their eyes set on something much higher and more distant. It would be a long time still before Fuuga's ambitions began to feel like a burden to him.

Fuuga turned and left the arena.

Hashim was waiting for him in the corridor on the way to the changing room. "That was superb, Lord Fuuga."

"Sure was. And now Zem belongs to me," Fuuga said, clapping a hand on Hashim's shoulder as his advisor bowed to him. "Now, how do we use this country?"

"Let's keep the nation as it is while arranging things so that we can make use of their powerful mercenaries. I believe it would be wise to appoint Moumei, the tournament's runner-up, as your viceroy and have him rule the country."

"Ah... So that's why you had Moumei participate too."

Moumei Ryoku was a mountain of a man who wielded a giant hammer and rode a steppe yak into battle. He also led Fuuga's infantry. And in a simple test of strength, no techniques or magic allowed, he rivaled Nata Chima for the title of strongest.

Hashim nodded. "There are those who view Sir Moumei as having nothing special beyond his strength. But he is an earnest man who will follow any mission he is given with simple honesty, and he also possesses mental flexibility. I am sure he'll be able to carry on ruling in the same style as Gimbal."

"And now I see why you *didn't* have Nata participate..."

"Indeed. We couldn't trust him with Zem."

Nata was always yearning to fight tough opponents, so of course he'd wanted to join the tournament, but Hashim adamantly refused. It was true that might made right in Zem, but leaving the country to a man with might and nothing else wasn't going to work.

Hashim raised his head and looked Fuuga directly in the eyes. "Now the preparations are complete. I would like you to show me where your next road leads."

"So to the Kingdom or to the Empire, huh?"

With the Lunarian Orthodox Papal State and Zem under his control, he'd been advised he needed to attack either the Kingdom of Friedonia or the Gran Chaos Empire. In order to secure his current gains and ensure he didn't lose momentum, he required administrators with experience running a large nation. For that, he had to force one of the two great powers to submit. The Empire had a massive population, while the Kingdom of Friedonia was allied with the Republic of Turgis and the Nine-Headed Dragon Archipelago Kingdom. Neither would be an easy opponent. However, Fuuga had no option to stop.

"Call up the commanders as soon as we return to the Great Tiger Kingdom. We'll discuss what's to be done at a council of war."

"Understood."

Upon returning home to his country, Fuuga gathered his retainers in the meeting room in Haan Castle.

In attendance were his wife, Mutsumi, the Wisdom of the Tiger; Shuukin Tan, the Sword of the Tiger—now viceroy of the Father Island of the Spirit Kingdom; Nata Chima, the Battle Ax of the Tiger; Gaifuku Kiin, the Shield of the Tiger; Kasen Shuri, the Crossbow of the Tiger; and Gaten Bahr, the Flag of the Tiger. Those present were commanders who'd distinguished themselves in the unification of the Union of Eastern Nations, as well as in the ongoing liberation of the Demon Lord's Domain.

Also here were Saint Anne of the Lunarian Orthodox Papal State; Lombard Remus—once a king in his own right—now administrator of a territory retaken from the Demon Lord's Domain; and his wife, Yomi Chima.

Aside from Moumei Ryoku, the Hammer of the Tiger, who was serving as viceroy in Mercenary State Zem now, all the famous retainers were gathered together.

Looking around at each of them, Fuuga said, "Mercenary State Zem is now in our hands."

"Congratulations, Lord Fuuga," Mutsumi said. The assembled retainers all congratulated him and bowed their heads as well.

Fuuga raised his hand, signaling for silence. "With this, our faction has gained enough land forces to fight anyone, even the Empire. For the past few years, we've steadily retaken land from the Demon Lord's Domain while stabilizing the situation inside the country and amassing power. You could say this was the result of all that... So, that being the case..."

He looked around the room once again.

"We are putting a temporary pause on retaking the Demon Lord's Domain from here on out."

"What?!" shouted Kasen, the youngest commander in the room. "Haven't we fought all this time with the goal of liberating the Demon Lord's Domain?! Many of the people believe that you will be the one to slay the Demon Lord and retake all the stolen lands! How can we stop here...?"

"Now, now. Settle down, Kasen," said the easygoing commander Gaten, who was sitting beside Kasen.

Fuuga continued on, undeterred by the interruption. "It's not that we're stopping. We're just pausing temporarily. Hashim."

"Yes, sire."

Hashim rose and went to stand in front of the map of the world that was behind him. Taking a pointer in hand, he traced the line of the Great Tiger Kingdom's current northern frontier.

"We have worked all this time to liberate the Demon Lord's Domain. Our efforts have led to the return of the refugees who fled south. It's a fact that positive reception towards being able to return home is part of the vocal support for Lord Fuuga."

"So then why?"

"The lands further north are desert, and not many people lived in them to begin with. Maybe a few nomadic tribes, at best. That means any advance north will bring us more land, but not more people. Ultimately, this would put a greater strain on our nation."

Hashim patted the palm of his hand with the pointer.

"Furthermore, if we continue north, we run the risk of making contact with the demons that are said to have wiped out the combined forces of mankind led by the Empire. I won't suggest that Lord Fuuga would lose, but as they are an unfamiliar opponent, it would only delight our neighbors to see us moored in conflict with them. That's the reason for this pause."

"Is that really okay?" Shuukin asked. "We've relied on inertia to expand our country as far as we have. It's because we were actively liberating the Demon Lord's Domain, people gathered to our cause, and the men were motivated. Suddenly going on the defensive goes against all that. I feel like it would be a bit of a shame."

As the second-wisest man in the room after Hashim, Shuukin had the other commanders listening intently. One of them, Lombard, raised his hand.

Hashim called on him. "Sir Lombard."

"I agree with Sir Shuukin's opinion, but...I think it may still be fine. It will take time to stabilize the territories we've taken, and if we were to keep charging onwards as we have been, one incident could cause the whole thing to fall apart."

"Yeah. I'm in charge of the Father Island now too. I can understand what Sir Lombard is saying," Shuukin said, momentarily agreeing. "But..."

Shuukin trailed off. After collecting his thoughts, he continued.

"It's easy to keep pushing a spinning wheel. But once the wheel grinds to a halt, it takes considerable power to restart movement. If we kill our inertia, it will not be easy to begin retaking the Demon Lord's Domain again."

"I'm sure you're right," Hashim agreed. "It's awkward to say this, but...the reason people idolize Lord Fuuga is, of course, in part because of his charisma. But it is also because they are fed up with the status quo. The refugees wish to be set free from their present situation, and those who find themselves disadvantaged inside the country want to become more prosperous... Their desires are in line with Lord Fuuga's grand ambition, and so they push him from behind. If we give them stability now, that will weaken Fuuga's ability to gather people to his cause."

It was as if Hashim was saying they mustn't let the people have peace.

"I never meant to say that much, though..."

"It seemed hard for you to say, so I said it for you."

Shuukin looked unhappy, but Hashim was unabashed. Hashim then turned his cold eyes to each of the other commanders.

"Lord Fuuga has been undefeated since he first raised his flag in Malmkhitan. We had a bitter stalemate against the Dragon Knight Kingdom, but fighting to a draw with them actually served to enhance his reputation. The people are in a frenzy. They believe that under Lord Fuuga, their country can expand infinitely—and that we may even unite the continent."

"Is that not...overconfident?" Mutsumi asked in a cautious tone.

It wasn't only the commanders who could grow overconfident and arrogant. The people of the country were also starting to think victory was assured. The soldiers and the general populace might become overconfident due to Fuuga's successes.

"Lord Fuuga has the blessing of Lady Lunaria. It's only a natural assumption," Saint Anne said as if it were obvious.

Her belief was everything to her, and the people's faith in Fuuga's victory was similar in nature. Mutsumi looked at Saint Anne as if she empathized with the state of mind the people must be in.

"Is it that you fear what may happen once we lose our inertia, Brother?" Mutsumi asked.

"Precisely. We must keep winning, keep advancing, and keep leading the people. But as I just said, taking any more land from the Demon Lord's Domain would bring little benefit and only increase our burden. I believe it is time for a change of direction."

"Then let's take the empty land between us and the Empire's border!" Nata, who wasn't interested in difficult topics, said eagerly.

Hashim looked at him coldly. "The vacant lands between our border and the Empire's are a buffer zone to prevent conflict. If we declare them our territory, we'll have a direct border with the Empire. That runs the risk of everything from skirmishes to the outbreak of total war. Did you suggest that with this sentiment in mind?"

"Of course I did! We've got the strength to take on the Empire now! I'm not the only one who thinks so either! Everyone in this country from the rank-and-file soldiers to the man on the street says so! The Empire has stopped moving. They aren't the ones who should lead mankind now—it's us, the Great Tiger Kingdom!"

Nata's words obviously came from a man with muscles for brains, but it was also true that the soldiers and people wanted to supplant the Empire.

Shuukin raised his hand. "Hold on, Nata. If we pick a fight with the Empire, it may not be just the Empire we end up fighting against. I hear that King Souma of Friedonia and the Empire's Empress Maria have been on friendly terms since the response to the Spirit King's Curse. It's conceivable that they have some secret ties we don't know about. No matter how strong we've gotten, it's not enough that we can take on both the Kingdom and Empire at once."

"No. There's no worry regarding that." Hashim contradicted Shuukin. "It's true that Souma and Maria seemed close during the summit in Balm. But their personal regard for one another doesn't extend to their people. I don't know if they have secret ties, but the Empire and the Kingdom are *not* allies."

"Well, yes, but..."

"I have the House of Chima's spies investigating public sentiment regarding the Kingdom and Empire in each nation. When Souma first ascended the throne, the Empire was forcing the Kingdom to pay war subsidies. Whether that money was used effectively is not at issue here. It's something the people of the Kingdom were not happy about. As for the people of the Empire, they take pride in being the greatest of mankind's nations. If they had to form an alliance to counter a rising power like us, it would deal a blow to their pride. Their soldiers worship Maria. They wouldn't take it quietly."

"You're saying they can't help each other due to public sentiment?"

"Exactly. Not in the present moment, at least."

According to Hashim's understanding, if Fuuga's faction grew and the Empire and Kingdom felt imperiled, the situation might change. However, under current conditions, even if they attacked one of the two countries, the other couldn't help them.

Hearing all this, Shuukin felt uneasy. "Sir Hashim, are you planning to pick a fight with either the Kingdom or the Empire?"

"Yes... That is what I've advised Lord Fuuga to do."

Hashim's words drew an audible gulp from all present, and they turned to look at Fuuga.

Fuuga nodded silently. Shuukin glared at Hashim.

"Have you grown overconfident yourself?"

"Hardly. My counsel is based in reality."

Hashim related what he'd told Fuuga about the domestic situation when they were in Mercenary State Zem. How the lack of administrators capable of running a large nation was holding them back, and that they could only gain them by forcing either the Kingdom or Empire to submit.

"It goes without saying, we do not have to act right this moment. Both countries will be troublesome opponents if their people are united. The Empire is powerful in its own right, and the Kingdom can use its allies in the Maritime Alliance. First, we should choose our target, find an opening or create one, and prepare to strike hard and fast when the time is right."

Nata slapped his knee happily. "Then let's fight the Empire!"

Hashim's eyes narrowed. "Dare I ask your reasoning?"

"If we're gonna fight, I wanna fight the stronger one! I saw Souma in the Duchy of Chima, and he looked weak."

"Rejected. It wasn't even worth listening to."

With a pained look on his face, Shuukin said, "Both countries helped us with the Spirit King's Curse. We owe them a debt of gratitude, so I just...can't get behind the idea of preparing to attack either of them..."

"I understand how you feel, but we must put Lord Fuuga's ambition first and foremost," Hashim told the hesitant Shuukin. "Souma said it himself back then. Disease isn't a problem for one nation. It's something the whole world needs to cooperate on. It's not as though we received any favor he didn't also benefit from either. Our cooperation prevented the disease from spreading all across the continent. I'm sure our people see it that way too."

"I question that argument..."

"Shuukin," Fuuga interjected. "I get where you're coming from. It's true we couldn't have contained the disease that quickly on our own. You might not have survived without their help."

Shuukin stayed silent, recalling his own battle with the Spirit King's Curse.

"But if we follow our sense of gratitude, we'll have nowhere to go. Those sorts of obligations are what tied up the Union of Eastern Nations, making it impossible for them to flourish. We were only able to come this far because we didn't have that stuff getting in our way. Don't forget that."

Hearing Fuuga's response, Shuukin had no choice but to back down. "Okay..."

In an effort to change the heavy atmosphere in the room, Kasen asked Fuuga, "So, Lord Fuuga, which of the two do you think it'll be easier to topple?"

"Yes. I'd like to hear your assessment too," Mutsumi added. "Of Sir Souma and Madam Maria."

"Hmm..." Fuuga stroked his chin. "Maria is a firebird. She charms people with her almost blinding radiance, and keeps her enemies at bay with scorching heat. But...the light she emits comes at the expense of herself. Maria must be exhausted. If she keeps pushing herself to shine, eventually she'll burn out, and all that will be left is ashes."

"I see. And Sir Souma?"

"Right. He's...a turtle, I guess?"

"Huh? A turtle?" Mutsumi was nonplussed.

Fuuga nodded. "The guy lacks ambition. He has no desire to attack anyone. He just wants to protect himself from the sparks that come falling his way. Souma doesn't have the beauty Maria has that allows her to charm people. He's plain and grows slowly."

"That makes him sound...awfully easy to beat, doesn't it?" Kasen said, but Fuuga laughed.

"You think so, Kasen? If he's a turtle, he's easy to beat?"

"Uh, yes. If he's a turtle, then—"

"What if I told you he's a turtle that's bigger than a mountain?"

"Wha?" For a moment Kasen thought this might be a joke, but Fuuga's face was totally serious.

"Souma's a turtle of enormous stature—bigger than a mountain. He's slow and lacks style, but once he starts to move, he can crush mountains and change the terrain itself. He has a bunch of snakes for tails too. Those snakes will whip out and attack anyone who means the turtle harm—whether he wants them to or not."

"He sounds like a monster..."

"Damn straight he is. If we take on Souma, that's the kind of monster we'll be facing," Fuuga said in a matter-of-fact way. "If he sets his mind to it, he can mobilize the Republic and the Archipelago Kingdom. His subordinates are all complicated and clever too. They take action for their country without Souma meaning for them to. Even Yuriga, who's lived there for years now, says she can't make heads or tails of the place. For my part... I'd rather he *not* start moving."

The assembled commanders listened to Fuuga's evaluation in silence. Souma was a man whom Fuuga himself was hesitant to fight. That alone made him worthy of caution.

After some time, Mutsumi asked, "So you're saying it's the Empire we should make submit?"

"Sounds about right. If we can just make them give in, Souma'll probably do what we say. If we can show him an overwhelming difference in power, he'll bend the knee without any pointless resistance. He's the type who'd put the safety of the people around him before his pride as a king."

Fuuga's words here decided the Great Tiger Kingdom policy. Treating the Empire as a hypothetical enemy, the Great Tiger

Kingdom would work to stabilize the country, prepare their military, and watch like a hawk for any opening to attack.

In the 6th month of the 1552nd year, Continental Calendar, Fuuga sent forces into the unoccupied territory between them and the Gran Chaos Empire. It was clear to all that he was trying to claim the region as his own, and that he was prepared to accept having a direct border with the Empire.

This report disturbed the higher-ups in the Empire. Empress Maria's policy had been to ensure their defenses against monster incursions from the Demon Lord's Domain were ready, but she had never broken her cautious stance when it came to retaking land. Her Mankind Declaration was in line with that policy, and it focused primarily on giving support to states bordering the Demon Lord's Domain to prevent its expansion. However, at the same time, Fuuga's Great Tiger Kingdom grew massively by liberating land from the Demon Lord's Domain, taking on the mantle of protector of mankind's nations against the Demon Lord.

Maria's Mankind Declaration was seen as having already outlived its purpose.

If Fuuga's forces occupied the buffer zone now, the Empire would be completely blocked off from expanding to the north. Many of the Empire's citizens felt threatened by that fact. They were firmly rooted in the belief that it had been their country's efforts that had defended the nations of mankind up until now—that theirs was the greatest country of all mankind. It was a source of pride...and of arrogance. Such people could not accept the current situation, where Saint Maria's presence faded as Fuuga won all the accolades. That was why members of both the military and bureaucracy began to voice the sentiment that they should send troops into the buffer zone. Those voices grew larger by the day.

In the audience hall of Valois Castle in Imperial capital Valois, a conversation was taking place...

"Your Imperial Majesty! Please, give us the order! To retake the northern lands from the Demon Lord's Domain before Fuuga Haan! I speak on behalf of all our griffon riders!"

"Krahe..."

At the bottom of the stairs to the throne, pleading with his empress, was General Krahe, the commander of the Empire's air force—the griffon squadrons. As a devotee of Saint Maria, he couldn't bear to see Fuuga getting all the glory.

"Restrain yourself, General Krahe!" shouted Jeanne, the Little Sister General, who was standing by Maria's side. "Her Imperial Majesty has already made her will known! We will not be expanding north, she says! Do not trouble her by asking the same thing time and again!"

"No, I cannot remain silent! More and more, the knights and nobility are dissatisfied with the way Fuuga runs wild across the northern lands! You are losing your authority as a saint! I—no, *we* want to fight for Her Imperial Majesty's glory! I would gladly be buried in the Demon Lord's Domain if I could fall in a battle to retake those lands as a sword of the Saint of the Empire!"

"It would be unthinkable to move our forces to satisfy your intoxication with my sister! Why can you not understand her desire to not involve the soldiers and people in such a battle?!"

Krahe and Jeanne's argument continued back and forth. Maria watched impassively. It wasn't that she was uninterested, but she was endeavoring, as empress, not to display any emotion.

Maria addressed him in a quiet voice. "Krahe."

Krahe bowed low before her. "Yes, ma'am!"

"I...do not desire to expand the Empire any further."

"B-but you can't mean that!"

"There is nothing to be gained from the abandoned lands to the north. They would only tax the treasury with the cost of revitalizing them. For those in the forces of Fuuga Haan, with nothing to lose but their lives, I am sure a meager lifestyle in the liberated lands will prove more than satisfying enough. But that does not hold true for our country. Whoever was appointed lord of those lands would request financial support, and I am sure they would resent us for it if they were not given enough."

"Then please, entrust the liberated lands to us! Those of the same mind as myself would rule them for you without a word of complaint!"

"I do not mean to say that they would request support out of their own greed. If they are truly considering the needs of the people who would be resettling those lands, it is only natural they would seek our aid. Even if the lord chooses to act stoic when he should not be, it does no good if the people are still facing hardship."

"Yes... But..."

With this well-reasoned explanation from Maria, not even the loquacious Krahe had any counterargument. Because Maria was the saint he worshiped, with the people always in her thoughts, he had no words with which to deny her.

The woman standing at Krahe's side spoke up. "A word, if I may..."

She had a bit of a baby face, but she was the sort of intellectual beauty who would have looked good in glasses. Although she was maybe a little over twenty years old, she stood upright with dignity and confidence.

"Lumi..." Jeanne murmured to herself.

The woman's name was Lumiere Marcoux. Despite her youth, she was one of the top bureaucrats of this country.

Maria turned her head to face the woman. "What is it, Lumiere?"

"With all due respect, given the power of our country, we could take possession of all the land between us and the Great Tiger Kingdom and support it with ease. If the people of the liberated territories have a hard life, then we can simply give them aid. It would only heighten your own fame as a saint. I'm in agreement with General Krahe on this."

"Lumi, not you too..." Jeanne was about to say something, but Lumiere held up a hand to stop her.

"Jeanne. General Krahe and I are giving our opinions for the sake of this country. I know you're my friend, but please don't interrupt me."

"Ngh..." This time it was Jeanne's turn to be silenced.

Maria looked at Lumiere with a pained expression on her face. "It's true... My country has strength left to spare, but that doesn't mean we always will. If we expand to take as much land and people as we can, we may not be able to respond in a crisis. That could very well set off the chain reaction that causes it all to fall apart."

"It is our duty as your retainers to do everything within our power to prevent that from happening."

"It is my job as empress as well. And it is also my duty not to make choices which can result in such risks unless I absolutely have to."

"But, ma'am—"

"I'm sorry, Lumiere. We'll have to end it there for today." Maria brought the conversation to a close and dismissed the two of them.

Once they had left the audience chamber, Jeanne's shoulders slumped. "Darn it, Lumi... She's totally become part of the hawkish faction inside the bureaucracy."

Maria set aside her persona as empress and talked to Jeanne as her elder sister. "You two were friends, right?"

"Yes, we've known each other since the military academy. But Lumi's shoulder was shattered in a training accident, and the lingering aftereffects of that disqualified her from becoming an officer. The surgeons we have now might have been able to do something for her, but medicine wasn't so developed back then, before Sir Souma came to this world..."

"I see... And that's why she joined the bureaucracy?"

"She's a hard worker by nature. Once her path to becoming a military officer was cut off, she couldn't simply sit around powerless and unmotivated. She did everything she could to make the transition to the bureaucracy, and she climbed her way to the top."

"She sounds wonderful."

"I respect her. Even now, I'm proud to call her a friend. But... maybe because she was originally a military person, she's hawkish even now that she's become a bureaucrat. She's become something like the leader to the bureaucrats upset with your passive strategy."

Jeanne looked like she had bitten into something unpleasant.

"She's serious and honest to a fault. It's hard to watch... I've asked her several times, as a friend, to try to understand your feelings...but it's just never worked..."

"I see..." Maria murmured sadly before rising from the throne. Turning around, she looked up to the Imperial flag hanging behind it. "For all this time, I've worked to unite the people of this country. And at some point, they started holding me up as the 'Saint of the Empire.' I never liked the name, but if it brings our hearts together... I thought I could live with it."

"Sister..." Jeanne choked, a pained look on her face.

With a sad smile, Maria responded, "But now our hearts seem to be drifting apart."

Jeanne could say nothing in response.

CHAPTER 3
The Shaking Empire

"**W**HY, MADAM MARIA?!" I exclaimed.

"Sire!" cautioned Hakuya from beside me. But I was in no state of mind to listen to him.

"I'm sorry... It's already been decided," Maria said apologetically.

Despite the melancholy look on her face, it wasn't going to change how unacceptable this was.

"You're getting ahead of yourself; I thought we had an understanding here. While it's possible our country can deal with it in our current state, the same cannot be said for the Empire. This was something that we were only able to do because Friedonia, the Republic, and the Archipelago Kingdom moved on it in lockstep."

"Yes...I thought so too. But there's immense pressure on me from below to do something because of Sir Fuuga's accomplishments."

"Even so, why does it have to be now?" I said, clutching my head. This was giving me a serious headache. "Why do you have to *abolish slavery* so suddenly?"

During our broadcast meeting here, Maria had told me she was going to abolish slavery in the Empire.

Now, just so I'm not misunderstood, I agreed with her that the buying and selling of people was a terrible custom. It was something that had to be wiped out for human history to move forward. I was in the process of taking steps towards abolishing it in my own country. But if we just did it all of a sudden, it would cause societal upheaval.

"Slaves are the downtrodden in society. Even if you abolish slavery and the slaves all go free tomorrow, they'll have nothing they own. They'll struggle to maintain any sort of lifestyle. If they don't have knowledge and skills, they won't be able to find new jobs. The men will have to sell themselves as cheap labor, and the women...in some cases, they may also have to sell their bodies."

"I suppose so..." Maria nodded in understanding.

"That's why—prior to formally abolishing the system—our country has been working to make it something that exists in name only. We made the slavers into public servants managed by the state, protecting the slaves from having their rights ignored or being used until they could no longer work. At the same time, we promoted academia through Ginger's Vocational School and set up learning centers where anyone could study for free. These will let the slaves be hired under more favorable conditions."

Maria looked at me as she intently listened to my words.

"We've had a shortage of personnel since we changed the way we evaluate performance. Many houses wanted to acquire capable slaves even if it meant paying them wages, and now that's becoming the norm. Thanks to Ginger and the others' teaching and hard work, even if people find themselves reduced to slavery for a time, we're building a system that will help them to crawl back up with enough hard work. Although, that doesn't apply to penal slaves."

"That's all wonderful. We've been emulating your policies here in the Empire too," Maria said with a smile. I didn't understand.

"Abolition in everything but name... Even if they're still called slaves, you have to work towards a society where slaves are not used cruelly. If you suddenly declare the system abolished, there will be those who push back. That is why you instead change society without them noticing. Ensure the rights of slaves, make it so they can own property. And then when they're no longer abused, you change the name for them, and suddenly there are no slaves who aren't also criminals."

Essentially: leave the word "slave" as is, but raise their status to the same level as a part-timer or contract employee. The priority was to protect the slaves' lives and safety.

If only the name is changed and not the reality, it's no different from if the system were still in place. The fact is that even after the American Civil War ended, inequalities like black people not having the right to vote meant that the conditions which resulted in discrimination continued for a long time after that. Though, even in my time, I wouldn't say things had been *completely* fixed...

It's like trying to stamp out discriminatory language. Even if you declare a word offensive and ban its use, then ban the next word that takes its place...all you're doing is piling up words people can't use.

I recall hearing that some of what Yoshitsune said at the Battle of Ichi-no-Tani in the *Tale of the Heike* is considered discriminatory, and in some editions, it's censored. That made me think that what needed to be clamped down on wasn't words, but the people and society that use them abusively.

I looked at Maria's reflection through the simple broadcast receiver.

"Was that not the Empire's understanding of the situation too?"

"Of course. That was our intention," Maria said, her expression somewhat exhausted. "However, there are people who've been shaken up by Sir Fuuga's rapid advance, and their demands of me have only escalated as well."

"Because of Fuuga?" I asked.

"Are you aware? These days, they call him the Liberator."

"The Liberator? Because he's liberating the Demon Lord's Domain?"

"It goes beyond that. It seems he's been freeing people from slavery as well. That's likely to increase the number of residents in the territories he liberates. He's made freemen of the slaves who belonged to nations that opposed him inside the Union of Eastern Nations, or those who fled there from other countries due to harsh living situations."

"He's doing something unreasonable again..."

I got what he was aiming for, at least. *They're like the tondenhei settler colonists...no, more like Cao Cao's Qingzhou Army of Yellow Turbans, I guess?* He was taking in people who had no place in society and using them to bolster the strength of his nation. The Great Tiger Kingdom wanted people to rebuild the lands they'd liberated, and they were ready to take just about anybody. If Fuuga freed them from slavery and gave them someplace to live, they'd be loyal to him. It was an effective strategy.

"*The strength of the Great Tiger Kingdom begins here,*" he could say. There were drawbacks too, of course. The most obvious being a decay in public order. There also would likely be friction between the old and new settlers. Accepting everyone meant risking that some of the people would be ruffians and criminals. That would be fine so long as Fuuga, with his overwhelming military might and charisma, was still alive and well. Those villains would be vanquished by his elite cavalry, forcing them to lay low.

But when Fuuga's time had passed, they might prove a source of turmoil for the Great Tiger Kingdom. Not that Fuuga was one to care about that.

"*The people who come after me can worry about what comes then.*" I could imagine him saying that with an undaunted smile.

"Recently," Maria began as I was lost in thought, "the people have been talking in the northern lands of the Empire. They say, 'Sir Fuuga is freeing slaves, but what is Maria, the one they call a saint, doing?' and 'She's a saint, so she should lead the way on liberating the slaves.'"

"That's not fair..." The people were being unreasonable. "Even if the Great Tiger Kingdom frees the slaves and gives them abandoned houses and fields, they don't have the wealth to support this. The newly freed slaves will simply be impoverished."

While true, compared to the oppression they'd faced, the slaves would still probably be grateful for that. But if you compared the situation of their freed slaves with our slaves who had been freed in all but name, there was no way they were more affluent. *But hold up... Isn't something off with this whole conversation?*

"I've never heard Fuuga called a liberator of slaves here in our country," I confided.

If that kind of talk was going around, the Black Cats would have reported it. The fact that they hadn't meant...

"Is someone spreading that rumor inside the Empire?"

After a brief pause, Maria nodded. "Yes...I believe so. People from Sir Fuuga's camp are likely doing it intentionally."

"Huh?!" I gasped. *Propaganda! That can only mean...*

"It must be his advisor, Sir Hashim," Maria noted. "He wants me to rush into abolishing slavery to breed chaos in the Empire."

"If you know that, then—"

"But I see this as an opportunity," Maria said, cutting me off.

"An opportunity? You don't mean..." As my eyes widened with surprise, Maria pressed a finger to her lips.

I knew what this meant and fell quiet. Beside me, Hakuya had a dubious look on his face, but I was going to ignore him for now.

I scrutinized Maria's expression as I asked, "You...really plan to do this?"

"Hee hee, your voice has lost its composure, you know?"

"Answer me, Maria Euphoria!" I pushed the question, my tone serious.

Maria silently nodded and said, "Yes."

"So that's how it is, huh..." I pressed a hand against my forehead. Her resolve seemed firm. "You've made up your mind... All right, then."

"Thank you. And I'll be counting on you, Sir Souma."

With that, Maria terminated the broadcast.

Hakuya immediately approached me. "What was that about at the end?"

"Something personal... For now, it seems Fuuga has set his sights on the Empire."

"That it does. The two countries are bound to collide eventually," Hakuya said, and I scratched my head.

"We're going to have to talk about the future. Call Excel to the capital for me."

"As you wish."

Some days later, an announcement was made inside the Empire abolishing the institution of slavery and liberating all of their slaves.

Because progress—even if it was less than in the Kingdom—had already been made towards abolishing the system in everything but name, there was no great effect on people who weren't slave owners or the slaves themselves. In fact, they were happy not to be called slaves anymore. However, the people who used those slaves worried that their own lifestyles might be in jeopardy.

The groundwork had already been laid for the protection of slaves' rights to ensure they weren't worked to the point of infirmity or death. Normally, this would only have been a change of terminology, nothing more, but that was where Hashim's agents began spreading their propaganda. Rumors spread that Maria was putting the lifestyles of the slaves first, neglecting those of the propertied class. That meant that the higher up you went in society, the more resistance you found against Maria.

That was when an incident occurred.

An independence movement began in two of the Empire's vassal states—north of the Star Dragon Mountain Range on the continent of Landia. The eastern one was the small Kingdom of Meltonia, bordering the Nothung Dragon Knight Kingdom. The western one was the Frakt Federal Republic, henceforth referred to as the Frakt Federation. These two states had secured their continued existence by submitting to the Empire early on.

In the case of the Frakt Federation, it was a region that once housed many small- and medium-sized states, like the former Union of Eastern Nations. But they chose to unite into one country to confront Imperial expansion back before the appearance of the Demon Lord's Domain. Their bonds were stronger than those of the Union, and the constituent nations were dismantled to be ruled as states, each of which sent a representative to the republic's senate. However, when the senate determined they could no longer resist the Empire, they chose to submit in order to nominally preserve their nation.

As for the Kingdom of Meltonia, they were vassalized by the Empire before the Frakt Federation. They were smaller and less powerful than the Dragon Knight Kingdom or Frakt Federation.

When they opposed the massive Empire, it was clear they were going to be reduced to cinders. For the Empire's part, they had just fought a bitter war with the Dragon Knight Kingdom that ended in a stalemate, and they wanted a buffer state. That was why they allowed the Kingdom of Meltonia to continue existing. Even now, the Meltonian royal family ruled over the country.

When these two countries first became Imperial vassals, there was friction between them. However, thanks to the high degree of autonomy afforded to them during the time of the former emperor—Maria's weak-willed and inactive father—and under Maria's own peaceful reign, they only rarely pushed back on things these days. In fact, because they were protected by the Empire after the appearance of the Demon Lord's Domain, relations between the three states were actually good.

However, the past few years had changed that.

The expansion of Fuuga Haan's forces had made it so that the Frakt Federation and the Kingdom of Meltonia no longer bordered the Demon Lord's Domain. This freed them from the worry of the demon waves and, in turn, put them beside the newly established Great Tiger Kingdom instead.

If the monsters were at their gates because of the demon waves, they could count on the Empire to send forces to protect them. But would that hold true if the enemy were the Great Tiger Kingdom? Would the Empire save them like before? The two countries began to have doubts.

It was certainly true that the Empire would not acknowledge the acquisition of territory by force. But their decisions were inevitably slower when it involved the other nations of mankind. This was shown by their inability to prevent the Principality of Amidonia from attacking the Elfrieden Kingdom. Furthermore, if the Empire and the Great Tiger Kingdom were to collide, these countries caught between them might be turned into a battlefield. This led to a debate among their people over which side to support.

Recently, there had also been an active independence movement. This was brought about by two disasters that occurred at roughly the same time.

One night at the end of the 6th month, 1552nd year, Continental Calendar, in a bar in the north of the Empire...

Rattle, rattle, rattle.

"Hm...?"

A drunk arched an eyebrow, and the guy sitting across from him cocked his head to the side.

"Huh? What's wrong?"

"Uh, I thought I felt something shaking..."

"Shaking? Oh, hey, you're right."

Rattle, rattle... Rumble!!!

"Whoa!"

The tremors grew larger as the shaking of the earth became audible. The tavern shook back and forth. Tables moved around, and the tableware fell and shattered to pieces. The quake went on for a long time and showed no sign of ending.

The shaking of the building grew worse, and cracks formed in the earthen walls.

"The tavern's not gonna make it! Get outside!"

"Y-yeah!"

The drunken customers scrambled outside just in time to watch one part of the city walls crumbling. Looking around, they saw houses with their roofs caved in and reddish smoke rising in the distance.

In every direction, they could hear people screaming.

"This is horrible..."

"Yeah..."

The two drunks' legs were quaking as they felt themselves sober up.

At the same time, in a town near the Frakt-Meltonia border...

"Hey, look! The mountain!"

"It's spitting fire..."

"The lava flow could come here! We need to hurry and run!"

The people watched as their mountain erupted. The rocky formation served as the border between the Frakt Federation and the Kingdom of Meltonia. Consequently, debris and volcanic ash from this eruption fell equally on both nations. Its damage to agriculture was especially heavy, forcing the governments in both countries to request aid from their masters in the Empire.

It was unknown whether there was a connection between the earthquake in the north of the Empire and the volcanic eruption that struck the Frakt Federation and Kingdom of Meltonia. However, one thing was certain—Maria couldn't send support to both her own people and her vassals at the same time.

In the coming days, Maria would summon her top bureaucrat, Lumiere.

"Let's send generous aid to the Frakt Republic and Kingdom of Meltonia first."

Lumiere furrowed her brow. "You realize our country also suffered major damage from an earthquake, yes?"

"Our people have the strength to endure for now. Theirs, however, do not. The situation there will only worsen."

"But there are limits to how much we have set aside for this. If we give the vassals too much support, reconstruction in the north will be delayed, resulting in discontent. It could roil the country."

"I know, Lumiere," Maria said, nodding. "That's why I intend to go to the Kingdom of Friedonia for assistance."

"Wha?! To the head of the Maritime Alliance?!"

Lumiere's eyes widened. Most Imperial retainers didn't know about the strong connections between Maria and Souma. In fact, now that the continent was divided into three factions, some people saw him as a threat to Maria's position, the same as Fuuga. Lumiere was one of them.

"The Kingdom of Friedonia...giving support...to us?"

"Sir Souma, the King of Friedonia, is an understanding sort. This was a natural disaster, so he'll likely be willing to offer support without concern for things like national boundaries. Of course, if the same happens to them in the future, we'll be expected to return the favor."

"But if you go to the leader of the Maritime Alliance for aid now—as Fuuga Haan sways the hearts of the people with his liberation of the Demon Lord's Domain—it will hurt your image! Would you please reconsider?!"

"Lumiere..." Maria looked on with sadness in her eyes. "My image doesn't matter. Our thoughts should be on how many victims we can provide succor to. Am I wrong?"

"Yes...that's true... But still! We take pride in serving *you*!" Lumiere shouted, her eyes filled with anguish. "I may not be as devoted as General Krahe, but I still serve you! The Saint of the Empire! Yet recently, you've treated that like it means nothing. What of... What about our pride, Your Majesty?"

Maria lowered her eyes. In a soft voice, she said, "I'm sorry, Lumiere."

"Your Majesty!"

"This is an order. Do I make myself understood?"

Lumiere didn't answer immediately. After a few seconds, she muttered, "...Yes, ma'am."

Maria watched Lumiere go with a sigh.

Thus, Maria provided support to her two vassals while requesting Souma's assistance inside her own country. Souma gladly accepted and immediately sent the *King Souma*, loaded with relief supplies, to an Imperial port. Word of this spread far and wide, improving the opinion of the Kingdom of Friedonia with the people of the Empire. At the same time, however, it bred discontent among those retainers who could not bear to see Maria standing in Souma's shadow.

Meanwhile, Fuuga Haan's advisor, Hashim Chima, smiled coldly when he heard this report.

"I see... So that's how Maria moved, did she?"

As soon as he'd finished listening, he gave orders to the agents he had brought with him from the House of Chima.

"Spread rumors in the Frakt Federation and Kingdom of Meltonia at once. 'The empress accepted relief supplies from the Kingdom of Friedonia, then kept them for the Empire instead of distributing them to her vassals.'"

While this was technically true, it was also a distortion of the facts. The Empire had been so generous with their aid to their two vassals that they had needed to go to the Kingdom of Friedonia for assistance. This was something they should have been thanked and not resented for, but the half-truth sprinkled into the rumors incensed the two countries. It didn't help that this came at a time when they were wavering between the Empire and the Great Tiger Kingdom. Because of this, the voices that said they should abandon the cruel Empire and turn to the Great Tiger Kingdom for protection grew by the day.

Of course, the higher-ups in both nations knew about the support the Empire had given them. Alas, the senators of the Frakt Federation went along with public sentiment in order to avoid looking weak themselves. The royal family of the Kingdom of Meltonia tried to mollify their people, but Hashim's agents whipped the populace into a frenzy that could not be contained, and the royals were forced to flee to the Empire.

They say God sends natural disasters as a sign that a country is coming to an end. However, that's not because the natural disasters destroy the country, but because they have deteriorated to the point they are unable to overcome them.

The sun was setting on the Gran Chaos Empire... That much was becoming clear.

HOW A REALIST HERO REBUILT THE KINGDOM

CHAPTER 4
Flowers Working Behind the Scenes

IT HAD ONLY BEEN A FEW DAYS since the Black Cats brought me the report saying that the Empire's vassals, the Frakt Federation and the Kingdom of Meltonia, had switched sides to join the Fuuga Faction. The Kingdom of Meltonia, which had expelled its royal family, was dismantled and annexed, and the Frakt Federation was allowed to maintain nominal independence but was effectively controlled by the Great Tiger Kingdom.

The Mankind Declaration did not allow the changing of borders by military force, but it also recognized the right of peoples to self-determination. In the event that a country's people decided they wanted to be ruled by Fuuga, the Empire had no choice but to accept it. They'd fallen victim to the same hole in the Mankind Declaration that we'd taken advantage of in the Amidonian War.

It was possible that Hashim, the instigator of all this, had been studying our methods. With their vassals leaving them, the Empire was still a great power, but the Mankind Declaration was no more. Meanwhile, if you included his allies in the equation, Fuuga had now expanded to the point where he had overwhelmingly more people and power than the Empire. His sphere of influence formed an ominous, warped crescent, and people said it looked like the maw of a wolf, ready to devour the Empire.

Even the common folk could see it was time for a showdown between the two.

With me in the governmental affairs office were Liscia, Hakuya, and Julius.

"Things moved faster than we expected..." I said, pressing a hand to my forehead.

"Yeah..." said Liscia with a nod, stroking her chin. "I didn't expect such momentum from the Great Tiger Kingdom, nor how fast Maria would find herself pushed into a corner."

"Part of that comes down to bad timing... They were shaken up by the sudden abolition of slavery, and then there were the natural disasters on top of that. It all piled up."

"Will our country be all right? Won't they try the same slavery trick here?" Julius asked.

"We should be fine," Hakuya replied. "The rights of our slaves are well protected. And if none of them are dissatisfied, there should be no one for them to stir up. They live better than the freed slaves in the Great Tiger Kingdom, and we've made that clear to the people using broadcast programs. Now it's just a matter of us moving together with the Republic and the Archipelago Kingdom to change what they're called. At which point, the system will be no more."

"Yeah, that sounds about right. Let's work with Kuu and Shabon to go forward with it," I said.

Julius crossed his arms and groaned. "The ability to spread news with broadcast programs... It's a powerful tool. I could sense that even when I was in Amidonia. I hated it when I was up against you, but now it's reassuring."

"Ah ha ha... I'll take that as a compliment," I said with a wry smile at the frowning Julius. "Anyway, if they were going to stir up trouble here, it would be with people in the Amidonia Region, not the slaves. But Roroa is still beloved by the people there, and Julius can keep the ones who don't care for her in line with the memory of Gaius. With you two on our side, I don't see the Amidonia Region getting out of hand."

That took the scowl off Julius's face. "Heh! It's not bad, hearing you say that," he said.

"For all your arguments, you two get along pretty well," Liscia said, sounding exasperated.

Julius and I both smiled wryly.

"That said...Souma? I know Fuuga Haan seems to have his eyes set on the Empire, but what would have happened if he'd come after us instead?"

"I had plans I was working on for if it came to that, but... Hakuya's read on the situation was, well... You tell her."

Liscia looked to Hakuya. He nodded.

"We wouldn't lose, but it would be a quagmire."

"Oh! That's how it'd be, huh?"

"In a defensive war, the terrain is on our side. Fuuga's forces are powerful, but we hold a technological advantage. We have a number of weapons, such as our wyvern cavalry equipped with simplified propulsion devices, that they don't know about. That's not something they would be able to deal with overnight. Their current strategy of lightning-fast advances wouldn't work here."

Having said this, Hakuya pointed to the world map behind the desk.

"And given time, our Maritime Alliance allies in the Republic and the Archipelago Kingdom would attack the Great Tiger Kingdom and their allies. If our fleet moves with the Archipelago Kingdom's, we would be able to fight defensively on land while also attacking the Great Tiger Kingdom from both the east and west coasts. Fuuga's forces would be forced to respond to this, further delaying their invasion. And if it dragged on for several years...something decisive would happen."

"Something decisive?" Liscia repeated, and Hakuya pointed to the upper area of the map.

"The periodic release of large numbers of monsters from the Demon Lord's Domain in the phenomenon we call a demon wave. As things stand now, the Great Tiger Kingdom is the sole nation keeping the domain in check. It will take some time still, but if things drag on for too long and a demon wave breaks out, the Great Tiger Kingdom will be forced to confront it alone. They've rendered the Mankind Declaration ineffective, and we'd be under no obligation to help the people who'd invaded us."

"I get it. You're saying they don't have time to attack us, right?"

"Yes, but we would also have trouble attacking them. So with neither side being able to win a decisive victory, the war would bog down. That's why it would be a quagmire."

"I'm sure Fuuga and Hashim know as much too. That's why they went after the Empire," Julius added helpfully.

"If Fuuga was going to pick a fight with the Kingdom, it would have to be after he's built his forces up enough to overwhelm the Maritime Alliance. He'll need to be able to place units all over to respond to our attacks before he can come settle things with us."

"Conversely, he doesn't want us to make a move until then."

Hakuya stroked his chin and grunted in agreement. "Mmm. He'll do something to keep us in check, I'm sure. To keep us from acting while he attacks the Empire."

"I agree, Prime Minister. I'd do the same."

"You would, would you?"

If Hakuya and Julius, my two great advisors, agreed on that, I had no choice but to believe it.

Some days later, I received word from Yuriga that Fuuga wanted to do a broadcast meeting with me.

It seemed Fuuga had gotten his hands on a number of dungeon cores in the process of expanding his territory. They'd learned how to use them for communication and broadcasting from Yuriga, who had experience with that in the Kingdom. Now he was set up to hold broadcast meetings with us like the Empire did.

Tomoe and Yuriga were in the room with me, watching as we prepared for the broadcast.

"Maybe I can make my reports to my brother over the broadcast instead of by letter from now on? It's been such a hassle," Yuriga said casually, earning a wry smile from Tomoe.

"I don't think so. This country isn't allied with the Great Tiger Kingdom, and there's no telling what you might say."

"But they haven't been censoring my letters anyway, right?"

"Oh, well...I guess it might be fine, then?"

As Tomoe cocked her head to the side, Yuriga suddenly let out a sigh.

Tomoe blinked repeatedly. "Are you feeling tense...?"

"Of course I am... I have no idea what my brother plans to say."

Fuuga hadn't told Yuriga what this broadcast would be about, only to get him a meeting with Souma. The lack of information made her think all sorts of things, and she felt uneasy.

Tomoe had a pensive look on her face, and she said, "They say he's going to war with the Empire..."

"Yeah... Augh, I don't want anything that makes it hard for me to stay here..."

"Hee hee, so you want to stay in this country now," Tomoe said.

Yuriga turned her head away peevishly. "Yeah, I do. I've been talking with my teammates about how we're going to win for sure."

"Oh, this is about mage soccer, huh? I know you've been doing really well."

"Me and this senior dragonewt girl on the team are the two top players... That's why it'd be tough being called back home so suddenly. The team's on a roll right now."

Yuriga's expression clouded as she said that. Tomoe subtly moved closer to her.

"...What?" Yuriga asked.

"Hm? Oh, I was just thinking if you went, I'd miss you too."

"Agh! Don't get cheeky with me, you little kid!"

"We're about the same height now."

Yuriga turned her head away, acting prickly. Meanwhile, Tomoe was grinning, her tail wagging back and forth.

While they were chatting, preparations for the broadcast meeting moved forward, and Fuuga and I were finally able to meet directly.

"It's been a while, Fuuga."

"Yeah. Long time no see, Souma."

After some meaningless pleasantries through the broadcast...

Fuuga suddenly looked around and called her name. "Yuriga. Are you around?"

"Ah! Yes, Big Brother." Despite her surprise, Yuriga stepped forward next to Souma.

Fuuga then told her, "Yuriga. I'm speaking to you as king of the Great Tiger Kingdom."

"R-right!" Yuriga stood at attention as Fuuga slowly opened his mouth.

"I will have my sister, Yuriga Haan, marry into the family of Souma A. Elfrieden."

"Fuuga!" I exclaimed.

After hearing his words, I couldn't help but raise my voice. He wanted Yuriga to marry me. It was a clear demand for a strategic marriage.

Using his sister as a political pawn... For a king in this world, and in these times, it was common sense for him to do so. My relationship with Liscia had started out that way too. Despite understanding this, however, it upset me that he was doing it so naturally. Furthermore, Yuriga had been living here long enough that I'd developed a familial affection for her.

I glared at him, and Fuuga looked straight back into my eyes.

"Souma. I'm considering an invasion of the Gran Chaos Empire."

I listened in alarmed silence.

"I'll defeat the declining Empire and show the world that the Great Tiger Kingdom is the one to lead the nations of mankind. With you married to Yuriga, you'll be family. If the leader of the Maritime Alliance is with me, mankind will be unified. The Nothung Dragon Knight Kingdom and what's left of the Spirit Kingdom of Garlan will have no choice but to obey. We can just ignore the Star Dragon Mountain Range. With mankind unified, we'll liberate the Demon Lord's Domain. I'm going to unify the world—something no one's ever been able to do."

He's talking nonsense... I thought, but there was a certain amount of logic to it.

If the Great Tiger Kingdom was able to take all of the Empire's land, not even the Maritime Alliance would be able to oppose him. If he sent Imperial troops to contain the Republic, Kuu wouldn't be able to act. Meanwhile, he'd invade us with his main forces from the north, and Zem and the Lunarian Orthodox Papal State to the west. Even if we had control of the seas, we'd be slowly ground down on land. We'd be left with little choice but to seek asylum in the Archipelago Union. And if it was going to come to that...I'd likely surrender early on. With all this in mind, Fuuga's read on the situation wasn't necessarily wrong.

"Is that your plan, Fuuga?"

"Yeah. So, while we settle things with the Empire, I want you to stay put. In exchange, I'll give you Yuriga."

"You'll give her to me? She's your family... You'd do that so easily?"

I glanced at Yuriga. She was standing up straight, looking at Fuuga. I couldn't read any emotion in her expression. Her eyes weren't dead, at least, but there was no great emotion. She was just calmly, intentionally, looking at Fuuga. *What does she think of all this?*

"I'm not doing this lightly," Fuuga said. "She's my darling sister, cheeky as she can be sometimes."

He didn't show even a hint of guilt.

"I've been running around with my buddies, working towards this grand ambition of unifying the continent, and the country's grown this big. The soldiers and the people lend me their strength in order to chase that dream. But...once it comes true, I'll probably be satisfied. I think I have the strength to take over the world. But I also know I don't have the talent to hold on to it once I do."

"What are you trying to say?"

"I'm thinking you're more fit to rule the world after I unify it. Once the world is all mine, I figure I'll hand it over to you."

"...?!" Everyone in the room gulped.

He's going to give me the world... Is he serious? In an old game, the Dragonlord said, "I'll give you half the world," but Fuuga was offering me the whole thing once he'd unified it.

"Don't say that so easily. Your subordinates and the people won't accept it."

"That's why you're marrying Yuriga. The kid she'll have with you can inherit the Great Tiger Kingdom. You can handle the rest of the personnel assignments. You're good at that stuff, right?"

"I've got a whole mountain of things to say about this, but... What if you have a kid with Mutsumi?"

"Hmm... I guess we'll go back to the steppes, or maybe become adventurers. Neither Mutsumi nor I want to manage a sprawling empire. And even if we do have kids, I wouldn't want them to inherit it."

I had no reply to this. And he probably wasn't lying. *This man is genuinely just interested in taking over the world... Damn it!*

Gathering myself, I then said, "Is this why you showed no sign of calling Yuriga back home?"

"I was leaving her with you until she was of age. My subordinates knew that was with a future marriage in mind."

"But Yuriga came to this country to study because she wanted to be of use to you."

"It was reading her letters that convinced me I shouldn't fight with you or the Kingdom. If she can stop our countries from getting into a war that's bound to turn into a total quagmire, she'll already have done more than enough."

When Fuuga said that, Yuriga stepped forward. "Brother. You took my letters seriously, then?"

"Of course. That's why I decided I should join hands with the Kingdom and subjugate the Empire."

"I see..." Yuriga spun around to face me. "I'm sorry to interrupt during an important talk between kings, but could I speak to my brother for a moment?"

"S-sure..."

"Thank you. Now then, Brother..." Yuriga looked directly into Fuuga's eyes. "In the time I've lived in this country, I've been thinking about it. If you fought them, what would happen? Could you defeat Souma? Could Souma defeat you?"

"Oh, yeah? And how do you see it?" Fuuga urged her to continue, seemingly interested.

Yuriga quietly shook her head. "I couldn't imagine Sir Souma being able to achieve victory."

"Mmm."

"But at the same time, I could never fully convince myself that you'd be able to conquer this country."

Fuuga's eyes widened. Yuriga continued, choosing her words carefully.

"As I wrote in my letters...this country's values are too diverse. Even if you're unmatched in martial prowess, that won't be enough to rule here. Your power comes from having the respect of all your people, but in a country with such diverse values like the Kingdom, one man couldn't possibly earn the respect of the entire country."

Fuuga looked at Yuriga, showing no sign of interrupting her.

"There are people who respect Souma for rebuilding this country with his policies, and those who love and respect Queen Liscia. There are people charmed by the songs of the Prima

Lorelei, Queen Juna Doma—warriors who aspire to have the strength of Queen Aisha. There are those of Amidonia, who love Queen Roroa, and the common people of Parnam who are friends with Queen Naden. Even with just the current king and his wives, there are all these different reasons...different views..."

Yuriga took a long breath before continuing.

"And despite all these groups, they don't form factions. Because this house is unified in their desire to keep the country together. That's why a system of rule like yours or Empress Maria's, where all of that respect is concentrated on one person, wouldn't work in this country. Even with your great majesty, it wouldn't be easy to capture the hearts of all this country's people. And that's why..."

Finally, Yuriga came straight out and said it.

"I accept your command to marry Souma."

"Come again?" I blurted out despite myself. *Huh? Is it really okay for her to accept so easily?*

Even Fuuga looked a little thrown off by this. "I was ready for you to pitch a fit..." he said.

"I won't be doing that. I more or less saw this coming. Although, I want to complain a bit about you bringing this up so suddenly."

"Right... Sorry."

"You'd better be. Still, if I'm going to marry Souma, you should understand that I'll be working on behalf of the Kingdom of Friedonia from here on. Because that will benefit you too."

"Hmm... What do you mean?" Fuuga asked dubiously.

Yuriga put her hands on her hips and thrust her chest out towards him. "I'm not convinced you're going to win. So I can't say for certain that you're not going to end up dragged before Sir Souma bound in ropes someday. When that happens, *I'm* the one who'll have to beg him to spare your life."

Fuuga was speechless.

"Whether Sir Souma listens to my pleas or not is going to hinge entirely on whether he loves me. I need to become a queen Souma will love and the people of this country will feel sympathy for. In order to do that, I'll serve this country with all my heart."

"Heh heh... Ha! Ha! Ha! Ha!" Fuuga roared with laughter. "So you decided to marry him on your own, not because I said to?!"

"Yes, Brother."

"I like it! You've really grown up in the short time I haven't seen you! You're not letting yourself be swept along by events—you're carving your own path! I regret letting Souma have you now!"

Uh... I didn't even know what was happening at this point.

After a hearty laugh, Fuuga looked at me. "Well, there you have it. Look after Yuriga for me, all right?"

"You can't just lay this on me..."

"There isn't a single lie in what I just said. This shouldn't be a bad deal for you people. You should talk it over with the Black-robed Prime Minister and Julius Lastania. So...I want you to stay out of this one."

War between the Empire and the Great Tiger Kingdom seemed inevitable. I had just one thing to say about that.

"Are you sure you're not taking Maria Euphoria too lightly?"

"I'm not taking her lightly at all. I intend to throw everything I have at her."

With that, Fuuga's image vanished.

We hadn't formally accepted the marriage yet, but they were probably going to announce it as an established fact. If I tried to drive Yuriga off and get out of it, I'd only be giving them an excuse I didn't have to.

As I was wondering what to do, I noticed Yuriga trembling beside me.

"Um... You okay, Yuriga?"

"...won."

"Huh?"

Yuriga was mumbling so I cupped my ear...

"I *won*!!!" she shouted out loud right next to me.

"Whoa?!" I stumbled backwards.

The others were looking at us, wondering what was up. But Yuriga paid no mind to them; instead, she thrust her right fist into the air. She was like a new champion who'd just taken the throne. And as if that wasn't enough for her, she thrust her left fist up too, holding both arms up in jubilation.

"I won my bet!!!"

Huh? Bet? Has she gone crazy? As I was thinking that, Tomoe ran over and tackle-hugged her.

"Congratulations, Yuriga!"

"Tomoe! Thank you!"

Yuriga and Tomoe jumped up and down, holding one another.

Seriously... What?

"She really pulled it off," Liscia said as she walked over to us.

"Do you know something about this?" I asked.

"She's been talking to me about it for a while. Come on, Yuriga. We have to explain to Souma."

"Oh! Sure thing, Lady Liscia."

Yuriga seemed to come back to reality when Liscia called for her. She let go of Tomoe and cleared her throat before slowly approaching.

"Erm... Uh... Where do I start?"

"How about with what you said about winning a bet?"

"Of all the potential futures for me, I was able to win close to the best one."

"Close to the best one? You mean getting married to me?"

"I mean, in my *position*. It was always a given that I was going to be thrust to someone for a strategic marriage."

Yuriga shrugged her shoulders and sighed.

"I mean, the Great Tiger Kingdom is rising rapidly, and I'm the younger sister of their king, right? People were going to want to marry me to get closer to my brother, and he was going to want to wed me to someone influential who could help him on his quest for dominance."

"Yeah...I get that."

"So, at that point, the only difference is *who* I get married off to. Having lived in this country for a few years now, I'm used to living here. I didn't even want to think about getting sent elsewhere. I want to keep playing with my mage soccer team. And as for having to leave behind my friends like Tomoe, Ichiha, Lucy, and Velza, well, um...I didn't want that either."

"Aww, Yuriga," Tomoe cooed, a huge grin on her face.

Yuriga turned her head away, refusing to look at Tomoe. "Um, that's why I wanted to marry someone who'd let me stay in this country and hopefully continue playing mage soccer a while longer. But when it came to who my brother would be willing to accept, you were about the only person who came to mind. Ichiha meets the first two criteria, but my brother wasn't going to settle for me marrying a vassal of yours. And besides..."

"Yuriga?" Tomoe called to her, still smiling.

"...Your little sister kind of scares me."

"Ah ha ha..."

Given these events, I was going to have to get Tomoe and Ichiha formally engaged too. They each seemed interested in the other, and a lot of other people were aiming for both of them, so making it official would nip that in the bud.

Yuriga looked at Liscia. "That's why I went to talk to Lady Liscia and the others. I needed to know if she could accept me as one of your wives, and I wanted help convincing my brother to give me the order."

"Wait... The other queens were in on this too?" I asked, looking at Liscia.

"Well, you could say our interests were aligned. Right, Yuriga?"

"Yep!"

Liscia and Yuriga high-fived one another, looking smugly satisfied.

"You said you wanted to avoid a war with the Great Tiger Kingdom now, right? And that we needed to convince Sir Fuuga not to fight with us. That's why when Yuriga came to me for advice, I said I'd accept her as one of your queens if she'd use her letters to make Fuuga less likely to attack us. We wanted to convince him to win us over instead of opposing. Juna was in charge of overseeing the letters, by the way."

"Oh... Well, damn..."

If she was getting tips from Juna, who'd learned from the experienced Excel—then yeah, of course she'd be able to make Fuuga cautious of this country. And since Yuriga was writing the letters of her own accord, he was unlikely to notice it. Well, that didn't guarantee Fuuga would make the decision they wanted, but... *Oh! So that's why it was a bet.*

I stared at Yuriga. "So you had him dancing in the palm of your hand?"

"Ah... What I said in my letters and what he told you just now were all true, you know? If a mighty warrior like my brother was going to fall, I think it would be to this country. And honestly, I do plan to beg for his life if it comes to that."

"That's some determination... But are you really satisfied with this? Having to marry me."

"Well, I do like you. Up until now, I would have been more into someone like Sir Shuukin, who's like another big brother to me. But I respect you, and I could see myself loving you."

"Y-you could...? You're being awfully pragmatic about this."

"She's like a past version of me, isn't she? I just couldn't leave her alone," Liscia said with a wry smile as I stared at them in awe.

"Oh, and one other thing..." Yuriga looked at Tomoe. "If I marry you, that makes Tomoe my little sister, right? I like the idea of that."

"Ah! But I'm the adopted daughter of the former royal couple, so this won't make me your little sister, Yuriga."

"Huh? It won't?"

"I only call Big Sister Liscia my big sister. I just call Big Brother Souma that because he's married to her. I don't call Aisha, Juna, Roroa, and Naden 'Big Sister.'"

"W-well, when I'm queen, you'd better show me respect! You're just a princess!"

"Okaaay," Tomoe said with a chuckle. "I've applied to be chamberlain, by the way. I'll do a good job scheduling your nights with Big Brother."

"Bwuh?! Oh, I can't *stand* you!"

"Ah ha ha ha ha ha."

Tomoe and Yuriga bantered back and forth.

Yuriga probably came up with this plot and found the determination to carry it out because she didn't want to lose this sort of interaction.

Hakuya and Julius were no doubt listening somewhere nearby, so I said, "A question for the brilliant minds that help run this country..."

"May we help you?" asked Hakuya.

"What is it?" followed up Julius.

"Did you two see this coming?"

When I asked that, they looked at one another and shrugged.

"No. I never anticipated the queens were backing her..."

"I doubt Fuuga or Hashim imagined this either. They might have expected you, me, or the prime minister to be planning something, but...they wouldn't have counted on having to consider the intentions of the queens as well. What a terrifying country."

"Tell me about it," I said with a nod.

These reliable, frightening women were working as a team. We were no match for them. If you looked at just the result, they'd pulled one over on both Fuuga and me.

CHAPTER 5

Crossed and Conflicting Intentions

With fuuga's sights set on the Empire and Yuriga's decision to marry me in the future, our country had managed to avoid conflict with the Great Tiger Kingdom for the present. That gave us a lot of time to work with. This wouldn't have been possible without Yuriga working to realize her own desires, and Liscia and my other wives helping her because of their common interests.

The day after the meeting with Fuuga, I was with Liscia and Yuriga explaining to my other wives—who weren't at the meeting—what had happened. That said, Yuriga had all of them in on it from the beginning, so I didn't need to explain her feelings to them, as they already knew more than I did. When I told them Yuriga would be marrying into the family, they all cheered for some reason, and Roroa and Aisha even clapped.

"Ya really pulled it off. Nice goin.'"

"You bent Fuuga to your will. Even warriors would have trouble doing that."

Naden, meanwhile, stood in front of Yuriga, hands on her hips and chest thrust outwards. "Now I've got a queen who's my junior. People have been treating me like I'm younger than I am, but now everyone will see they can't treat me like a kid anymore."

"Hmm... But don't you see that Yuriga is already taller than you?" Juna pointed out.

"Whuh?" gasped Naden, and her eyes widened. Her body hadn't changed much since we met, while Yuriga's figure had filled out, giving her a more womanly form. If you asked me which of them was younger...I'd have had to go with Naden too.

"I-It's okay, Lady Naden! I'll show you the respect you're due as my senior!" Yuriga hurriedly reassured her before she could get too depressed.

"You mean it?" Naden asked, eyes upturned, and Yuriga nodded vigorously.

"Oh, my. But when Yuriga marries into the family, she'll be a primary queen, won't she? As secondary queens, aren't we the ones who have to show her the proper respect?"

Naden's shoulders slumped as Juna pointed this out too.

"Juna..." I said, looking at her reproachfully.

"Hee hee!" Juna playfully stuck out her tongue.

I gave Naden a hug and a pat on the head to raise her spirits. "Yuriga wants to keep playing mage soccer, and it'll probably still be a little while before the wedding. If Fuuga announces the engagement, I just plan to confirm it for now. So she's just my fiancée for the time being."

If we maintained a loose relationship status, it would be

possible to break things off if the situation called for it. Should Yuriga decide later that she didn't want to marry me, I wasn't going to force her. But saying that now would trample on her determination, so I kept it to myself.

I bowed my head to all my wives. "If Yuriga does join our family, I want all of you to be good to her."

"Of course," Liscia said, hugging Yuriga tight. "If anything happened to her, Tomoe would cry... And, I mean, Yuriga is like a little sister to me too. I couldn't make any of my sisters cry."

"L-Lady Liscia..." Yuriga said, blushing.

Yeah, they're going to be fine. As I was thinking that, Roroa suddenly crossed her arms and groaned. *What's she going to say?*

Roroa glanced at Yuriga. "Is it okay to assume Yuriga's on our side? Is she gonna keep makin' reports to the Great Tiger Kingdom?"

"Ah! No!"

Yuriga slipped out of Liscia's arms and placed her right hand over her chest.

"If I'm going to marry Sir Souma, I need to put *this country's* interests first. My obligation to report to my brother ended with yesterday's meeting. If you tell me to send him false information, I would be hesitant to the idea, but I won't tell him any of this country's secrets that I might learn! Because, if I do anything that hurts this country, I won't be able to beg for his life!"

Hearing all this, Roroa then glanced at me. She was probably checking to see whether it was okay to trust her. I nodded, and Roroa seemed satisfied.

"Well, in that case, I'm not gonna hesitate to talk. We may be fine with all this, but the problem's the Empire, right? Fuuga Haan's goin' after the Empire, so won't you gettin' engaged to his sister shock them?"

"Yeah, you have a point there..."

Unlike us, who had been given a little extra time thanks to Yuriga, Maria and Jeanne's Empire was about to face the moment of truth.

"I've got Hakuya contacting Madam Jeanne about it right now. He'll be telling her about everything, including Yuriga."

"Madam Jeanne...gets along pretty well with Hakuya, right?" Liscia mumbled to herself. "This must be difficult for him..."

Yeah... I knew it was his job, but maybe I'd pushed an unpleasant task onto him.

At the same time, in the room with the broadcast jewel...

"I see... Sir Souma, with Sir Fuuga's little sister..."

"Yes..."

Black-robed Prime Minister Hakuya and Little Sister General Jeanne were talking over the Jewel Voice Broadcast. He had just finished recounting what had happened during the broadcast meeting between Souma and Fuuga yesterday.

"That Yuriga girl sounds pretty competent, starting a fight with her own brother in order to get what she wants... Compared to the way we've been on the back foot against him lately, it's satisfying to see that happen."

Jeanne let out a self-derisive laugh. Hakuya's expression grew concerned.

"You're on the back foot?"

"Yes. With the Great Tiger Kingdom's rise, the support for our own country and our vassal states after the natural disasters, and the sudden abolition of slavery...our country is in a state of disarray. Now, on top of that, if we have Sir Souma getting engaged to Madam Yuriga—thus creating a familial bond between the Kingdom of Friedonia and the Great Tiger Kingdom—that will only breed further confusion. That man...Hashim, was it? Fuuga's advisor is sure to spread word of it far and wide."

"I'm sorry to cause you additional trouble..." Hakuya apologized, but Jeanne shook her head.

"No. You did what you had to. It's only natural to put your own country first... Even if we're on the back foot, in the past, my sister would still have been able to do something about it. The fact that she can't now is a failing of our country."

"Is Madam Maria...the same as always?" Hakuya asked hesitantly.

Jeanne nodded. "As always, she's slow to act. She only responds to issues as they arise..."

"I see..."

"Honestly... I don't know what she's thinking..." Jeanne muttered, a pained look on her face. She shook her head. "I'm speaking in a personal capacity... Please, ignore what I'm about to say... To my eyes...it looks like my sister has lost the will to be Empress. I know she's been enduring the weight of responsibility all this time. But if that's true...then this country is..."

Hakuya looked at her, speechless, and Jeanne let out a weak laugh.

"Ah ha ha... I shouldn't be like this. The commander of the Empire's armies mustn't think like this. No matter what decision my sister comes to, I will protect her."

"Madam Jeanne... I..."

"Don't worry about it. You are the prime minister of the Kingdom of Friedonia. You should act on behalf of your own country. Don't strain yourself on our account."

Jeanne rejected him with a smile on her lips.

"If the worst should happen... Sir Hakuya. Please, stay well."

There was nothing more Hakuya could say.

Step, step, step. Prime Minister Hakuya walked the halls of Parnam Castle, lost in thought. His face was as calm as ever, but in his mind he was playing out simulation after simulation, giving no attention to his surroundings. Bureaucrats greeted him, guards saluted him, but Hakuya just kept walking, unnoticing.

His mind was occupied by two things: Jeanne's pained face on the other side of the broadcast as she rejected his help, and simulations of how the Kingdom of Friedonia should act from here on. Brilliant mind that he was, Hakuya had a firm understanding of the situation. If the Kingdom of Friedonia was going to prepare to deal with the growth of the Great Tiger Kingdom, it was *in their interest* for the Empire to be destroyed.

If the Great Tiger Kingdom and the Empire fight a total war, the Empire will almost undoubtedly lose, he thought. *The Empire's knights and nobility are torn on whether or not they support Madam Maria right now. Unless they unite as one, not even the Empire can fend off the fierce attacks of the Great Tiger Kingdom. But she still has the overwhelming support of the rest of her people.*

Step, step, step.

If the people who worship Madam Maria as the Saint of the Empire have an almost religious belief in her... If Fuuga were to kill Madam Maria...the whole Empire would rage. Their massive territory would become an unstable region with frequent rebellions. When they put down one rebellion, the resentment will remain and fester once more. He won't be able to say, "Today the Empire, tomorrow the Kingdom of Friedonia," and invade us next. He'll need a great deal of time and effort to solidify his position in the Empire.

Step, step, step.

Fuuga and Hashim must know this. Once their victory is assured, they'll call on Madam Maria to surrender. If they can make her submit without killing her, they can keep her believers under their control. But Madam Maria won't submit. She wouldn't make her people follow a man as bellicose as Fuuga, and she would defend them as long as she's still alive to do so.

Step, step, step.

In the event that Fuuga goes to war with the Empire, he can only end the war with their total annexation. That means ruling over a vast and restive territory. During the meeting, Fuuga said that once he united the continent, he would give it to His Majesty... In a way, that's true. Once he unites the continent and amasses all the enmity that will earn him, Fuuga won't be able to maintain the unified nation.

Step, step, step.

So...if you think about it from just this country's perspective...our best move is not to get involved in a conflict between the Great Tiger Kingdom and the Empire. It's not impossible that His Majesty could assume control of everything without shedding a drop of our blood. But...that means abandoning Madam Maria and Madam Jeanne...

Step, step, step.

As prime minister, I have to advise His Majesty to do that. His Majesty is a rational man, and he cares deeply for his family and those who are close to him. He'll surely want to save Madam Maria and Madam Jeanne, who were our allies. I...have to stop him...because, on the day he hired me, I swore to myself I would support him.

"Oh, hey..."

Urgh... I mustn't waver. I'm the prime minister of this country. I need to work for the benefit of this nation without letting myself be trapped by my own personal feelings. Madam Jeanne understands that. It's why she turned me down. I mustn't let my emotions sway me from my duty. If I were to abandon my role and act on Madam Jeanne's behalf, that would sadden her...

"Hey, are you listening?"

But... Even so! Even so...in my heart, I want to...

"Hey! Hakuya!"

There was a sudden pull on his shoulder, and Hakuya turned to find Souma standing there. Aisha was behind him too.

"Your...Majesty? And Lady Aisha too."

"Jeez, what's got you so worked up? I called out to you, but you didn't even respond."

"Ah! My apologies. I've been thinking..."

"Yeah, I'll bet. Your face looked scary with all those wrinkles on your forehead," Souma said with a shrug, and Hakuya turned his face away from him.

Souma sighed, patting him on the shoulder with the hand he'd been using to hold it.

"Let's take this conversation somewhere else. Follow me."

"As you wish..."

The three of them went to the governmental affairs office.

"Aisha, keep people away."

"Yes, sir! Understood!"

Souma posted Aisha at the door to the office and went inside with Hakuya. Instead of using the desk, this time they sat down facing one another on the sofas in the reception area.

Once they had relaxed a moment, Souma said, "I know why you've got that look on your face. It's Madam Jeanne, isn't it?"

Hakuya was silent, but his expression spoke for itself.

"Ha ha ha, you're unusually easy to read for once."

Seeing how Hakuya was shaken to have this pointed out, Souma smiled wryly.

"You had a meeting with Madam Jeanne, right? War between the Empire and the Great Tiger Kingdom is inevitable at this point. You know what will become of Madam Maria and Madam Jeanne...so you offered to help, and Madam Jeanne refused... Is that about right? Or could you not even voice your desire to save her?"

It was the latter. But Hakuya didn't say a word. He told himself that a prime minister must not get his personal feelings involved in his work—Souma already knew, though.

"Even if you want to help Madam Jeanne, the best thing for this country is to abandon the Empire... That's what you're thinking, right? If we're going to take on the Great Tiger Kingdom, it's simply better for us if we do it when he has to deal with an unstable Empire that's lost Madam Maria."

"You understand me well..."

"We've been working together a long time," Souma casually responded.

Hakuya gave in and spoke up. "What I should advise you is that...rather than let our momentary emotions get the best of us, we should stay out of the fight between the Empire and the Great Tiger Kingdom."

"Even if that means abandoning Madam Maria and Madam Jeanne?"

"Indeed."

"You think we should stay neutral?"

"Yes. Whether Sir Fuuga means to keep his word to you or not, he will not be able to fully capture the hearts and minds of the people of the Empire. Once they annex the Empire, the Great Tiger Kingdom will surely lose steam. Should we choose to join hands with them or fight them, it will be easier then."

"You're naive..." Souma muttered.

Hakuya snapped back to his senses and looked up at him. That was when he realized Souma was staring at him critically.

Souma told Hakuya, "Your understanding is naive. That's not like you, Hakuya."

"What do you mean...?"

"'Declaring yourself in favor of one party against the other will always be more advantageous than standing neutral.' Those are the words of Machiavelli, the political thinker I always refer to when making decisions as a king."

Souma was paraphrasing the twelfth chapter of *The Prince*, "How a Prince Should Conduct Himself So as to Gain Renown."

"To explain what he means, imagine there are two countries, A and B, in conflict. If C remains neutral, the winner will view C as weak, and they'll be the next target. The loser will resent C for being heartless and not coming to their aid, so if the winner attacks C, they won't be willing to help defend them. This is the harm that comes from choosing neutrality."

Hakuya listened intently to Souma's words.

"Now, if they declared themselves in favor of one party... Let's say C sides with A. If A wins, they'll share in their joys, and that will build a bond between the countries. Conversely, if A loses, A will still be grateful for the help, and if they recover at some point in the future, they'll be a reliable ally. The winner, B, will respect C for standing by their beliefs—be wary, and if possible, try to become allies with them...or something like that."

Machiavelli served as a diplomat in the Italian Peninsula when it was divided between many scheming principalities, so you could see his distaste for ambiguous positions. In fact, the Florentine Republic, which Machiavelli served, remained neutral in the conflict between their long-standing ally France and the Holy League of Pope Julius II. As a result, the government of the republic was thrown out by the House of Medici with the backing of Spain, a member of the Holy League, once the French withdrew from the Italian Peninsula.

Souma told Hakuya, "If I were going to go in the direction you've suggested, I should align myself with Fuuga outright from the start. I could even send our troops in with Fuuga's vanguard and help them destroy the Empire. If we don't go that far, we won't have a say in how things are settled after the war."

"But we couldn't—"

"Yeah. I don't want to do it either. But if we aren't prepared to go that far, we won't be able to survive under Fuuga's rule."

Souma was thinking of Tokugawa Ieyasu.

Ieyasu was renowned for his patience, having endured serving under other powerful figures. When his ally Oda Nobunaga called for reinforcements, he fought as hard as the Oda. Even when they lost to the Takeda, he was strong in his commitment to the Oda alliance, and he bowed his head to the next ruler, Hideyoshi, too.

If the Hidetsugu Incident hadn't made the Toyotomi government such a mess, Ieyasu would likely have remained a loyal ally. However, after Hideyoshi's death, he had to take over to stabilize his house and the country. This is the Ieyasu who is hated by those who are fans of the commanders of the Western Forces at the Battle of Sekigahara—like Ishida Mitsunari, who died for loyalty to the Toyotomi government—or of the commanders on the Osaka side of the Siege of Osaka, like Sanada Yukimura.

He wasn't a commander Souma liked before, but now that Souma had become king, he was finally able to see just how great Ieyasu was. If you were to ask him if he thought he could do the same, he didn't think so.

Hakuya was looking down, a hand pressed to his forehead.

"Still... I can't see it. I can find no other way."

"Hakuya..."

"It is impossible to protect this country and maintain the Empire. If we recklessly try to defend both, it will turn into a quagmire. No matter how I think about it...I can't find the answer I want."

Hakuya hung his head. Souma was quiet for some time before opening his mouth.

"————"

Hakuya's head snapped up at what Souma had said. He looked at Souma, as if trying to check whether what he said was true.

Souma nodded. And then, rising to his feet, Souma gestured for Hakuya to follow him.

They went to the second war room, a place that was hardly ever used.

In the center of the gloomy room, which relied on candlelight because it had no windows, a number of tables had been pushed together with a huge map of the continent on top of them. Present was a distinguished group consisting of Liscia, Aisha, Juna, Roroa, Naden, National Defense Force Commander-in-Chief Excel, Vice-Commander Ludwin, and Julius the White Strategist. There was also Tomoe, Ichiha, and even Fuuga's little sister Yuriga.

"I don't believe I was ever told this war room was in use…" Hakuya said, sounding confused.

"Yeah, because you weren't," Souma replied with a shrug. "You were our representative in talks with the Empire, and you have feelings for Madam Jeanne too, right? Excel said it was best to hold off on telling you."

"They say love makes men blind," Excel said with a chuckle, hiding her mouth behind her fan.

Hakuya felt a mixture of confusion and consternation, but he set those feelings aside for the moment and stood in front of the big map. Souma stood beside him, putting a hand on his shoulder.

"Now then, Hakuya. I have high regard for your intelligence… The board is ready. The pieces too. All that remains is you. In light of everything we just talked about, here are your orders."

Souma gestured broadly towards the map with his right arm.

"I want you to use that head of yours to devise the optimal future for us."

Meanwhile, there was a military council being held in Fuuga's camp as well...

The Great Tiger King, Fuuga Haan, sat with the Partner of the Tiger, Mutsumi Haan, seated on one side of him, while the Wisdom of the Tiger, Hashim Chima, was seated on the other.

At the seats lining the luxurious carpet that stretched out in front of Fuuga were his wise and brave commanders: the Sword of the Tiger, Shuukin Tan; the battle-crazed Battle Ax of the Tiger, Nata Chima; the veteran Shield of the Tiger, Gaifuku Kiin; the commander of the archers, the Crossbow of the Tiger, Kasen Shuri; and the gaudy Flag of the Tiger, Gaten Bahr.

Further away were newcomers like the Saint of the Tiger, Anne, sent by the Lunarian Orthodox Papal State, as well as Lombard Remus and his wife, Yomi. It was a who's who of Fuuga's subordinates.

The only one not present was Moumei Ryoku, the Hammer of the Tiger, who was currently serving as viceroy in Mercenary State Zem. Fuuga had determined their next target was the Empire, and now Hashim was explaining the strategy they would use against them.

"We must strike quickly and decisively," Hashim said, pointing to the map of the continent in the center with a pointer. "If you include our allies, we have twice as many soldiers as the Empire. However, the Empire is still a more powerful nation. If this turns into a protracted war, we'll likely have a hard time."

"We can't maintain our supply lines?" Shuukin asked, but Hashim shook his head.

"That is not a major concern. Fortunately, our forces are more mobile than those of other armies. When the Kingdom of Friedonia was experiencing a food crisis, I heard that they rolled out a transportation network to bring food from places that had it to places that didn't. We can do the same. We have a lot of mounts in our forces, so we'll have no shortage of overland transportation options. With the current strength of our country, we can wage war for a few years. The Empire also has a transportation network, perhaps modeled after the Kingdom's. That will help us to move faster as well."

"Introducing good ideas even if they were developed elsewhere... It speaks to Madam Maria's broad-mindedness," Mutsumi said, sounding impressed.

"Yeah, sure," Fuuga replied with a laugh. "It seems the Kingdom and the Empire are more connected than we thought... Come to think of it, Souma was saying we shouldn't underestimate Maria."

"Indeed. That is why we must go at this with everything we have," Hashim said with a polite bow.

The youngest member of the group, Kasen, raised his hand. "Sir Hashim. If we don't have to worry about our supply lines, why do we need to strike so fast and decisively?"

"It's simple. We run the risk of losing our all-important 'momentum,'" Hashim said, tapping his left hand with the pointer. "Lord Fuuga has expanded the country this far by winning every battle he's fought. The people supporting him believe Lord Fuuga cannot lose. It's the same for us soldiers, isn't it?"

"Of course," Kasen said with a nod. Hashim nodded in return.

"Right now, if Fuuga says we are going to fight, the people will have no doubt victory is assured. When Lord Fuuga takes to the field, our enemies tremble. However, if we struggle against the Empire, we will lose that advantage. Once our abilities come into question, this smooth expansion we've experienced up until this point will no longer be possible."

"So, basically, if we say we're gonna fight, we've gotta win or we're finished," Fuuga added.

Hashim nodded in response. "Indeed. There is no need to occupy the entirety of the Empire; we just need to move quickly to the point where they concede. We can strike down Empress Maria and her sister Jeanne to destroy the House of Euphoria, or we can take the Imperial capital Valois... Perhaps make Maria surrender so that people see she's lost her authority and impress upon them that Lord Fuuga has won."

"Hmm... You're talking about destroying the House of Euphoria, but they have that other sister, what's her name, in the Kingdom, right? Can we leave her alone?"

"You mean the third sister, Princess Trill. Opinion of her in the Empire is low. They talk about how she was shipped off to the Kingdom because even Maria couldn't keep her in line. Even if King Souma were to trot her out later, no one would follow her."

Hashim said this as if it were no big deal. Shuukin arched an eyebrow at that.

"We owe the Kingdom and Empire for their help in suppressing Magic Bug Disease. So, I don't know about this talk of destroying them..."

"Hmm. It's not to your liking, Sir Shuukin?"

"They did save me, after all."

Seeing the pained look on Shuukin's face, Hashim said with cold eyes, "We must prioritize Lord Fuuga's great work. Or am I wrong?"

"I know that... When the time comes, I'll kill my emotions and fight like a demon."

"If you're not keen on it, you can leave it to me. I'll send those Imperial losers packing!" Nata, the battle-crazed lunatic, said with a hearty laugh.

Men as simple as him make for easy pawns, Hashim thought, but he didn't say it out loud. He pointed to the map.

"What we need is speed. There are two routes from our territory for a fast attack on Valois. One heads through their former vassal states, the Kingdom of Meltonia and the Frakt Federation in the northeast. The other heads straight west from our allied nation, the Lunarian Orthodox Papal State, and Mercenary State Zem now ruled by Sir Moumei."

"Let all be as Holy King Fuuga wills it." Hearing the name of her country, Saint Anne bowed her head.

Anne was of the Lunarian Orthodox Papal State but had been taught to submit to the ruler she served, so she would never oppose anything Fuuga did.

Looking at those routes, Lombard cocked his head to the

side. "Wouldn't the route south from the former buffer zone be shorter?"

Hashim shook his head. "I would prefer to avoid routes near the coast. We can't be sure that the Maritime Alliance won't intervene."

"I see..."

As things stood, there was no nation that could equal the Maritime Alliance in terms of naval power. Even with their incredible momentum, Fuuga's forces couldn't handle even just the Kingdom on its own at sea. Thus, an inland route was of utmost importance here.

"I gave him Yuriga and told him to stay put, though..." Fuuga said with an exasperated shrug.

Mutsumi furrowed her brow. "Are you saying the Kingdom will align itself with the Empire?"

"Looking at how strong their connection ended up being, he might be considering protecting Maria and helping her escape... Yuriga's going to be acting as Souma's queen from here on, so we can't count on her to keep him out of it. But that's why we're making a strong offensive, right?"

Fuuga turned to Hashim, who nodded.

"Indeed. If we let her escape, all we need to do is loudly spread the word that Maria abandoned her people. Depending on how we do it, we might even be able to make it so that Souma abducted her in the confusion. If we can hurt their opinion of the Kingdom, they will reject Maria if she tries to come back with the Kingdom's support."

"Harsh," Fuuga said, half appalled, then looked at the map. "If we want to hit them hard and fast, dividing our forces is a bad idea. Do we choose one route and go with it?"

"No, we attack using *both*. We also make the Empire aware we will be attacking by these two routes. That will force them to spread their forces to defend them."

"Oh-hoh..."

"However, on one route, we will only make a token effort while we focus on the other. That means we will be making a primary and secondary attack. We'll break through their divided defenses all at once with our main force. But while the secondary attack is not a serious one, we still need to act in a way that makes them think it will be the primary one."

"Hmm. So, north or east? Which side do we make the main one?"

"This one," Hashim replied, pointing to the route through the Orthodox Papal State and Zem. "If they learn we intend to attack by two routes, the Empire will assume one must be the primary invasion force. The logical thing to consider, then, is how well we can coordinate with our allies, Zem and the Orthodox Papal State. It's only natural to be suspicious of a country you haven't been allied with for long. Therefore, the Empire will assume 'They will invade through the north, as it's closer to the Great Tiger Kingdom's main force, and the east will only be a token effort from Zem and the Orthodox Papal State.'"

"I get it. That's how we trick them, huh?" Fuuga crossed his arms and grunted.

Hashim gave an exaggerated bow. "Indeed. Even if the Empire does predict that this is the primary attack, they still need to position forces on the northern route. The mental strain of having a border with the Great Tiger Kingdom up north should be considerable for them. I think that our forces, together with those of the Orthodox Papal State and Zem, will be able to break through."

"Got it."

Fuuga stood up and drew the sword at his waist, holding it backhanded as he swung it down at the Imperial capital on the map. It went through both Valois and the table.

"We're going with Hashim's plan. Everyone, prepare for war!"

"Yes, sir!"

His vassals all rose from their seats and saluted him.

While Fuuga was preparing to invade the Empire...

The Empire had noticed the moves he was making. Jeanne, the commander of the Imperial forces, went to her sister Maria to ask how they should respond. She had her soldier face on as they stood with a map of the continent between them.

"The Great Tiger Kingdom is preparing to invade us. One route is from the north through the Federal Republic of Frakt, while the other is through their allies in Zem and the Orthodox Papal State to the east. His forces are large, and many of the soldiers are recently recruited, so I expect they will aim to strike fast and decisively. No matter which route they take, we can expect them to come straight for Valois."

"How much greater are their forces?"

"With the loss of the Frakt Federation and Meltonia, our forces now amount to less than 250,000 men. If you include his allies, Fuuga has 400,000. That's less than twice as many as us."

"I see..." Maria said, nodding. "Then there's no chance they'll split their force perfectly in two."

"Agreed. If they had double our strength, that would be one thing, but without it, they run the risk of being defeated in detail. The steep mountains of the Star Dragon Mountain Range lie between the two routes, so it will be hard for them to communicate. I can't imagine that Fuuga or his advisor Hashim would employ such an amateurish plan."

"Yes, I agree... That's why I think one of the two must be a ruse while they focus their forces on the other. And this will be their real target." Maria pointed towards Zem and the Orthodox Papal State on the map.

"They'll attack through their allies, not closer to their homeland...is what you're saying?" Jeanne asked.

"Sir Fuuga trusts in his strength, while a schemer like Sir Hashim doesn't trust others very well. He won't think his allies would put up a good fight without him there to command. That said, Zemish mercenaries are experienced at acting as a diversion, and the Orthodox Papal State has a sizable military too. Without those two countries, they wouldn't have considerably more forces than we do, right?"

"Well...even without them, they'd still have slightly more."

"Then he'll want them under his control so he can use them to his advantage. To do that, he needs them to join up with the main force. That's why he'll choose this route."

Maria spoke confidently, but Jeanne was still unsure.

"It's true if he takes this route, he can secure the men he needs. However, if he brings men who are not marching at the same pace with him, his advance will be slowed. Is it not entirely possible that he will use his allies as decoys while attacking from the north with a force purely of his own men?"

Jeanne presented her doubts, but Maria quietly shook her head.

"I'm sure that's what Sir Fuuga expects us to think. It's certain that if his goal is to destroy us and become the greatest power on this continent, that plan would work. But Sir Fuuga has grander ambitions. He intends to strike into the heart of the Demon Lord's Domain, and perhaps to have a showdown with the Maritime Alliance to unite the continent. Which means..."

"He doesn't want to use up his soldiers fighting us," Jeanne said bitterly. "We're being taken lightly..."

Maria didn't respond right away. Instead, she placed a pawn on the border with Zem. "That is why I will have you and Sir Gunther lead the majority of our forces to the east. Please, do everything you can to hold back Fuuga's forces as they come in from Zem and the Orthodox Papal State."

"Yes, ma'am! Understood." Jeanne clicked her heels together, stood up straight, and saluted. "But what will we do about the northern route?" she asked.

"I have Sir Krahe defending us with his personal forces there. He will join up with the knights and nobles who have land in the north. That should be enough to deal with a decoy army."

"In the north...?"

Maria's comments made Jeanne look hesitant.

"Jeanne?"

"Oh, no... Sir Krahe is an odd one, but his loyalty to you—or his faith, rather—is abnormally strong. It's just...Lumiere and all of them have their lands in the north."

Lumiere was the Empire's young and talented top bureaucrat. And she had also repeatedly objected to Maria's policies on domestic issues. Ever since Maria rejected her advice that "the Empire should take part of the buffer zone too" as the Great Tiger Kingdom was seizing the territory, she had secluded herself in her own domain.

"It's not just Lumiere. The northern regions were confused by your sudden abolition of slavery, so many of the knights and nobles are pushing back against that."

Jeanne's comment made Maria nod sadly.

"Yes... That's why it's best to have them focus on defending their own lands. We'd be in trouble if they collaborated with Fuuga's forces on the front lines. It's my fault for not doing a better job of keeping them attached to us, though."

"Sister..." Jeanne couldn't help but address her not as a soldier, but as a family member.

Maria smiled at Jeanne as she stood up and walked to the

window. "Hey, Jeanne? What do the soldiers think about fighting the Great Tiger Kingdom?"

"Everyone is highly motivated! They want to fight for the country, and for you! Many of the knights and nobles criticize your policies as being too passive, but those of lower birth understand! They know it's your politics that have protected their families!"

Jeanne spoke from the heart, but Maria's expression was unchanged.

"Then...what of the common people?"

"They love you, Sister! I...never really respected you for it, but the way you sang and danced on the broadcast made a fine lorelei that everyone loved! They're prepared to endure any hardship for you!"

"I imagine they are," Maria murmured, running her fingers along the window glass. "The one the people love, getting them caught up in a war... It's almost as if...I've brought the war upon us."

"No! That's absurd!"

"Jeanne." Maria walked over to Jeanne, took her hand, and wrapped both her own around it. "No matter what happens, I want you to survive. You are not allowed to throw your life away."

"Sister...!" Jeanne gritted her teeth and pulled her hand away. "I will protect you, Sister! I will protect you and our country to the end!" Then, saluting, Jeanne said, "Excuse me," and left the room.

Left behind, Maria dragged herself to the bed and collapsed into it. She turned onto her side, clenched the sheets, and mumbled. "Sir Souma... I really..."

CHAPTER 6
Collision

IN A DARK ROOM at night in Haan Castle, Hashim was pushing pins into a map spread across a desk. One by one, the pins spread across the Empire. At a glance, it was unclear what they might represent. Then...

"Go."

With that curt word from Hashim, a person standing in the shadows silently disappeared. They were a spy in the service of the House of Chima, one who supported Hashim in his plots.

After the figure was gone, Hashim let out a long sigh.

"...Brother," a voice hesitantly called out to him from behind.

"Mutsumi?" Hashim turned to see his younger sister, Mutsumi, the wife of his master. "No, should I call you 'Your Majesty'?"

"Call me...whatever you like." Mutsumi shrugged, pulling up a chair and sitting down next to Hashim. "Is your plan to invade the Gran Chaos Empire going well?"

"Yes. Without a hitch." Hashim smiled coldly as he stroked the map. "Heh heh... I'm grateful to Lord Fuuga. He's let me devise plans I never would have had the chance to see while living in the Duchy of Chima. The men, materiel, and allies I have access to are on an entirely different scale. As a strategist, I couldn't be more excited."

"I'm glad to see you're satisfied... And this is why you cut Father loose?"

"Heh, of course." Hashim laughed at Mutsumi's question. "I made the decision that Father would have in his younger years. This is how the House of Chima has always survived and built our name. I'm sure...when Father died, he entrusted that dream to me."

"Knowing Father, I'm sure he was content with that..."

Given that their father Mathew Chima's last act was to pass Hashim a list of capable people in the Union of Eastern Nations, he likely recognized his son's abilities and was satisfied dying the way he did. Still, Mutsumi felt it was wrong that Sami and others had to be sacrificed, but she wouldn't say this. Her beloved Fuuga had benefited from those sacrifices, so she didn't feel she had the right to object.

Mutsumi shook her head and returned to the matter at hand. "You're using a lot of spies, aren't you? Are their activities going well?"

"Everything proceeds apace. I will seize the initiative with my first stroke."

Seeing the bold smile on his face, Mutsumi said, "I'll be counting on you, Brother."

Broadly speaking, Souma had taken three military actions since he'd been given the throne.

First, there was the series of wars involving the traitors Georg Carmine and Castor Vargas, as well as the Principality of Amidonia. He'd fought against the former of the two differently than he did the latter, but because it all happened in a connected series of events, it was understood to be one military action.

Second, there was his dispatch of troops to the Union of Eastern Nations during the demon wave.

And third, there was his dispatch of the fleet to the (then) Nine-Headed Dragon Archipelago Union to put down Ooyamizuchi.

One thing that proved useful on these three occasions was a type of broadcast that used jewels. In the war with Amidonia, he broadcast his defeat of Georg and the rebels to reduce confusion in his own country and to declare war on Gaius VIII, pulling him onto a well-prepared battlefield. This allowed the forces of the Kingdom to use their greater numbers to overwhelm those of the Principality.

In Souma's third action, the dispatch of the fleet to the Nine-Headed Dragon Archipelago Union, he used the broadcast to hold talks with Nine-Headed Dragon King Shana in front of all the soldiers on both sides. Then, with the "convenient" appearance of Ooyamizuchi, the two countries formed a joint front to slay the massive unidentified creature. If not for those broadcast talks, there would have been a delay in coming to a common agreement, and the soldiers from the two countries wouldn't have been able to coordinate their efforts.

Truly, broadcasts had a major role in Souma's battles. When word of this spread to other countries, there were people in those countries who studied the great impact they could have. You could even say Maria's activities as a lorelei were part of that. And this wasn't limited to the rulers of countries like the Empire, the Republic, and the Archipelago Kingdom that were friendly to the Kingdom of Friedonia. Hashim Chima, advisor to Fuuga Haan of the Great Tiger Kingdom, was also a student of Souma's use of broadcasts.

1552nd year, Continental Calendar.

"People of the Gran Chaos Empire..."

In the fountain plazas of cities small and large across the Empire, the projected image of Fuuga began to speak. It was a clear day. His voice was heard in towns, cities, fishing villages, the mountains, military bases, and Valois Castle.

"I am Fuuga Haan, king of the Great Tiger Kingdom of Haan."

Hashim's first strike was a broadcast jack. The jewel broadcasts ran on a sort of magic frequency, and any jewel could project images on receivers around the continent. This meant that, with an insider who knew the Empire's frequencies, the Great Tiger Kingdom could broadcast throughout the Empire using their own jewel.

That night, Hashim had been sticking pins in the map to show the locations of broadcast receivers, and he had used a sizable portion of his resources on making this broadcast possible.

"People of the Empire. We have risen up to rid mankind of the threat of the Demon Lord's Domain."

The image of Fuuga was addressing the Empire's populace.

"I have unified the Union of Eastern Nations and thrown myself into the struggle to liberate the Demon Lord's Domain for years now. I am sure you all know the task is more than half done. The Great Tiger Kingdom's reach has spread far to the north, and we are now the sole nation shielding mankind from the monsters of the Demon Lord's Domain. However! What has Maria, who issued the Mankind Declaration—claiming the nations of mankind must unite against the Demon Lord's Domain—been doing all this time?"

Fuuga pumped his fist into the air as he made this impassioned speech.

"If I was feeling generous, I could say she was fortifying her defenses. But the fact is, she did nothing to further the liberation of the Demon Lord's Domain! Without proper equipment, we took in the weak and dispossessed, and we reclaimed a huge swath of land with our passion alone! There's no way that the Empire, the largest and most powerful of all mankind's nations, couldn't have done the same! And yet Maria did nothing!"

If Souma were listening, he'd have said "Framing is everything." Yes, Maria could have liberated those territories, but it would be costly to maintain them. Making other regions foot the bill for this would have bred discontent. If the Empire were a group of people with nothing, like Fuuga's forces were, then the people would be used to austerity and think nothing of it. However, under Maria's rule, the people of the Empire had enjoyed a life of stability, so there was great risk in dissatisfying them that had to be avoided. That was why Maria had worked with other nations to fortify their defenses and ensure things didn't get any worse. But for those who didn't understand this, Fuuga's words only stirred their emotions.

"She took in refugees, but she never tried to take back their homelands! She trampled on the feelings of those who longed to return north! This is idle complacency! *We* are trying to fully liberate the Demon Lord's Domain and truly save mankind, but for as long as someone so complacent rules this great nation, mankind can never be united! The people of the north have endured and endured! But they have limits! They can wait for Maria to act no longer!"

Fuuga thrust his fist forward.

"That is why we will raise an army to pull the complacent empress down! This is a battle to remove Maria and bring the Empire under our command. If the Empire follows us, the Maritime Alliance will too. I've wed my own sister, Yuriga, to Souma, leader of the Maritime Alliance. If the will of the people is focused on conquering the Demon Lord's Domain, then Souma—as a man who sees the flow of the times—will go with us too. All mankind can embark on the conquest of the Demon Lord's Domain! Our allies in the Lunarian Orthodox Papal State and Mercenary State Zem have already raised their troops to fight with us!"

When he said that, Fuuga stepped aside and Anne, dressed as a Lunarian Orthodox saint, appeared in his place. Anne put her hands together in front of her and quietly spoke.

"Empress Maria of the Empire has falsely assumed the title of saint. Yet, despite this, she has done nothing against the Demon Lord's Domain. Lady Lunaria would never forgive such a person. Faithful believers of Lady Lunaria, please return to the correct path. I beg you, give your strength to the holy king, Lord Fuuga."

These plainly spoken words were a powerful blow against the Empire.

Unlike how the Kingdom of Friedonia, the Empire had yet to sever the believers in their country from the Lunarian Orthodox Papal State. Because of this, the faithful inside the Empire were confused as to whether or not they should heed Anne's call. And the nonbelievers had to question whether those believers might be collaborating with their enemies. Hashim had used Anne to hammer a huge wedge into the Empire.

The image changed again as Fuuga took Anne's place once more.

"We will march on Valois, where Empress Maria is, with our allies. People of the Empire! If you would join us in this great endeavor, we will welcome you! If you would reject and resist us, then we will answer you with our swords! The choice is yours!" Then, raising his voice, Fuuga declared, "The Great Tiger Kingdom of Haan, the Lunarian Orthodox Papal State, and Mercenary State Zem hereby declare war on the Gran Chaos Empire!"

The combined forces of the Great Tiger Kingdom of Haan, the Lunarian Orthodox Papal State, and Mercenary State Zem (hereafter referred to as Fuuga's forces) crossed the border and invaded the Gran Chaos Empire. Their forces totaled roughly 350,000 men.

Of those, 200,000 were from the Great Tiger Kingdom, 80,000 were Zemish mercenaries, and 70,000 were from the Orthodox Papal State. Because of the size of this force, they could boldly march down roads large enough to accommodate rhino-saurus trains, but they came to a stop at the Empire's Jamona Fortress.

"Hmm, in front of us, the fortress is like an iron wall. And far to our rear is a river, huh?" The Wisdom of the Tiger, Hashim, was at the very front of Fuuga's forces, giving them orders. There was an open area in front of the fortress where he could deploy a great army.

However, the river was not far, and they would need to cross it to invade. Jamona Fortress, which had been built to repel invaders, was nestled between steep mountains, and they had changed the flow of the river to make retreat difficult for their enemies. It was an impregnable fortress with nature itself on its side.

This fortress was constructed because the Empire had been prioritizing expansion to the north at the time—not into the infertile lands of the Republic of Turgis and Zem, or into the Orthodox Papal State, whose religious authority made them difficult to handle. Jamona Fortress was there to keep the nations of the east from interfering as they expanded north, so it was the hardest point in the Empire's defenses.

This also meant they were fully reliant on this fortress to deal with invasions from the east, so they didn't have any defensible positions behind it. If the enemy ever broke through here, they could walk through essentially empty plains all the way to Valois.

Jeanne's 200,000 soldiers had come to the fortress to fight off Fuuga's forces. They had somewhat fewer troops than Fuuga, but many of them—like Gunther—were loyal supporters of the Euphoria sisters, and morale was high. Although Hashim's broadcast jack had shaken up people inside the Empire, it hadn't had that effect on these forces.

A messenger rushed into the forward camp where Gaten, the Flag of the Tiger; Moumei, the Hammer of the Tiger; and Nata, the Battle Ax of the Tiger, were serving with Hashim.

"I have a message! The Imperial forces have come out of Jamona Fortress!"

"What?! They're coming out to meet us?! Awesome!" Nata hefted his ax bravely, but the messenger hurriedly shook his head.

"No! The Imperial forces have come out and are forming into ranks! It looks like they plan to face us on the field instead of in a siege!"

"Huh? They aren't settling in for a siege even though we outnumber them?"

Nata looked perplexed by this report. He'd expected the Empire to shut themselves up inside the fortress because they were at a numerical disadvantage. However, contrary to most expectations, Jeanne had led her soldiers out of the fortress to fight a field battle.

"Ha ha ha! The Imperials sure are bold!" Gaten, the showiest man in Fuuga's forces, said with a jolly laugh. "What do you think they're playing at, Commander?" he asked Hashim, who was beside him, looking through a telescope.

Hashim had been entrusted with commanding the front lines by Fuuga, so he was in charge of the brave and fierce warriors assembled here. He set his telescope down and snorted. "Now I'm sure of it. This area in front of the fortress is too wide open. Normally, the road would narrow as you approached a fortress like this, but this place has enough room for two great armies to clash. And the river is too far to serve as a natural moat."

"So that means?"

"The terrain lets them fight a field battle before the fortress is attacked. And if the attackers are defeated and try to retreat, the river will be in their way. It's a well-designed layout."

"Do they think we're not worthy enough opponents that they need to use the fortress?" Gaten asked, and Hashim patted the telescope next to him.

"There's nothing strange about that. Like us, the Empire has expanded by invading other countries. Their recent rulers have been on a defensive footing, but they understand an army is most valuable on the field of battle."

"I see. They're not good at defending, then?"

"No, I couldn't say one way or the other. But they must be confident in their ability to fight a field battle. They may be thinking that rather than holing up, they'll be able to defend better if they can beat us once on the field of battle first."

"That's how it is, huh... We really can't afford to underestimate them." Gaten crossed his arms and groaned. "So, Commander, how do we attack?"

Hashim smirked. "Let's make this straightforward at first. We'll face them in a straight-up skirmish."

"Oh-hoh. I trust you'll let me lead the vanguard."

Despite the show-off's request, Hashim shook his head. "That, I can't do, I'm afraid. It would be foolish to send you, who won't underestimate the Empire. We must have our men who are underestimating them learn what we're up against."

"So deliberately let them feel the pain?"

"Exactly. After winning all our battles, we're becoming arrogant. They think Fuuga's forces are invincible, we have double the enemy's number, and the Empire is an Empire in decline, unworthy of their fear."

"And you see it differently, Commander?"

"This skirmish is to teach them otherwise. Although, it would be best if we could simply tear through them... Sir Moumei."

Hashim called over Moumei, who was leading the Zemish soldiers on Fuuga's behalf. This mountain of muscle, riding a giant steppe yak and swinging a giant hammer, looked like he had dumped all his stat points into power, but he was also learned enough to be trusted to rule in Zem. He was a talented commander and the best example of not being able to judge a man by his appearance in all of Fuuga's forces.

Once Moumei slowly walked over, Hashim told him, "I want Zemish mercenaries in the vanguard. But you—you're not to get too far forward."

"So you mean to teach them to fear the Imperial soldiers..."

"Precisely. Of all our forces, the Zemish mercenaries are the most likely to underestimate the Empire. They probably still think of themselves as swords for hire. To them, the vain Imperial soldiers are no more than a source of money."

"You must be right. I understand what needs to be done." Moumei bowed and walked away with lumbering steps.

At this point, Nata stood up, unable to sit still any longer.

"Hey, Hashim, my bro. You don't mind me going too, right? I wanna have a go with some Imperial soldiers!"

"We had another idiot here..." Hashim sighed, waving at his brother dismissively. "Oh, very well. Go and do as you please."

"Aw, yeah! I'm gonna scatter those Imperial losers!" Nata grinned now that he had the go-ahead. He hefted his ax and left in a jovial mood.

"Was that all right?" Gaten asked as he watched Nata go.

"Even the finest doctors have no cure for idiocy," Hashim said bluntly. "It will do him good to almost die at least once."

"Ha ha ha..."

Even Gaten, who was known for his raucous laughter, could only smile wryly when he heard that.

Getting back on track, Hashim gave orders to the waiting messenger. "This is a message for all non-Zemish units! We will be fighting a battle with the Imperial soldiers in front of us. When the mercenaries make contact with the enemy, we will support them! However, this is a skirmish to determine the enemy's strength, so don't move too far up! Steel yourselves for battle!"

Thus began the first battle between Fuuga's forces and the Empire.

"Let's cut into the Imperial forces! Show those soldiers from the Empire, the Great Tiger Kingdom, and the Orthodox Papal State the might of Zemish mercenaries!"

"Yeahhhh!"

Moumei, the Hammer of the Tiger, gave the order, and the Zemish mercenaries eagerly charged towards the Imperial forces. To support their charge, the archers and mages of the Great Tiger Kingdom and the Orthodox Papal State let loose on the Imperials as well. The Imperial forces returned fire on the Great Tiger Kingdom and the Orthodox Papal State, starting a long-range battle.

"Have at 'em, boys!"

Meanwhile, the Zemish mercenaries left the shooting to their allies and rushed headlong at the Imperials, polearms at the ready. They blocked the hail of arrows with the bucklers fastened to their arms and prayed that the magic wouldn't strike them as they ran forward.

An infantry charge. It looked reckless, and a cavalry charge would scatter them in an instant, sending them fleeing in defeat. However, the Zemish mercenaries were expecting that cavalry charge. Because, as mercenaries, the cavalry was their golden goose.

There was a sharp glint in their eyes as they looked at the Imperial forces.

"I want someone real showy to come at us!"

"Because the higher their rank, the more ransom they pay!"

"The Empire's wealthy, so we'll make a killing!"

"They'll probably pay good money just to get the heads back!"

"Their weapons and armor'll sell for a good price too!"

"If we can't get ransom money, we'll sell them as slaves. And if we catch any female knights... Ga ha ha!"

"Maria's little sister, Jeanne, was it? She's a fine woman! I wanna capture her!"

The mercenaries made their money on the battlefield. Half of what they were paid went to the country, but whatever they could plunder in terms of weapons, armor, and prisoners was theirs to keep. Career soldiers made money even in peacetime, but mercenaries wouldn't be paid until they moved on to their next battlefield. Their need to earn enough to support themselves during peacetime made them fight harder and act more fiendishly.

In Machiavelli's *The Art of War,* he said of mercenaries, "War makes thieves, and peace hangs them." When people are unable to make a living any other way and are unable to find someone to hire them as soldiers, they become highwaymen in peacetime. That's why the Republic of Florence, which Machiavelli belonged to, worked to establish an army of the people when they attacked the city-state of Pisa.

When she saw these rapacious mercenaries coming at her, Jeanne's face remained calm. "We know how Zemish mercenaries fight. And their weaknesses... Sir Gunther."

"Yes, ma'am!"

As Gunther stood tall at her side, Jeanne gave him his orders.

"Take command of the Magic Armor Corps and crush the Zemish mercenaries. However, if they begin to flee, don't over-extend to pursue them. Just chasing them off for now is fine."

"Yes, ma'am."

With that short acknowledgment, Gunther donned his helmet and shouldered his big shield before quickly walking away. Jeanne watched him go before looking back to the battlefield.

"Fuuga's forces are sacrificing the mercenaries, so we will sacrifice them too."

The Zemish mercenaries specialized in clustering together with long spears, surrounding their enemies to defeat them. In a way, they were a sort of highly mobile phalanx. The magic armor soldiers of the Empire's Magic Armor Corps wore heavy mail that was stained black. They clustered close together with similarly stained black shields and pikes, marching towards the enemy in a neat formation that was either a proper phalanx or a push of pike.

Strangely, this had turned into a battle of polearms versus polearms.

"If they're clustered that tight, we can't surround them! Split 'em up!" the mercenaries shouted when they saw magic armor soldiers on the front line. Those who had bows or could use magic moved forward and began unleashing on the magic armor soldiers.

Countless ranged attacks rained down on the magic armor soldiers. But...

Plink, plink!

"Wha?!"

They could hear their attacks make contact, but the magic armor soldiers continued unfazed—their steps beating a steady rhythm. When they saw this, the mercenaries finally understood what they were facing.

"Magic and arrows don't work on these guys!"

"There's no mistaking that black armor! They're a heavy infantry unit meant for anti-magic combat!"

"The shields of the Empire...the Magic Armor Corps?"

The Magic Armor Corps all wore armor enchanted to nullify magic and marched forward with iron defenses, trampling the enemies of the Empire underfoot. While their march was slow, it was said to be impossible to stop them with ranged attacks.

Gunther, who was in the center of their formation, lifted his spear and said, "Crush them."

"Yeahhhh!"

With his command, their raised pikes swung sharply down on the mercenaries who were looking up in shock.

"Gyargh!"

"Gwugh!"

The pikes didn't stab them; they bludgeoned them to death with a heavy mass of iron. The strikes were powerful enough to cave in their iron helmets, and many mercenaries fell, bleeding from their heads. The magic armor soldiers then marched over the bodies or kicked them out of the way as they advanced.

"If they split us up, we're done for! Form up and push back!" one mercenary shouted.

The other Zemish mercenaries massed together in a line of spears to match their opponents. Many of them had muscles for brains, so it was easy for them to jump on the first suggestion someone made in a rapidly developing situation. This did mean they weren't thinking for themselves, but you could say that it allowed them to work together efficiently. In fact, by forming a line of spears, they were just barely able to stop the magic armor soldiers' advance.

However, once they were massed together... *Boom! Ka-blam!* Suddenly, a black mass came down on them.

It blew apart the mercenaries at the point of impact before digging into the ground. The mercenaries who escaped peered into the newly formed hole to see a cannonball there. The moment they processed what had happened, they felt the ground vibrate under their feet.

They looked up to see a number of creatures with armaments mounted on their backs lumbering towards them. It was the Empire's cannon rhinosauruses—a seemingly self-propelled artillery. The cannon rhinosauruses accompanied the infantry and provided supporting fire.

The mercenaries couldn't have known this, but when Souma was occupying Van, the capital of the Principality of Amidonia, he and Hakuya didn't know what to do when they saw the magic armor soldiers and cannon rhinosauruses surrounding the city. Those were the same cannon rhinosauruses that Jeanne had sent along to support the magic armor soldiers.

After being bombarded with cannonballs when they were already under pressure from the magic armor soldiers, the mercenaries couldn't take any more. They were ready to flee at any moment.

"Out of my way!"

Suddenly, a big man charged through the mercenaries to the front. Then, using his big ax, he came out swinging at the magic armor soldiers.

"Take this!"

Simply put, he swung the ax with all his might. However, with that one strike, he struck first blood against the as-yet-unharmed magic armor soldiers, knocking some backwards and sending them colliding with ones positioned in the rear.

"Oh. You're just hard, that's all."

Shouldering his ax and glaring at them was Nata, the Battle Ax of the Tiger. The magic armor soldiers swung their pikes at Nata, but he deflected them with a powerful swing of his ax, and his next strike sent more of them flying.

"You're relying on how hard your armor is? That's not gonna stop me!"

When Nata swung his ax down, his blows were powerful enough to deform their armor, even if he couldn't cut it clean in half. It was horrible enough that whoever was inside couldn't survive. Because the magic armor soldiers advanced in formation, it was difficult for them to take on a single opponent. The rhinosaurus cannons that were supporting them couldn't target an individual either.

If you looked at the larger picture, the magic armor soldiers were pushing back the mercenaries, but there was a strange indentation in their formation where Nata was.

Elated to finally have the chance he'd wanted to let loose, Nata roared, "Who's next?!"

"I won't let you do this."

Clang! Gunther knocked Nata's big ax away using only his shield. The deflected blow tore into a mercenary who happened to be in its way.

"Gwargh!"

"Damn it! Who are you?!"

"Gunther... The Euphoria sisters' shield."

Having answered Nata's question, Gunther cast aside the pike he was holding and drew his sword.

Nata watched him with the eyes of a predator. "So you're a renowned general. This is gonna be fun! I'll take you on!"

"You cur."

The sound of the impact echoed as Nata's ax and Gunther's shield collided. Gunther used his shield to redirect Nata's ax, looking for an opening to strike back with his sword—which Nata avoided as he kept on swinging. With each swing of Nata's ax, Gunther's shield became more and more crushed. The power between these two men was incredible.

"Sir Gunther!"

"Ngh?!"

A person appeared behind Gunther and used his shoulders as a springboard to leap over Nata's head and get behind him.

"What?!"

Before Nata could turn and swing, the person in question had closed in, placing their palm on his muscular torso.

"Hahhhh!"

With a cry of exertion, they unleashed a bolt of lightning. The stabbing pains that raced through Nata's entire body made him grunt and stumble as he tried to cut his assailant down.

Gunther held up his battered shield and charged in, knocking the larger Nata away. Standing with the person who had arrived safely behind him, he said, "Madam Jeanne... What did you come here for?"

"Because I'd be in a tough spot if anything were to happen to you so early in the battle!"

The person who'd intervened was none other than the Little Sister General of the Empire, Jeanne Euphoria.

Jeanne saw this first exchange as no more than a skirmish for them to gauge each other's abilities, but Nata had charged in despite it being that early stage. When she saw Gunther struggling against him, she'd rushed in to prevent the worst from happening. Although Gunther was angry at her recklessness, he restrained himself.

"When we return, I'll have Lady Maria give you a talking-to," Gunther said.

"Normally, it's the other way around. I wouldn't mind something different for a change."

Jeanne smiled, but she didn't take her eyes off Nata. Her point-blank lightning and Gunther's powerful tackle had hit Nata hard enough that he still couldn't move very well yet.

"Damn it all!"

He might have broken a rib. However, he was still eager and willing to fight.

"I'd say it's about time..."

Meanwhile, Moumei, who had been watching from the rear, decided the mercenaries had seen enough to instill a proper fear of the Imperials in them.

He raised his hammer aloft, and shouted, "We're done here! Everyone, retreat! And don't forget to retrieve Sir Nata!"

With the order to withdraw given, the mercenaries fell over one another fleeing. Some mercenaries were slow to retreat and ended up taking a magic armor soldier's pike in the back, but the scattered withdrawal actually made it harder for the slower magic armor soldiers to give chase. As Moumei, Nata, and the mercenaries fled, the forces of the Great Tiger Kingdom and the Orthodox Papal State pulled back too.

After watching this, Jeanne and Gunther pulled their own forces back into the fortress.

It was fair to call this first exchange a victory for the Empire.

The battle between Fuuga's forces and the Empire's raged on. The once enthusiastic Zemish mercenaries grew cautious after their initial loss, and followed Moumei's (and by extension Hashim's) orders. In a winning battle, mercenaries were courageous in order to maximize their profit and accomplishments. But in the face of a tough opponent, saving their own lives took priority. They wanted money—just without risking their lives for it. They were just being true to that natural human instinct.

Nata the battle maniac was sent to the rear with the heavy wounds he took on the first day, so there was no one left on the front line to charge in like a barbarian. The attackers didn't overextend, and the defenders were careful. In a straightforward battle like this, it was the forces of the Orthodox Papal State that proved most effective.

"This is a crusade for Holy King Fuuga," Anne, the saint of Lunarian Orthodoxy, said to her countrymen. "Defeat the pawns of the false saint Maria and offer victory to our Lady Lunaria."

Anne wasn't large, but her voice carried well. Her expression was unchanging—her tone bereft of emotion, as if a doll were speaking, but in a way that lent her an unearthly air.

To the believers, her words were a literal message from the heavens.

"Ohh! Victory to our Holy King! And to our saint!"

"The blessing of Lady Lunaria is upon us! What do we have to fear?!"

"Even if we die, we will be taken to Lady Lunaria's side!"

The forces of the Orthodox Papal State included many volunteers in addition to the regular military. They were peasant soldiers without proper equipment, but they lived for the faith and would gladly die for it too. They attacked the Imperial forces prepared to do so.

"Here they come! Defend!" Gunther ordered the magic armor soldiers.

The Empire's magic armor soldiers were terrifyingly strong, and Fuuga's forces would not forget the terror of that first day. But the Orthodox Papal State's forces charged in without hesitation.

"Bring God's judgment on the evil Empire!"

"For Lady Lunaria! For the saint!"

The people who shouted these things—carrying equipment that paled in comparison to the mercenaries'—rushed heedlessly onward until they were impaled on a wall of pikes. They believed dying here would let them go to Lady Lunaria's paradise.

The two main pillars of Lunarian Orthodox teaching were mutual support and helping the weak. It was simple and easy to understand. And yet, religious leaders interpreted the teachings to their own benefit, creating a system of holy war and believers who would fight for the faith. Their religious zeal meant they didn't fear death. That was why they would charge in regardless of who they faced, like the Ikko-ikki of Japan's Sengoku period.

Naturally, the Orthodox Papal State's forces took heavy losses. It looked like a massacre or even a mass suicide. However, faced with these men who, unafraid of death, climbed over the dead bodies of their brothers-in-arms to attack them, the elite magic armor soldiers were worn down and pushed back.

The battle was at a standstill. The attackers couldn't push through, but the defenders couldn't push back. It was a war of attrition.

Saint Anne was watching it unfold from the Orthodox Papal State's main camp. The men she'd stirred up fought, shed blood, and fell dead. She had simply performed her role as a saint and as a tool. But as she stood there, unable to do more, she heard a voice that was still echoing in her ears.

"Do you understand the fate that awaits you?"

They were the words of Mary, who had fled the Orthodox Papal State.

Anne remembered their brief meeting in their homeland. She recalled the mixture of sadness, hesitation, and pity in Mary's eyes as she'd regarded her. Anne didn't understand why Mary looked at her that way. She'd been chosen as a saint, so she would fulfill her duties as one.

Even now, Anne was doing as people expected of her, assuming the attitude of a saint. Her voice delighted the believers, allowing them to cast aside their fear of death and go to the battlefield. She was being useful. It gave her a reason to exist. For Anne, an orphan who'd had no place in society, this was something to be happy about. Yet, why had Mary looked at her that way?

"Once you see the broader world... In the Kingdom, you'll be able to find a life other than as a saint."

That was what she'd said as she extended her hand to Anne.

But Anne couldn't see the value in what she was proposing. After that, Mary had left the Orthodox Papal State with a large number of other saint candidates. They were excommunicated, but the church of Lunarian Orthodoxy in the Kingdom of Friedonia took them in.

If I took Mary's hand then, would it have changed anything?

That was what Anne pondered in the copious amounts of free time she had after sending the soldiers to the battlefield. Though, think as she might...there was no answer forthcoming, so she stopped.

As she did, a soldier, pale of face and bleeding from the chest, was carried in. He must have taken a serious wound on the battle-field.

"Ah! Your Grace!"

"Please, leave!"

Ignoring her bodyguards, Anne approached the wounded soldier. He groaned in pain, but his joy was evident when he saw Anne's face.

"Ohh... Your Grace... I'm sorry to show myself before you in this piteous state..."

"There is nothing piteous about it. You have fought well as a believer in Lady Lunaria."

"Thank you for your kind words... Now, will I be able to go to her side...?"

He reached out his right hand, seemingly bloodied from holding his wounds, towards Anne. The guards tried to come between them, but Anne held her ground, taking the man's hand without hesitation and unconcerned as the sleeve of her white raiment was stained crimson.

"Yes. Lady Lunaria sees everything you have done," Anne answered in a calm voice.

The man seemed satisfied with this. He smiled and said no more. Anne placed the hand she'd taken gently on the man's chest, and then he was carried away.

Anne clutched her bloodstained sleeve. The man had looked so incredibly peaceful. As a saint, she had sent him to his death. As a saint, she was able to grant him salvation. Both were her job as a saint. However...Anne neither regretted nor relished any of it. She had merely played the role she had been given.

"Lady Anne... Do you require a change of clothes?" one of her guards said, unable to watch her just stand there.

"This is the blood of a noble spirit who fell for our faith. How is that unclean?" Anne said, looking to the battlefield once more.

Souma struggled with the title of king, and Maria with the title of saint. But despite this, they never stopped thinking as normal people. Even if the weight of their positions nearly crushed them, their love for their countries made them hold back at the brink, never falling into just playing a role.

Anne, on the other hand, shut her heart off, committing to the role of saint entirely, in order to protect herself. So that even as she got blood on her hands, she could continue to be a saint.

One night, after several days of fighting...

"Well, the Empire sure knows how to put up a fight," Gaten said with a hearty laugh.

Inside a large tent with a campfire, Hashim, Gaten, Moumei, and Kasen were holding a council around a model of the battlefield and the surrounding terrain.

"Their defenses are hard, and their morale high. None of them are intimidated by Lord Fuuga's glory. They're definitely the toughest opponents we've fought so far."

"It's nothing to laugh about, Sir Gaten," the serious Crossbow of the Tiger, Kasen Shuri, remonstrated him.

"Their tactics are precise too. We tried to send a detachment around the back of the fortress, but were intercepted by troops who'd anticipated the move. They're limiting their losses while gradually grinding us down. I thought that maybe the Empress's little sister got her post through nepotism, but she's no ordinary general," Kasen said, frustrated because he was the one to lead that detachment.

Jamona Fortress was built on naturally defensible terrain, making it remarkably resilient against a frontal attack, but there were narrow gaps in the mountains that looked like they went through to the other side. Kasen's detachment had used those narrow paths to try and attack the fortress from the inside, but there had been enemies lying in wait, forcing them to retreat.

The experience had given Kasen an idea of what Jeanne's goals were.

"She's left gaps deliberately because she knows the narrow paths well. It's easier for her to do damage to a small detached force than it is against a full-frontal assault by the main army."

"On top of that, she has the guts to charge in solo like Nata. She's a great general with both brains and brawn." Moumei offered a few words of praise for Jeanne.

Gaten shrugged in exasperation. "I guess that makes her like our Shuukin? Could we have Sir Shuukin come here from the rear?"

Shuukin was in the rear, defending their supply lines. He'd been placed there because the debt of gratitude he felt towards the Kingdom and the Empire for saving him from Magic Bug Disease raised concerns that it might blunt his willingness to fight. Hashim was unwilling to trust someone hesitant to manage the front lines, and Fuuga didn't want to lose Shuukin to any blunders caused by that hesitation.

However, that conservative decision had proved effective.

Hashim shook his head and said, "The Empire never misses an opportunity. If we neglect to defend our rear, they will target us there in no time. If our supply lines are cut, we would struggle to maintain such a large army without food. We need a great general like Sir Shuukin defending them."

"In other words, we have to do something about the front line ourselves," Gaten said, shrugging again.

"Oh, it won't be much longer now," Hashim retorted, a smirk forming on his face.

"I have a report!"

As if spoken into existence, a messenger came up. They saluted, then approached Hashim to whisper in his ear. As he listened, the corners of Hashim's mouth turned up to form a shape like a crescent moon. That deranged grin sent chills down the other three commanders' spines.

Hashim rose to his feet and told them, "The preparations are complete. Let's go put on the finishing touches."

To make tomorrow's sun the setting sun of the Empire.

The next day...

Jeanne and Gunther stood on the walls of Jamona Fortress, surveying the camps of the Imperial forces.

"We're pushing them back...for now," Jeanne said to Gunther, who was beside her. "Their assault is fierce, but if we keep knocking them back, they're the ones who'll run out of breath first. We need to hold out as long as we can and wait for their morale to decrease."

"That is the only way we can win, after all," Gunther said gravely. Maria had called for a common front between all of mankind, so she had no intention of counterinvading the Empire. That forced them onto a defensive footing.

At the same time, as the mightiest of all nations, they had no allies they could ask to support them. Even the Kingdom of Friedonia, with whom they had a secret pact against the Demon Lord's Domain, would have had trouble moving against the Great Tiger Kingdom. If the Empire was going to win this and achieve something in this war, they had to win the battle of attrition, then pursue the enemy as they fled and deal major damage.

Jeanne crossed her arms and touched her chin. "What concerns me is that no one has seen Fuuga yet. I heard he was a wild man who enjoys fighting on the front lines..."

"Would it not be a bad idea for the commander-in-chief of a composite force like theirs to go too far to the front?"

It was true that while Fuuga was used to fighting alongside the soldiers of the Great Tiger Kingdom, there were also Zemish mercenaries and soldiers from the Orthodox Papal State in his current army. If he ventured to the front and went down like Nata did on the first day, that would be a major hit to his forces' morale. Were Jeanne his advisor, she'd have told him in no uncertain terms that he absolutely should not go to the front. Nonetheless, it still concerned her.

"Fuuga's forces sent a diversionary force to the north too, right? I'm suspecting that Fuuga could be with them..."

"Given the intensity of their attacks, I'd say the bulk of their forces must be here."

"Agreed. I don't doubt this is their main force."

Even if Fuuga was with the diversionary force, he wouldn't be able to lead a vastly inferior army to any great military victory. Krahe alone ought to be enough to deal with him.

Still, Jeanne couldn't wipe her concerns away. And they would prove to be well-founded.

On that day, even once the sun rose, there was no attack on the fortress. Jeanne was wary, wondering what was happening. In the afternoon, she saw a massive water ball forming over Fuuga's camp.

Jeanne ordered her forces to remain alert as she glared at the ball.

They must mean to use the broadcast again, she thought.

Before this battle, Hashim had used it to sow confusion inside the Empire, so Jeanne expected more propaganda.

But what are they going to broadcast now...?

Now that the broadcasts had been used to sow confusion once, if the Empire was shown information they already knew, the viewers would simply think, "This again?" The effect wouldn't be as strong the second time around, nor would it cause the same chaos as before.

Does he have another trick up his sleeve?

Suddenly—

"Ah?!"

When they saw the scene projected on that ball of water, Jeanne and every other person in Jamona Fortress gulped. It was a shocking image, but there wasn't pandemonium. That was because the scenery they were shown was unbelievable.

"This is absurd! Fuuga's main army is here!" Jeanne shouted, punching the edge of the fortress wall.

Gunther's eyes were wide too. For the image projected in the water ball was Valois, surrounded by a massive force...

HOW A REALIST HERO REBUILT THE KINGDOM

CHAPTER 7

Falling Flowers,
Flowing Water

WEEKS BEFORE the capital was surrounded...

"Oh, *why*, Your Majesty?!" lamented Krahe Laval, commander of the Empire's main air force—the griffon squadrons.

With Fuuga's forces on the verge of attacking, Krahe, who venerated Maria as a saint, had been in high spirits. He thought the time had finally come for him to fight invaders for his liege. However, Maria's orders to him were to join the knights and nobles of the north to intercept Fuuga's forces. The former vassals in the Kingdom of Meltonia and the Frakt Federation were being used to invade the Empire itself.

The Empire's prediction was that the main force would attack from the Lunarian Orthodox Papal State and Mercenary State Zem, so the forces in the north were merely a diversion. This meant Krahe had been excluded from the decisive battle. He felt betrayed.

"Oh, Your Majesty! Why will you not let me fight for you?! General Gunther and half of our griffon squadrons are fighting in the decisive battle, and yet I am not granted the same honor?! I, who would throw my very life away for you without hesitation!"

Krahe shed tears as he repeatedly punched the table. He might have been hitting it too hard because his knuckles were bleeding.

Someone silently approached Krahe from behind.

"Ah—! Who's there?!"

Krahe drew his rapier faster than the eye could see, leveling it at the person who was behind him. With the tip of his blade at the person's throat, they calmly raised both hands.

"It's me, Sir Krahe."

"Madam Lumiere...? I apologize."

After realizing who it was, Krahe sheathed his rapier. Before him was Lumiere, the Empire's top bureaucrat. She had a domain in the north and was a former military officer, so she had joined Krahe's forces with her personal troops.

Lumiere shook her head. "No, I shouldn't have crept up on you. You seemed tormented by something, so I thought a little surprise might help you to loosen up..."

"Thank you for your concern..." Krahe thanked her, then looked away.

"I understand how you must feel..." Lumiere whispered to him. "You're afraid, aren't you?"

"Ah! What are you talking about, Madam Lumiere?!" Krahe sounded wounded by the accusation. "I am the sword of Saint Maria! No matter what opponents I face, no matter how great their numbers, I will show no fear! I shall slay them and offer my victory to Lady Maria!"

"That's just it," Lumiere said in a quiet voice. "I'm sure that you fear no enemy. What you're afraid of is something different. Something close to the root of your pride. In other words..." Lumiere pointed her index finger at Krahe. "Maria becoming an ordinary person."

"Wha?!"

Krahe was speechless. He mulled over what Lumiere had meant, trying to come up with a response. But he came up empty-handed and said nothing.

Lumiere looked at Krahe as she continued. "It's true that you're Her Majesty's loyal knight. You would rise against any enemy for her, even cast your own life aside. However, that is because she is a saint, respected by the people, and you take pride in protecting that saint. In short, you need her to shine so that you can shine yourself. If something caused her to lose her radiance, you would have nothing to fight for. You're afraid of that. Afraid of not being the saint's knight anymore. Am I wrong?"

"Madam Lumiere. You..." Confused, Krahe thought, *Why would you say that?*

He felt like her assertion got to the core of his recent struggles. If she was right, it would explain all his tormented feelings up until now.

But why choose now to tell me?

As he wondered, Lumiere seemed to look off into the distance.

"I've felt the same thing, Sir Krahe."

"Madam Lumiere?"

"I was originally seeking to become a military commander. In childhood, I talked with my friend Jeanne about how I wanted to join her and use our martial abilities to support her elder sister. However, a training mishap cut off that path for me, and I was forced to retrain to become a bureaucrat instead. That was fine. If Her Majesty would smile and say, 'I'm counting on you,' I was ready to do my best for her, even if I was taking a different path from Jeanne. And so I rose to the top of the bureaucracy."

After saying all this, Lumiere shook her head, sensing she'd gotten too heated.

"However, Her Majesty has been too passive about everything recently. Our actions against the Demon Lord's Domain are purely defensive, and even after Fuuga began making a name for himself by liberating those lands, we did nothing. The Maritime Alliance grows steadily stronger, but she doesn't sense a threat—she even turns to them for support in times of crisis. Wasn't she a saint who could lead people? I wanted some sense that I was serving the right ruler, even if it was as a bureaucrat."

With all of that said, Lumiere looked straight into Krahe's eyes.

"What about you, Sir Krahe?"

"What...do you mean?"

"Can you bear to see Her Majesty fall to nothing more than an ordinary human like this? Even if we manage to fend off Fuuga's forces now, I doubt she'll do anything like launching an offensive into the Great Tiger Kingdom. Rather than settle things, she'll take a conciliatory path, trying not to make things any bigger than they already are. No different from how she has been."

Krahe looked at her, unable to answer.

"Can you accept that? Even though it means losing her radiance?"

"I..."

"Sir Krahe, here's a thought for you. If Her Majesty is going to become an ordinary person...perhaps it's her knight's duty to end her while she's still a saint."

Lumiere's words sent a shudder down Krahe's spine.

Not of fear, however. No, of *excitement*.

He could end Maria while she was still a saint. Let the liege he'd wanted to shine end while she still did. These were sweet words to Krahe's warped sense of loyalty. He was prepared to give his life for Saint Maria. No matter the shame it may bring him, he was prepared. He could become any sort of villain for Maria's saintly radiance. He didn't care if the people who loved Saint Maria hated and abhorred him. If Saint Maria could remain a beautiful legend, he would welcome being killed, his grave defiled, and his bones scattered in the field for wild beasts.

This is it! My duty!

Krahe felt like he'd received a sign from heaven.

Seeing the ominous light in Krahe's eyes, Lumiere continued. "Many in the north hold a grudge against the House of Euphoria. If you and I go to persuade them, it would be easy to make them switch sides. If we take that army to join up with Fuuga's, we can encircle the capital. If even that's not enough to awaken Her Majesty to her role as saint, well..."

"You would have us lower the curtain on her ourselves, yes?" Krahe said with a dignified expression. Anyone could see he'd totally lost it.

It may have seemed strange to say his loyalty hadn't faltered in the slightest, but Krahe really was doing this for Maria. He would kill Maria *for* Maria. In his mind, this wasn't a contradiction.

That went well...

Lumiere was relieved at his reaction. She was still clearheaded compared to Krahe. There was no lie in what she'd told him, but what Lumiere desired to serve was not a passive empire but a great power that was doing things. With the path of becoming an officer in the military closed to her, she had been afraid that if she couldn't shine now, her whole life would be summed up as unfortunate.

That was why, when Hashim sent her the plan, she immediately accepted. To give her life meaning.

I feel bad for Jeanne... But I'm going to follow my own path.

Even if that meant parting ways with her friend forever.

And so, Krahe and Lumiere moved into action. They took only those who would go along with their plans to meet Fuuga's forces in the northeast.

The north of the Empire was upset with Maria's handling of the natural disasters, and many of the knights and nobles were unhappy with the House of Euphoria to begin with, so most joined the pair. Some houses wouldn't join them in their scheme, but they ignored them and didn't include them in their forces.

With that, an Imperial force composed only of those who agreed with them joined Fuuga's forces in the northeast instead of blocking their path, and together they headed down the road to the Imperial capital.

This was how Valois came to be surrounded.

Falling Flowers, Flowing Water

(1) Depicts the end of spring. The flowers fall and drift away in the water. By extension, refers to rot and decline.

(Four-Character Compound Dictionary, Gakken Educational Publishing)

In the violent currents of this era, a flower was about to fall...

The Imperial capital of Valois was surrounded by a combined force of 25,000 troops consisting of a detachment from Fuuga's army and the forces of the anti-Euphoria faction from the lords of the north led by Lumiere. The Imperial defenders numbered only 3,000, so it was clear that they could not hold. The battle had been decided the moment Krahe, who had gone to intercept Fuuga's detachment, switched sides.

Fuuga and Mutsumi were with the Great Tiger Kingdom's forces, as was the venerable commander Gaifuku, whom they had brought as a bodyguard. Their principal allies and elite warriors had gone to attack Jamona Fortress, but the three came with this group because they knew from the beginning that it was here that the war would be decided.

"I never thought we'd be attacking the capital so quickly..." Fuuga said, looking half impressed and half disappointed.

"Ga ha ha! I'll bet!" Gaifuku replied with a big nod. "We were just a little country on the steppes in the Union of Eastern Nations, and now we've got a sword to the throat of the largest nation on the continent. The things you see when you live to my age... I wish I could have shown this to your father, Lord Raiga."

"So do I... It's a bit of a letdown for me, though."

Fuuga had been imagining tearing through the Imperial soldiers that blocked his way to the capital as his sharp blade approached the Empire's throat. But the reality was that he passed through largely unobstructed, making it all the way here without so much as increasing the pace his troops were marching.

Mutsumi smiled wryly at his reaction. "It must be thanks to my brother finding Madam Lumiere. He focused his efforts on her, and she became essential to the plan."

"You've got a point..." Fuuga grunted, crossing his arms. "She not only brought together the lords who were opposed to the House of Euphoria, but she's also the top of the Imperial bureaucracy. That means she has experience managing a great nation, and many of the people she's trained will be highly capable too. She's exactly the person we needed to fix our shortage of administrators."

Having said this, Fuuga gave an exasperated shrug.

"This expedition was already more than successful enough for us when we got our hands on her. Even if we take the capital now, it's just an added bonus."

"Hee hee, if you say something like, 'I took the Imperial capital, but taking Lumiere was far more rewarding,' they might put it down in a list of your famous quotes."

"Ha ha ha! I like it! Have the chronicler write that down!" Fuuga said with a jolly laugh.

"You're too kind," said Lumiere, who had arrived with Krahe at just that moment.

They knelt before Fuuga, heads lowered, then Lumiere spoke up again.

"I thank you for allowing us to serve under your banner and trusting us to persuade the lords of the north. From here on, I will risk my life in service to your great work, Lord Fuuga."

"Hmm. That's a good show of determination, but don't you care about Maria?" Fuuga asked.

Lumiere raised her face and looked him in the eye. "I believe she was a good ruler, but...our views did not match. She had everything she required to take the whole of the continent, and yet she's remained passive. I advised her on many occasions that she should be more proactive towards the Demon Lord's Domain, but she rejected my advice and continued wasting time. I couldn't bear to see the people's burning passion for a world without the Demon Lord's Domain dying, and see the flames of my own passion dying with it. That is why I chose to place my bets on you."

"Makes sense…"

He could see the fire in Lumiere's eyes.

If Maria could have done anything about the Demon Lord's Domain, she no doubt would have wanted to. But she and Lumiere had disagreed on the amount of time needed to solve the problem. Maria wanted to address it slowly, as the issue of the Demon Lord's Domain was one that could destroy her country. She wanted to keep losses to a minimum and solve it in due time. She had been laying the groundwork so that even if it wasn't resolved during her reign, it could be during the next one or the one after that.

Lumiere, meanwhile, thought they should act to solve the problem immediately.

If the refugees were suffering as they watched, and if there was an unknown threat to the north, they needed to do something right away. Even if that meant drastic action, the kind that would strain the nation, she wanted to do something with her own hands. There was a slight desire for personal fame in that wish, but that was something everyone had to one degree or another, and it wasn't something to be faulted for.

This difference in opinion created an irreconcilable rift between the two of them. There was no way, at the present moment, to know who was right. In fact, even later generations wouldn't be able to tell. It was all in the world of "what if," and it could be that both were right or that both were wrong. Other than that, it was just a matter of personal preference—and Fuuga's forces preferred the latter.

Fuuga snorted and turned up the corners of his lips. "It looks like I won't need to warn you not to betray me. As long as you have that passion and keep your spirit burning, you're never going to want to leave us."

"Indeed."

"Ha ha ha! I like you. You're a good fit for my forces," Fuuga said with a laugh, then turned to Krahe. "And can I assume you're going to serve me too?"

"I don't want to see Lady Maria fall and become a mere human. That is why I want to take her life now, while she can still remain a beautiful memory."

"That's some darkness in your eyes..."

Looking into Krahe's eyes, Fuuga sensed the man was a mass of dark emotions, but they spoke to a strong will. For that reason, he could be sure Krahe wouldn't betray him. Although, once Maria was dead, that passion would be lost, and he might be left as no more than an empty husk...

Fuuga nodded to the two of them.

"Got it. Both of you work hard for me from here on."

"Yes, sir!" they replied in unison.

"All right, Lumiere. Hashim told me to ask you what happens next."

"Right. After conferring with Sir Hashim, this is what I've prepared to do," she replied, then raised her hand.

Seeing this, her men brought over a broadcast jewel to them.

"A jewel, huh?"

"Indeed. First, we will broadcast these images of us surrounding the capital to the entire Empire—which is the same as us having won a strategic victory. That includes the main army fighting at Jamona Fortress, of course. Sir Hashim will be gathering water mages and preparing to show them. I'm sure it will deal a heavy blow to Jeanne and the other defenders."

Lumiere rose and extended her hand towards Valois.

"And we will call on Maria to surrender. If she agrees, we win. If she does not, we will destroy her. After seeing that, if Jeanne tries to return to the capital, Sir Hashim and your main forces will strike her from behind."

"Layers upon layers of traps. Impressive..." Mutsumi said, and Fuuga nodded.

"If Souma has Hakuya and Julius, then I have Hashim and Lumiere."

"Hee hee. That will go down as one of your famous quotes too." Mutsumi laughed and shot him a mischievous smile.

And that is how the image of the capital surrounded came to be broadcast at Jamona Fortress too.

The sight of it threw Jeanne into disarray. She punched the edge of the fortress wall repeatedly. Fighting the urge to question if it could even be real, she shook her head and resolved to do *something*.

"Damn it! I must go save Sister at once!"

"Calm yourself!" Gunther shouted, causing Jeanne and all the soldiers nearby to stop.

When the usually taciturn general raised his voice, everyone stopped and paid attention.

Gunther brought his hands down on Jeanne's shoulders. "If you lose your presence of mind, our forces will collapse on the spot! The enemy before us won't allow our forces to abandon the fortress and return to the capital! They would attack us from behind. Even if we arrive before the city falls, it will be impossible for us to save them if we're bloodied from that sort of battle!"

Jeanne gasped. The feeling of Gunther's grip on her shoulders brought her back to her senses.

"But if we don't act, my sister is doomed... What can we do?"

"Well..."

Seeing that Jeanne had calmed down a little, and reassured that she wouldn't run off all of a sudden, Gunther let go of her shoulders.

Then, looking at the image of the Imperial capital, he said, "Saving the capital will be impossible. We could never make it in time. If Her Imperial Majesty could just escape and come join us, we would have options..."

"She'd never! My sister couldn't abandon the people of the capital..."

Jeanne pressed a hand to her forehead and hung her head. She couldn't imagine Maria, with her saintly kindness, leaving the citizens of the capital behind when they were at the brink of facing the fires of war. If anything, Maria might willingly give up her own life to avoid getting the people caught up in the conflict. That was the kind of woman she was.

The soldiers began to raise a ruckus. Jeanne looked up and saw Fuuga's image being projected.

"This is a message for Saint Maria of the Empire!" Fuuga's image began. "The Imperial capital is already surrounded. Most of your forces are at Jamona Fortress and likely aren't gonna make it back here in time. At the swing of my arm, my forces will storm the capital, reducing its historical townscape and citizenry to ash. That's not what you want, Maria! Open the gates and bravely surrender! I swear on my own name, Fuuga Haan, that the unarmed people will go unharmed!"

This was an ultimatum from Fuuga.

"There's no point in arguing who's right and who's wrong here. This war happened because we have two irreconcilable viewpoints. You want to protect the present, while I am trying to win us a future. And my side is about to win this fight! Many of your own people who couldn't abide by your views are with me. My being here right now is their answer to you! They support *us*!"

The moment Fuuga said that, a great cheer erupted from the Great Tiger Kingdom's forces in front of the fortress. They must have felt certain of their victory.

The Imperial soldiers in the fortress, on the other hand, were silent, as if the wind had been knocked out of them. They were beginning to feel that, struggle as they might, there was no turning this one around.

"I'm counting on you to make the smart choice—"

Just as Fuuga was finishing his ultimatum, his image vanished. The scenery changed, and a woman was projected instead.

A beautiful woman in a dress standing on a balcony of some sort high up in the castle.

"Sister!" Jeanne cried out despite herself. It was indeed her, Empress Maria Euphoria.

"First, to General Jeanne, who I am sure is watching this... I have an order for you and for the soldiers at Jamona Fortress. Please, put up a water ball so you can hear me clearly."

The moment Jeanne heard this, she gave the order. "Have our water mages prepare a water ball at once!"

"Yes, ma'am!"

This was likely in case Fuuga's forces dispelled the water ball in their camp.

Sister is about to tell us something important... Jeanne sensed. The soldiers hurried to obey her command, and soon there was a water ball above the walls of Jamona Fortress as well. The ball raised by Fuuga's forces and the ball raised by the Imperials both showed the image of Maria.

After a short delay, Maria continued. "The Great Tiger Kingdom used the broadcast to send a message demanding surrender all across the Empire. That being the case, this message should reach everyone in the country too. I ask all people of the Empire, and of the Great Tiger Kingdom, to lend me your ears for a moment."

Maria looked straight at them as she spoke.

"It is fair to say that I have been passive in my approach to the Demon Lord's Domain. That is because of the great loss that was suffered by the combined forces of mankind more than a decade ago. It was my father, the former emperor, who led that force, and we were all so confident then that with so much power amassed we could crush any enemy. This resulted in the annihilation of our combined force. With our forces massively weakened, we were unable to resist the monsters that came south. Many countries were destroyed, creating refugees."

Maria spoke quietly and eloquently, and the soldiers of the Empire, and even those of the Great Tiger Kingdom, listened without heckling. Then Maria brought her hands together in front of her chest in a gesture like she was praying.

"When inertia is on our side, we tend to feel like we can do anything. We think that with the winds at our backs, no enemy can stand in our way. The more powerful our country is, the stronger this tendency becomes. However, this creates a trap for us. We have no way of knowing how far that inertia will last. People can never know when the winds of the era will turn because we are not gods. Even so, if we assume everything will be fine, we are guaranteed to get tripped up at some point. Yes, just as the combined force did..."

Maria trailed off, allowing some time for those watching to absorb her words.

"That is why I did not actively attack the Demon Lord's Domain... Instead, I focused on creating a framework for all of mankind to cooperate against it. I wanted to ensure no more countries were destroyed—no more refugees were created. It is true that my methods did not solve the fundamental problem. It may be right to call that negligence on my part."

"No!" Jeanne shouted despite herself. "You tried to change the situation! You sought to find a path peacefully—cooperating with other countries—and to walk it steadily, step by step! You were not negligent!"

This was especially frustrating for Jeanne. Having held broadcast meetings with Prime Minister Hakuya of the Kingdom of Friedonia and taken responsibility for their diplomacy with the Kingdom, Jeanne knew everything Souma and Maria had done together. Now people who didn't know any of that were calling Maria negligent, and she felt she couldn't blame them for it.

Maria continued on, not addressing Jeanne's feelings on the matter. "I can see from here that Lumiere, who supported me by managing our nation domestically; Krahe, the commander of our griffon squadrons; and many lords and knights from the north of the Empire are all collaborating with the Great Tiger Kingdom."

Maria's words sent a worried murmur through the troops.

"No, not Lumiere…"

"Sir Krahe! I can't believe he, of all people, would do this…"

Jeanne and Gunther were equally shocked. Jeanne had known Lumiere was ambitious but still believed her to be a friend, and Gunther knew of Krahe's insane love and respect for Maria, so neither could hide their surprise at these defections. And yet, at the same time, they understood. The capital was completely surrounded because those two, along with the knights and lords of the north, had all flocked to Fuuga's banner. It was the same for people across the Empire watching the broadcast.

"Lady Maria! Oh…"

"Ah... This... This can't be happening."

"Somebody, anybody, save her!"

The people watching the broadcast wailed in despair.

There were those among the knights and nobles who did not look fondly on the House of Euphoria, but Maria was loved by the people. Everyone watched in confusion and panic, wondering how they might save her. But, unarmed as they were, there was nothing they could do. Nothing but cry.

Even so, Maria continued speaking with a brave face.

"You asked for concrete measures against the Demon Lord's Domain, but I never nodded my head. No matter how vast the Empire's domain is, we do not have the strength to do anything and everything. If we push ourselves to the limit, we will have no margin for failure—any unexpected occurrence could leave us paralyzed. That can happen at any time, like with the earthquake and volcanic eruption in the northern regions. That was what scared me. Not being able to extend a helping hand to those who needed it. That's why, even if it was possible, I didn't want to overextend by advancing into the Demon Lord's Domain. That is what led the people now surrounding the capital to lose hope. If I was unable to keep them on my side, that is a failing on my part. It may be the will of Heaven saying that I am no longer necessary."

"What are you saying, Sister?!"

As Jeanne watched, the image of Maria carried a nearby chair next to the railing. And then, unbelievably, she then climbed on the railing using the chair. Jeanne was speechless. If Maria leaned forward even a little, she would fall straight down.

Maria's dress flapped in the wind, indicating how precarious her current situation was.

"This could be bad..." Hashim murmured to himself in the camp outside Jamona Fortress.

"Is something the matter, Sir Hashim?" Gaten, who overheard him, asked.

Frowning, Hashim replied, "Sir Gaten, and the rest of you. Prepare your forces to fight at once."

"But why? The capital looks ready to fall at any moment."

"Maria may be planning to die," Hashim said, glaring at the image of her as she stood on the railing. "If Maria dies now, there is the risk that the Imperial forces in Jamona Fortress will turn into absolute fiends. They might come at us like martyrs, prepared to die in the name of avenging her... If we take them on directly, we'll take considerable losses."

Hashim's prediction had been that, with the capital surrounded, Maria was sure to capitulate. He had been calculating that Maria, being the gentle soul that she was, could not bear to see the Imperial capital burn and its people be trampled. As a result, she would turn herself over instead.

However, if she killed herself on broadcast, with the whole nation watching, that changed things. Her supporters would all fight for vengeance. Not just the soldiers in Jamona Fortress, but each and every one of her people would come to hate Fuuga. The revolts would be ceaseless, and the land would be restive even after the war.

You've found the most effective way of harassing us, Maria Euphoria, Hashim thought.

"We...may not need an empress anymore. If this title—if my very existence—is what has brought this war upon us...then... I will cast my life away."

Hashim glared as Maria continued speaking.

"Is there no one there who can stop my sister?!" Jeanne shouted pleadingly as she realized that her sister meant to die. She prayed, *Someone, anyone, pull her back from the edge!*

And with a peaceful look on her face, Maria said, "I would give my life to keep the people who live in this empire from being hurt... I have always been ready to, and I still am. That is the kind of empress I am. Please, everyone, stay well..."

With that, Maria slowly leaned back. For Jeanne and the others, she seemed to move much more slowly than she did. Her body leaned, then was dragged down by gravity. As she vanished from view, Jeanne screamed.

"Noooooo!!!"

She was falling. The wind growled in her ears, and it felt as if it was pulling on her from inside her own body.

Oh... This feels more unpleasant than I expected, Maria thought, still seemingly clearheaded as she fell.

She had been through some hard times since becoming empress. There were nights she went to sleep absolutely spent. The pressure was almost crushing, and there were days when she threw up because the excessive praise and criticism made it hard to keep meals down. There were even times when she'd felt an urge to hurl herself from the balcony of her office.

That said, she'd never gone so far as acting on it before now, so she was learning for the first time how unpleasant the experience was.

In a few more moments, her body would slam into the ground below, splattering it with her red blood. And yet, Maria was thinking about it like she was watching someone else experience it. This was probably similar to the mental state Souma ended up in during the Amidonian War. She understood her role, and could no longer feel the weight of life. Even so, the weight of Maria's life was rapidly getting closer to the ground below.

"Even if I failed...I did my part..." Maria murmured, closing her eyes.

"I won't let that happen!"

Maria felt a sideways impact. She slowly opened her eyes, only to see the face of King Souma of Friedonia right before her. When their eyes met, there was momentary relief, which rapidly turned to anger, and he bashed his forehead into hers.

"Ow!"

After that headbutt, Maria held her forehead as tears filled her eyes. That was when she realized that she was cradled in Souma's arms and they were riding on the back of a massive black creature. It was probably the queen she had heard of, Naden the ryuu. Maria grasped that Souma had used a headbutt because his hands were occupied with holding her.

"You jumping wasn't in the script!" Souma said, giving her a look of anger and exasperation.

Maria looked at him in blank amazement. "Oh...! Um...I'm sorry."

"Ah... Well, it all worked out in the end... Thank goodness."

When Souma said that, relaxing as he did, Maria finally felt the fear of dying. It was strange that she felt it not when she jumped, nor when she was falling, but now that she had been *saved* from death.

Maria threw her arms around Souma's neck and cried, "I-I was so scared!"

When her true feelings leaked out, Souma sighed. "Of course you were... Naden, could you take us up?"

"Uh, sure. Roger that."

After directing Naden to ascend, Souma gently told Maria, "That's enough ad-libbing. I'll take it from here, like we planned."

"Yes... Please do."

With tears in her eyes, Maria buried her face in his shoulder. Souma hugged her tighter.

Falling Flowers, Flowing Water

(2) A man and woman in love. The man is the flower, and the woman is the water. If the man wished to entrust himself to the water's current, the woman will want to keep the fallen flowers afloat.

(Four-Character Compound Dictionary, Gakken Educational Publishing)

CHAPTER 8
The Maritime Alliance Gets Serious

"**N**O... SISTER..." Jeanne fell to her knees after seeing her sister jump.

The scenery behind her had been familiar to Jeanne—it was the balcony of Maria's office. Knowing the location and how high it was, Jeanne was absolutely certain of her sister's death. Gunther, meanwhile, was still staring in disbelief.

"...Huh?! What?!" Gunther gasped.

It was a strange reaction, and Jeanne, who had gone quite pale in the face, looked up at him.

"Sir Gunther?"

"Just now, something large and black flew by in the projection."

"Something...black?"

Jeanne looked where Gunther was pointing in the water ball. It showed the skies of Valois now that Maria was gone. And in that image, a coiled, black creature was suddenly climbing upwards. Her eyes widened seeing the figure—that of a dragon, yet different.

I know what that is, she thought. *And if it's...who I think it is...*

Before her head found the answer, someone jumped down from the back of the creature, their black cape swishing in the wind as they descended to the balcony. Held in their arms was Maria, who had fallen.

"Sister!"

Jeanne leaned out over the edge of the fortress wall without meaning to. She squinted at the image, but saw no evidence of any injury on Maria. The empress had her dainty arms wrapped around her savior's neck. Jeanne said a name she knew very well.

"Sir Souma..."

The figure in the projection was King Souma A. Elfrieden of Friedonia.

He adjusted his grip on Maria with a grunt, and she squeezed her arms tight around his neck. With that gesture, everyone watching the projection realized that Maria had survived. This time, a cheer erupted from the Imperial side, and it was the Great Tiger Kingdom's forces' turn to be silent.

Then, Souma spoke to the empress in his arms. "Proud and noble Empress Maria, it is absolutely not true that the times we live in have no need of you! As proof—I learned of your peril and came across the continent for you."

His performance was a touch theatrical, but that actually had the effect of relaxing and delighting the people of the Empire who were watching. Souma, who couldn't have seen their reactions, turned and addressed the viewers.

"Hear me, O soldiers of the Gran Chaos Empire and Great Tiger Kingdom of Haan! We, the three nations of the Maritime

Alliance, have begun an intervention to stop the Great Tiger Kingdom's invasion of the Empire!"

"So this is where you make your appearance, you slow turtle!"

At that same time, Fuuga was in the main camp of the army surrounding Valois, glaring at the projection. Despite the harsh look in his eyes, his voice was bounding with joy. He was excited, as if he were watching the climax of a movie.

Lumiere, meanwhile, showed immediate shock and anger. "The King of Friedonia?!" she screeched. "Why is he here?! Why now?!"

Yeah, why now...? Something seemed off to Fuuga.

Souma's appearance seemed far too well-timed. He appeared the moment Maria leapt from the balcony and made a dashing entrance after saving her. This broadcast was being shown across the Empire as part of Hashim's plan. The people who loved Maria were probably bawling their eyes out with gratitude about now.

Still, it seemed a little strange to Fuuga. If this was all following Souma's script, it wasn't like him. Even if he'd been planning to save her, he wouldn't have let Maria throw herself from the balcony. He'd have been too scared of what would happen if he failed to catch her. A cautious man like Souma would never let her take such a risk.

That means this script is someone else's...

Maybe Hakuya the Black-robed Prime Minister or the newly joined Julius would have proposed something like this. But they were Souma's subordinates. No matter how good he was at delegating things to his trusted comrades, Souma was still bound to reject a risky plan like this.

Well, who was it then...? Fuuga thought. Suddenly, the words Souma had said to him that day came flooding back. *"Are you sure you're not taking Maria Euphoria too lightly?"* Oh! So that's it! I get it now!

Fuuga stomped the ground.

"You sure got me, Maria Euphoria!"

Fuuga looked up at the skies above Valois to find the parachutes of the falling dratroopers opening like blooming flowers. They had been carried in and dropped by the wyvern cavalry. The countless parachutes descended to the castle, floating in the wind like cotton fluff.

"Urgh... This is terrible."

Also, at the same time, in the camp before Jamona Fortress...

Hashim bitterly ground his teeth. He was one of the few who instantly understood the situation.

Gaten looked suspiciously at Hashim.

"Why the grim look, Sir Advisor?" Gaten asked. "He doesn't appear to have shown up with that many reinforcements... Won't Lord Fuuga flatten Souma and his troops?"

"It can't be that easy..." Hashim shook his head. "Souma said he was intervening not just with the Friedonian military, but with the Maritime Alliance. That means the Republic of Turgis and the Nine-Headed Dragon Archipelago Kingdom will be getting involved in earnest. He only showed up with a small number of soldiers there, but the number that he still has in reserve is far greater. They'll be moving into action all across the continent."

"That's...frightening." Gaten gulped as it finally dawned on him what that meant.

It wasn't hard to imagine that Souma's forces were already on the move the moment he appeared. Hashim was certain that the Souma being projected there would soon say as much. Because that's what he himself would do to break the morale of the Great Tiger Kingdom's forces.

And, as he predicted, the projection of Souma spoke.

"What you see here is but one of the pieces I've played. I've left the deployment of the remainder of the Kingdom's troops to Hakuya, the Black-robed Prime Minister. I will let him explain the situation across all regions to you now. If you intend to continue this war after hearing all this, then...I'll take you on," Souma asserted, loud and clear.

At the same time, in a walled city in the south of Zem...

"Wh-what's that?!" shouted one of the mercenaries keeping a lookout from on top of the southern walls.

The mountains that demarcated the border with the Republic of Turgis looked as if they were squirming. At a distance, it appeared the trees were falling. The soldier thought it was an avalanche, but it wasn't the season for snow to have accumulated, and the squirming things were *brown*. Whatever was happening was most assuredly abnormal.

He hurried to fetch a telescope, only to discover the writhing mass was thousands of numoths—animals trained as riding beasts in the Republic of Turgis.

"It's the Republic! The Republic is coming!"

As the mercenary cried out, the others began rushing around.

There were only 8,000 men in this fortress now. The stronghold had been built as the first defensive wall against an attack from the Republic. So even with 80 percent of their forces having been sent to join Fuuga's, they still had a significant garrison here.

Yet, the onrushing forces of the Republic looked even greater in number. If there were thousands of numoths, then that meant there were tens of thousands of Republican soldiers nearby.

The mercenary commander of the walled city gave the order immediately. "Send a messenger to the Mercenary King, Sir Moumei, who is accompanying Fuuga's forces! We're no match for a force that large, and there's a high risk they'll strike deep into Zem! He needs to come back before it's too late!"

"Yes, sir!"

Once the order was given, the mercenary commander glared out towards the forces of the Republic. "We may have no choice but to abandon this city. The Republic fights well in the snow, but they're bad at holding territory they capture. If we make them stretch out their supply lines, they'll be easier to strike, and recapturing what they take will be simpler."

As the mercenaries were running around, the sound of rumbling gradually increased. Thousands of numoths were stampeding down the side of the mountains overlooking the fortress city. These would be the numoth cavalry, a category of troop equivalent to war elephants from Souma's old world. They had far more power to break through the enemy than ordinary cavalry, but were smaller and could make tighter turns than rhinosauruses. Because they were creatures from a frigid region, the numoths had the ability to cross ice and snow. However, they became weaker as they moved north and the temperature rose.

These numoths were accompanied by 50,000 beastman soldiers belonging to the Five Races of the Snowy Plains. These were all of the forces available to Kuu Taisei, the Head of the Republic.

Kuu rode atop a numoth at the front of the charge, shouting to his men. "Ookyakya! All right, we're close enough the sound should reach them! Band, let's give them a real show!"

On Kuu's orders, the band riding on a howdah atop the back of one of the lead numoths began to play their instruments. They paid no mind to harmony, instead focusing on making a whole lot of noise. They played as loudly as they could so as to not be drowned out by the stomping feet of their numoths and to show the grandeur of the Republic's forces.

"Urgh... It hurts my ears..."

Kuu's second wife, Leporina, who was riding with him in the same howdah, covered her bunny ears. She'd been able to bring earplugs because Kuu had informed her in advance about the plan, but her race's excellent hearing was making the cacophony unbearable.

Kuu held Leporina's head against his own chest.

"Wha...! Master Kuu?"

"If I don't do this, you won't be able to hear me, right?"

"Ohh..." Held close, with her husband whispering in her ear, Leporina turned bright red.

"What're you two flirting for when we're on the march...?" groaned Nike, an exasperated look on his face.

He'd nimbly jumped up on their numoth at some point and was sitting on the edge of their howdah. Leporina became flustered when she realized they were being watched and tried to get up, but Kuu wouldn't let her go.

Cackling like a monkey, Kuu then said, "Looks fun, doesn't it? Why don't you find a wife for yourself too?"

"Yeah, yeah, I'm so jealous," Nike said flatly. "You've got your other cute wife Taru waiting for you back home too."

Kuu smiled wryly. "I'm amazed you can say that. I hear you're even more popular with the ladies than I am. Bet you're getting more tail than you know what to do with, am I right?"

Nike had been famed as a beautiful young spearman in the Union of Eastern Nations, so he'd been looked at affectionately by many women of different races since coming to the Republic. Kuu became jealous when he noticed, and his wives called him

out for it—Taru with silent fury and Leporina with a teary-eyed lecture. The two of them had learned how to keep their man under their thumb while they were in the Kingdom.

"I prefer to be the one making offers, not receiving them," Nike said with a shrug. "If there was someone well-tempered and dignified like my sister Mutsumi, I just might go after her."

Now it was Kuu's turn to look at Nike in dismay. "They've got a word for people like you in bro's world, you *siscon*."

"Siscon? What's that? Some sort of title?"

"You know what, forget it... More importantly, you know what we're doing next, right?" Kuu asked, regaining his composure as the head of the Republic.

Nike also snapped back into serious mode and said, "Yes. We keep intimidating them as we close in on the city, yeah? Making as big of a show of it as we can."

"Yeah. Zem's got something like 100,000 troops in total, but most of them are out supporting Fuuga. When you consider that they need to have troops on their border with Friedonia too, even if that place is one of their key defensive positions, they can't have left even 10,000 guys in there."

"And that's why we'll be able to intimidate them—acting like we could crush them underfoot easily and getting them to run away, right? If our enemies are smart, they'll likely pull back their defensive lines to concentrate their forces."

"...Basically." Kuu let out a mischievous chuckle. "Bro and his prime minister only ordered us to intimidate them. If the enemy there tells their guys who are out supporting Fuuga that their homeland's under attack, they'll get antsy and want to go home. That'll be our job done."

"Then is there any need to force an attack?"

"What do you mean? If I'm coming out all this way, then there's no problem with having a city or two to show for it."

With a boyish grin on his face, Kuu continued.

"Let's call in Taru to turn the cities we take into impregnable fortresses. She's got all these ideas that she had to give up on because of the pushback there'd be if we did them in one of the Republic's cities. But a city we took off the enemy? We can remodel it all we like and they won't be able to complain much. This place looks like it's got potential for agriculture too... Oh, I know! We'll drill a tunnel through this mountain and hook it up to the Republic! That'll make maintaining our supply lines easier too!"

Nike's eyes widened as he realized that despite the innocent look on his face, Kuu was steadily thinking through how he'd rule the area after the war. As carefree as he might seem, Kuu was fit to stand at the top of a nation, and Nike now served him.

"Well, I don't see a problem with that," Nike replied, subconsciously tightening the grip on his spear. He was too proud to let it show on his face, so he deliberately remained aloof in his response. "I know I'd prefer to be somewhere less cold. That city looks like it'd fit the bill."

"Sure would. If the mercenaries defending the place put up a resistance, I'll be counting on you to show us your stuff. Let's race up the walls together and send them packing."

"You're going to the front line too, Master Kuu? If you don't hold back a little more, Lady Taru is going to get upset, you know?"

"Ookyakya! Well, keep it a secret from her!"

In the middle of their friendly banter...

"Jeez! Would you two stop talking like I'm not here?!" Leporina protested, still in an embarrassing position.

Also at the same time, on the eastern edge of the Great Tiger Kingdom, countless ships appeared in the open sea next to a port city on the coast...

These vessels of varying sizes, towed by sea dragons and horned doldons, belonged to the Nine-Headed Dragon Archipelago Kingdom's fleet. Responding to changes in naval warfare, the Archipelago Kingdom had worked with the Kingdom of Friedonia to augment their existing fleet of wooden and ironclad ships with steel battleships like the *Albert II*. These new ships could carry large cannons and anti-air repeating bolt throwers.

Incidentally, Shabon had said to Souma, "I would like an island-type carrier. I will pay for it, so would you please give us one?" but obviously he had to refuse. However, Shabon had learned to negotiate from Kuu, and she was far more persistent than Souma and the others expected. To that end, they had agreed that once enough new carriers were built and it was time to retire the originals, she could have one. Shabon was currently developing into a determined and stubborn queen.

Nine-Headed Dragon Queen Shabon was on the bridge of the largest, most impressive battleship in her fleet, the *New* ...*g*.

...are far too defenseless... Did they never consider that ...attack by sea while Sir Fuuga is away?" Shabon said ... her royal consort and prime minister. She watched ...s of the port city run around willy-nilly in response ...al of the fleet.

...w no can blame them?" Kishun said in response. "Sir Fuuga's people are of the steppes, masters of war on land. They have never been attacked from the sea, so they cannot be expected to be wary of such an event. I am sure that he simply left the task of ruling this port city to its former lord when they submitted to him."

"Just like Sir Souma told us, then?"

In the past two years, Souma had explained the importance of sea power to Shabon, as well as Fuuga's presumed lack of awareness about it. This meant that the only country on this continent other than the Kingdom of Friedonia and the Archipelago Kingdom with a proper understanding of sea power was the Gran Chaos Empire. And he'd explained this to Shabon, who, due to the geographical makeup of her country, best understood the importance and was able to build her forces to take advantage of it.

If he had kept it secret, he could have built the Kingdom's naval forces into a power unmatched by any other country's, but that would have led to pushback and likely the breakup of the Maritime Alliance. If the Archipelago Kingdom would become hostile to him and start engaging in piracy, that would be incredibly tough to deal with.

Instead, Souma and Hakuya had decided it was best to explain it to her from the beginning and arrange things so that they both benefited. Even if the Kingdom's fleet was not absolute, so long as they had the strongest fleet in the Maritime Alliance, they could maintain peace at sea.

Shabon smiled a daring and regal smile. After having given birth to two children, she was developing a dignified presence that rivaled Juna's or Excel's.

"Then we will have to show them what it means to fight at sea."

"Indeed." Kishun nodded. "We will teach them the importance of being able to make and act on decisions immediately."

Shabon swung her arm towards the port city. "As planned, our first target is the artillery battery in the port. Our second is the military ships in port. Let us neutralize them before they can come out. All ships, open fire."

"Roger. All ships, open fire!"

Boom! On Shabon and Kishun's orders, the *New Dragon King's* guns roared.

With that as their signal, the rest of the fleet began bombarding the port with their cannons, lion-dog cannons, and other gunpowder armaments. The countless shells all slammed into the battery that had been built to protect the entrance to the port. These were not explosive shells but ones that relied on pure kinetic force, so there were no showy pillars of flame or smoke.

Still, as the buildings in the artillery battery crumbled, it was clear to see that it had been neutralized. That was when the ships left port, possibly to intercept them, or perhaps to flee.

"Much too slow. They lack training."

Shabon ordered her fleet to continue firing, and the *New Dragon King's* main cannon roared once again. Its cannonball slammed into the largest enemy battleship—likely their flagship. Even at a distance, they could clearly see its bridge collapsing and falling like a crumbling tower.

"Excellent." Shabon gave a satisfied nod. "Our gunners are superb."

"Indeed. Ours have far more experience than theirs do, after all... Now then, Lady Shabon. Our task from the Kingdom's prime minister was to 'destroy Fuuga's military vessels,' which he expected to be gathered here, correct?"

Nodding, she replied, "Yes. As well as the destruction of any warships under construction. Even if they failed to understand sea power, Sir Fuuga and Sir Hashim would not be amused that we seized control of the seas. So they had to be building a fleet at their port city on the east coast. We were directed to seize or destroy it."

"And we do not have to take this city?"

"They have a land connection to it, after all. We would struggle to hold it when Sir Fuuga returns," Shabon said with a shrug before pointing to the west. "More importantly, this city is near Sir Fuuga's homeland on the steppes, so now that we have threatened it..."

"I see. It should serve to shake up the old hands among Fuuga's forces." Kishun let out a groan of admiration. "Then what do we do now? Their defenses are neutralized; if we are not going to occupy the city, should we at least destroy their storehouses?"

"No... It would be unwise to incur too much ire from the people who support Sir Fuuga. If all we attack are their military facilities, that will create a difference in the emotional response from the military and the civilian population. Treating them equally will only serve to unite our enemy."

"Very true."

"It would be best not to touch their food stores, lest people starve. I forbid any looting that targets civilians as well, of course. See to it that everyone has strict orders to that effect."

"Yes, ma'am! It will be done."

"However..." Shabon stuck her tongue out and smiled mischievously. "Let us help ourselves to the weapons and ammunition that they have no doubt stocked at the base. If possible, I would also like to drag back the warships that are under construction, as well as ones that have been neutralized. And all the resources they have for building more too."

Kishun stared blankly at her for a moment before smiling wryly.

"You've become quite merciless..."

"Does that hurt your image of me?"

"No, it is most reliable."

"Hee hee, good, then. I think we will have some nice souvenirs for Sharan and Sharon."

"You mean to give the children warships as presents...?" Kishun gave an exasperated shrug.

Their children, Princess Sharan and Prince Sharon, were currently in the care of the former Nine-Headed Dragon King, Shana, who had been entrusted with the rule of the Twin Islands. They'd indeed both smiled wryly when they saw how the stern face of the former monarch softened and he became a doting grandfather.

Shabon clapped her hands and said, "Now, let us do as a pirate fleet should and help ourselves to everything we can."

Having become a queen and the mother of two infant children, Shabon had become highly reliable.

At the same time, as Mercenary State Zem and the port city in the east of the Great Tiger Kingdom were being thrown into chaos, there was great confusion unfolding in the Lunarian Orthodox Papal State...

Thirty thousand forces from the Friedonian National Defense Force had appeared at their border. People screamed and ran about in terror, and all signs of life vanished from nearby cities and towns. They were all terrified by the forces of the Kingdom and piled into the holy city of Yumuen as refugees. Overrun by incoming people, Yumuen was left unable to send the defenders they had left there to the border.

Meanwhile, the source of that chaos—the Friedonian army composed of 30,000 soldiers mainly from the National Land

Defense Force—made no attempt to cross the border. They were not firing so much as a bolt of magic or an arrow into the country. They acted as if they were "just passing by" as they assembled there, displaying their might to the Orthodox Papal State. And yet, what terrified the people—the true source of such pandemonium—was the general leading this force.

They screamed his name as they ran.

"I-It's Julius! Julius is here!"

"The bloody prince Julius?! W-we have to flee, quickly!"

Everyone from the common folk to rank-and-file soldiers was shaken by news of his arrival, and things devolved from there. They dropped everything and ran like people who'd panicked after encountering a bear in the mountains.

With an indescribable expression on his face, Julius watched this unfold from the main camp of the Kingdom's forces. It was like he'd bitten into an unpleasant food...but with a far-off look in his eyes like he had resigned himself to something.

"The people of the Orthodox Papal State are awfully frightened of you, Sir Julius," called out an easygoing voice from behind him.

Julius slowly turned to see Mio Carmine standing there in her armor. Because they were mainly using the National Land Defense Force, they had called in Mio and assigned her to be Julius's second-in-command.

Incidentally, when she got the order, she and her fiancé, Colbert, had this exchange:

"Finally, a chance to serve as a warrior again! I have to participate!"

"Hold on, Madam Mio! What about the Carmine domain?!"

"I'll leave that to you, Sir Bee, my beloved fiancé!"

"Since when did fiancé mean slave?"

"I hear people talk about being a slave to love all the time."

"No, that's not very witty, okay?!"

Julius looked at Mio with dead fish eyes. "Oh, it's you... Madam Mio."

"Yikes! You look even more dead inside than usual. What happened?"

"Oh, it's nothing. I'm just realizing how much it hurts to have things pushed in my face from when I was less experienced..." Julius sighed and looked towards the Lunarian Orthodox Papal State. "It was after I took over the Amidonian throne from my late father... I ruthlessly suppressed the believers who the Orthodox Papal State stirred into rebellion against me. My infamy must have made its way back to the Orthodox Papal State proper."

"Ah... That would explain how scared they were, yeah." Mio clapped her hands together as she made the connection.

Julius sighed. "I thought it was my only option then, and I still don't think I was wrong, but...then Tia's face flashes through my mind. I imagine her being saddened by the blood of all those I trampled beneath my feet."

"Perhaps... But there's more to her, isn't there?" With a deliberate smile, Mio patted Julius on the back. "Tia looks innocent, but she's got a level head on her shoulders. Even if she learned about your bad reputation, she has the capacity to accept it and keep it close to her heart. She's not just going to sit around being sad."

"Madam Mio... Heh." Julius finally cracked a smile. "I never would have thought a daughter of the House of Carmine would say that to me... To think I had fought against them in the past."

"Well, us military folk need to take the good with the bad. That's what my father always told me. If you'd left the rebels to do as they pleased, someone else would have been hurt instead, so we can't say your actions were all bad. And, look. Thanks to your infamous reputation, we've been able to stir the Orthodox Papal State without fighting."

"Using everything he has, including my bad reputation... The prime minister comes up with some nasty ideas."

It was Hakuya who ordered Julius to lead 30,000 troops to go stand at their border with the Orthodox Papal State. In light of his past suppression of their believers, Hakuya judged this would be enough to shake them, and it was why he'd given firm orders not to take the troops across the border. Because there was no need to invade, all the troops—except Julius and a number of soldiers like Mio who had been sent to guard him—were so weak, they might as well have been cardboard cutouts.

Mio looked at him quizzically. "But are you sure we shouldn't go in? The plan is for the Republic to attack from the south, the Archipelago Kingdom from the east, and us from the southeast.

Meanwhile, His Majesty leads a unit to join up with the Empire in the west, right? If all four prongs of our attack were serious, wouldn't Fuuga's forces fall to pieces?"

"It would end in a quagmire..." Julius said, crossing his arms with a pensive look on his face. "If the Maritime Alliance were to launch a serious attack just as Fuuga was about to destroy the Empire, we could likely deal him a crippling blow. However, were we to do that, Fuuga's supporters would deeply resent Souma. They'd see him as the worst kind of person, marrying Fuuga's sister on one hand, then actively obstructing his brother-in-law's dream on the other."

"That's a rather selfish interpretation of it, especially when they've gone and destroyed Madam Maria's dreams themselves."

"Well, that's just how people are. Fuuga and Hashim would no doubt make a lot of noise about how unfair the Kingdom's been to them. And from there it would turn into a quagmire— an endless war that went on until one faction or the other was destroyed. Although, Hashim likely diverted all his forces to the Empire on the assumption that Souma would never do something so foolish..."

"I see..."

Julius let out a sigh.

"This is likely where the real challenge starts for the Black-robed Prime Minister."

"What we need in this war is not victory. In fact, it would be unnecessary."

At this point, Prime Minister Hakuya was in the castle at Parnam, in front of a map of the continent, explaining his strategy to Tomoe, Ichiha, and Yuriga.

"If we prevent Sir Fuuga's conquest of the Empire while dealing him a major blow, that will earn us the enmity of those who lionize him. Once that happens, even if we take a city, it will not be stable, and Sir Fuuga will easily be able to show up to retake it. And to keep Sir Fuuga from invading us, the Maritime Alliance would need to constantly keep sending troops to areas Sir Fuuga is not in, forcing him to repeatedly take them back in a game of whack-a-mole."

That was almost like the final stages of the Three Kingdoms period in China. In order to avoid being destroyed by the more populous and powerful Wei, Shu and Wu took turns attacking them, making them split their forces between the east and the west. There are those who believe that this is why Zhuge Liang and Jiang Wei continued the Northern Expeditions despite Shu having little strength as a nation.

"It would be a quagmire. The era would grind to a halt, and all factions would be exhausted. If a demon wave were to come from the Demon Lord's Domain then, none of our countries would be able to recover. It would be impossible for our exhausted nations to absorb the fresh waves of refugees while fighting a defensive war. We need to give people...the impression that Sir Fuuga won."

"That's why you didn't order them to take any of the cities, right, Mr. Hakuya?" Ichiha asked.

"Exactly," Hakuya answered with a nod. "It might be fine to take one city, but if we reach for any more, it will give the impression we were victorious over Sir Fuuga. What we are looking for is to give Fuuga's forces a Pyrrhic victory. The equivalent of him winning by decision."

Hakuya pointed to the Empire on the map.

"What the Great Tiger Kingdom wants now more than anything is the Empire's bureaucrats. These are the people who know how to run a large nation. If he can get his hands on them, then the vast lands of the Empire are only an added bonus. That's why I expect he'll use an insider to quickly assault the Imperial capital and force Madam Maria to surrender. In fact, it would be a problem for him if Madam Maria were to die. Should that happen, he would invoke the wrath of her supporters and the newly acquired Empire would be unruly, leaving him unable to assign his new administrators to positions in the Great Tiger Kingdom. He's going to want to take the citizens of the capital hostage in order to force Madam Maria to surrender. However, anyone who knows Madam Maria knows that is wishful thinking. She is the type who would choose her own death over surrender if she thought that was what was best for the people of the Empire."

"That's what Big Brother said too," Tomoe interjected. "He said that's the kind of person Maria is."

Hakuya nodded. "Yes. If that happens, Sir Fuuga and his people won't be able to get what they want. The Great Tiger Kingdom and the Empire will both be harmed, and no one will benefit from it."

"Yeah. That's why I decided to cooperate with Sir Souma," Yuriga said, crossing her arms and scratching her cheek. "I told my brother, 'If I'm going to marry Sir Souma, I need to put the Kingdom's interests first,' but I don't want either country to get hurt. I want to do everything I can to ensure that both sides benefit. That said, after listening to Mr. Hakuya, I think my brother shouldn't completely destroy the Empire right now."

"Yuriga... Are you okay with this?" Tomoe asked, worried, but Yuriga nodded.

"My brother needs to learn. There are some things you can't get by winning all the time."

"It may be that we would benefit from both their countries collapsing... With the Empire destroyed and the seeds of unrest sown in the Great Tiger Kingdom, that would serve to elevate the importance of the Maritime Alliance."

When Hakuya said this, Tomoe blinked at him. "No...! Then we'd be abandoning Maria and Jeanne. You and Big Brother have been friends with them all this time, haven't you?"

"We have. But even as a prime minister, I may be pushed to make such decisions at times. Madam Jeanne understands this. That's probably why she told me I didn't have to strain myself on her account. I...couldn't find a way to save the Empire in its current state. That being the case, I couldn't put my own feelings first and send our people to intervene in a war because of my personal affection for her."

"Mr. Hakuya..."

Seeing the pained look on Tomoe's face, Hakuya suddenly smiled.

"But one word from His Majesty changed the conditions entirely."

The day Jeanne had rejected his help...

"It is impossible to protect this country and maintain the Empire. If we recklessly try to defend both, it will turn into a quagmire. No matter how I think about it...I can't find the answer I want."

As Hakuya hung his head, Souma told him this: "There's no need to keep the Empire perfectly intact. Maria wants the Empire to shrink."

When he heard that, Hakuya snapped his head up, eyes wide with surprise.

Souma continued. "Maria is exhausted with the current situation where she is the only person supporting an empire that's far too massive. All this time, she's wanted to find a way to peacefully dismantle it. She opened up to me about that back when we met in Zem."

"I can't believe the Saint of the Empire would say that..."

"Listen, Hakuya. You said it was impossible to maintain the Empire, but if there's no need to, then we can choose a slightly better future, right? After all, we've got Fuuga, who wants more land and people, and Maria, who wants to cut some land and people loose. I'll bet you could find a way to make this work out in a way that saves Maria and Jeanne, couldn't you?"

Then, moving to another place and showing him the preparations he'd been making, Souma said this to Hakuya: "I want you to use that head of yours to devise the optimal future for us."

CHAPTER 9

The Fruit of Two Years

SOUMA SET MARIA DOWN and looked towards the viewers. "This is the situation on all fronts. As I speak, 150,000 soldiers from the Kingdom of Friedonia are coming ashore at the Empire's western port. With the Empire's transportation network and my own nation's shipping capacity, they will have gathered at the Imperial capital in about two days' time. If you insist on continuing this war, then as I have already said, we will take you on. Consider that carefully before you make your decision."

Following his words, the image of Souma vanished. Through this broadcast, Souma had informed the entire Empire of the current war situation. Supporters of Maria cheered at each thing he said, while Fuuga's supporters were overcome by a sense of frustration. And larger than either of these groups were the ones who were doubtful that this could really be happening all across the Empire. However, those who knew the kind of person Souma was, the kind of nation the Kingdom of Friedonia had become, and what exactly the Maritime Alliance meant could tell that he spoke the truth.

In front of Jamona Fortress, Hashim was grinding his teeth. "To think...he'd get so deeply involved in this..."

"What do we do? The soldiers from Zem and the Orthodox Papal State are demanding we let them return home."

Hashim snorted at Gaten's question. "Let those who wish to return home go. So long as we don't let our guard down, we can face Jamona Fortress with the forces of the Great Tiger Kingdom alone. If they want to retreat *without permission,* then we can have them take responsibility for that after the war."

Seeing Hashim's smirk, Gaten cocked his head to the side. "After the war...? Is it fine to start thinking about that already?"

"This war ends here... Out of an abundance of caution, Lord Fuuga and I discussed what to do if the Maritime Alliance showed up. I doubt either Souma or the Black-robed Prime Minister want to get into a serious war with us. There won't be anything more than minor skirmishes."

"Hmm... If you say so, then I'm sure you're right," Gaten said with a shrug.

Hashim glared towards the camps of Zem and the Orthodox Papal State. "Lord Fuuga described Souma as a mountainous turtle with countless snakes for tails. I've also thought he's a monster, but it's a monster's fate to be slain by a great man. I was sure Lord Fuuga would strike Souma down with ease, but...great as Lord Fuuga is, he can't do it with a patchwork coalition of riffraff. Only once he's able to move all the parts of our national body himself will he truly be able to become a great man."

Seeing the dauntless smile on Hashim's face, Gaten understood it was about to rain blood in the Orthodox Papal State and Zem. The realization sent an uncharacteristic shudder down his spine.

Meanwhile, in Fuuga's camp outside Valois...

"That's the end of this war..." Fuuga murmured to himself. The words made Lumiere's eyes go wide.

"Why?! If it's as King Souma said, we still have two days before Friedonian forces reach here! Even with the additional troops that just dropped into Valois, it's not a significant change! If we attack with the forces we have, we can take down both Maria and Souma in one strike!"

"That's not the point," Fuuga said, scratching his head as Lumiere ranted. "Souma's the furthest thing from reckless or haphazard. Unlike me, he doesn't enjoy the thrill of living on the edge of life and death. If Souma himself is out here, it means he has a chance of beating us. One that's good enough it won't be easy to overturn."

"Even so..."

"Besides, from the sound of it, if we back off now, Souma's gonna let us walk away with a victory."

"Huh?"

"Madam Lumiere, try to remember what Sir Souma said." Mutsumi began to explain as Lumiere stared blankly at them.

"Sir Souma said if we were to continue the war, he would take us on. That means he only wants a cessation of hostilities—not to have us pull out of the Empire entirely. In other words, we can keep the territory we've already taken. We'll still have defeated the Empire. However, if we continue fighting, we face an all-or-nothing gamble against Sir Souma."

"And what's wrong with that?! Why are you so cautious?! This isn't like you, Sir Fuuga!"

Despite Lumiere's impassioned words, Fuuga just laughed with a hint of self-derision. "Being a little cautious is just right. Against an opponent like Souma, at least. He's not so easy that I want to be taking him on at the same time as Maria."

Lumiere couldn't accept this and retorted, "Then attack with only the forces of the Empire that submitted to you! We'll take the capital by ourselves!"

"Madam Lumiere!" Mutsumi was about to chastise her, but Fuuga held up a hand for Mutsumi to stop.

"Well, I don't see a problem with that. Let them try."

"Wha?! Lord Fuuga?!"

"Thank you." Lumiere saluted him before striding off.

Mutsumi stared at Fuuga's face. "Is that really all right...? They probably can't win."

"I'll bet not." Fuuga crossed his arms and chuckled. "Consider it a lesson. The guys who surrendered could stand to learn how hard it is to fight Souma. I'm sure a little pain will make them listen better later."

"Yes, you're right... And having them attack the Imperial

capital will make it harder for them to return to the Empire later...
is what I'm sure Big Brother Hashim would say."

"Ha ha ha, no doubt... And besides..." Fuuga said, stroking his
short goatee as he looked towards Valois. "I kind of want to see
what Souma's gonna pull. He's probably got some kind of secret
move we'd never think of. Let's kick back and enjoy the show."

Meanwhile...

"Heh heh heh..."

Krahe, who had been standing by with his personal forces,
trembled with glee.

"Ha ha ha... Ah ha ha ha ha!"

At first, he had been holding back his laughter, but finally, he
reached his limits and burst out into a hearty guffaw.

"I... I have received a sign from Heaven!"

Krahe thrust his fists into the air as he shouted.

"I knew I was right! This is my role! In becoming Maria's enemy, I brought back her radiance as a saint! The love of Heaven
has returned to her! Did you see, men?! My fellow lovers and ad-
mirers of Lady Maria! She threw herself from the high balcony!
Normally, she would have been dashed against the ground below,
a bloody flower blooming where she struck! Yet Lady Maria did
not die! King Souma rode in on his black dragon to save her!"

Krahe's eyes shone with ecstasy and madness.

"King Souma is a divine servitor, sent from Heaven to rescue
Lady Maria! Her salvation here is proof that she is a true saint!
And we are the ones who led her to it! We who stand here as her

foes! Because we opposed Lady Maria, she was able to shine as a saint! We are the foes of the saint! We stood against her like the Demon Lord, and in so doing, made a saint and a hero appear in this land! We have played a truly heavenly role!"

Krahe drew his rapier and pointed it towards Valois.

"Now my heart is unclouded! With this sign from Heaven, I will face the saint as her enemy with all my might! The greater my evil, the more Lady Maria will shine! What greater joy could there be?!"

Just as he said this, a messenger ran up to him. "I have a message! Madam Lumiere says to attack the capital!"

"It shall be done!"

With that response, Krahe leaped onto his griffon's back.

Standing before his personal troops, he raised his rapier above his head and shouted, "Now, let us fight! Until our lives end!"

"You did your job admirably, Piltory," I told Piltory Saracen, my ambassador to the Empire, following the broadcast address from the balcony of Valois Castle. He'd been the one directing the mages who were controlling the broadcast jewel since the start of Maria's broadcast. Such a fine detail really illustrated how planned this was between the Kingdom and the Empire. I'd been able to stop Maria's fall because I was already close at hand.

"You stayed in the Imperial capital, working even as the fires of war drew near. Thank you."

When I said that, Piltory put his hands together in front of his chest and bowed. "No, I only did my duty as a retainer. As no order to return home had arrived, I was certain you would defend the Imperial capital, sire."

"Thank you... I'm glad *you* believed in me."

I looked at Maria, who I'd just saved. My smile had a hint of anger in it.

"*Right,* Madam Maria?"

"R-right..."

"Why did you jump? That wasn't part of the plan."

"Um... When I was standing out there, I found myself overwhelmed by my emotions..." Maria let out a troubled laugh. "And so many of my vassals left me, including Lumiere and Krahe. My name as Saint of the Empire is ruined now. I won't miss it, but if I was going to comfort and unite those who've still decided to stay with me, I needed a little of that divine aura—like miraculously surviving against all odds."

"Oh-hoh... So it was all an act?"

"Yes..." she muttered, averting her eyes.

I placed my hands on her shoulders and smiled gently at her.

"Um? Sir Souma?" Maria's expression twitched.

I looked her in the eye, pulled my head back, and... *Bonk!*

"Ow!"

I gave her a good, hard headbutt.

Maria held her smarting forehead as her eyes teared up. "Oww, that hurts. You're awful."

"Hmph, that's what happens to liars!" I said, my voice raising in anger. I couldn't hold it back right now. "Don't give me that crap after looking like you didn't have the slightest care for your own life! If I hadn't made it in time, you'd have been fine with it! Your life would have ended the war, and you'd be set free from your responsibilities as empress!"

"Urk... You understand me well..."

"I've been there myself on several occasions."

Being forced to play a role by my position, and then that role taking control of me. I have experienced it many times. It had nearly killed my heart before...

"You said it yourself, didn't you?! 'I want to be a person, and I want to be loved as a person!'"

"Ah...!"

Maria had talked about it in the past.

I may be an empress, but I'm still just a human being. Instead of being worshiped as a saint, I want to remain a person, and to be loved as a person.

It was a declaration that she wouldn't flee into her role as an empress and wouldn't lose her humanity.

"Do you have any idea how many people would grieve if you were to die? You, who have lived as a person and are loved as a person. Sure, the people who worship you as a saint may think that martyrdom will only make you holier, but those of us who love you as a person—those whom you've loved as people—would never want that for you!"

Large teardrops spilled from Maria's eyes. Without the time to let her voice out or the need to think about why she was sad, the tears overflowed from some natural, unconscious part of her being. Maria herself was visibly surprised when she noticed them streaming down her cheeks.

"Huh? That's strange... Why won't they stop...?"

Maria wiped them away several times, but the flow wouldn't end.

Her tear ducts were open now, after being held shut by force of will for so long. Understanding the size of the burden she'd been carrying, I renewed my decision to shoulder it with her from now on. Obviously, I wasn't very strong myself, but I'd get my friends and family involved too, and we'd all bear it together.

"Souma! The traitors from the Imperial forces are on the move!" reported Hal, dropping out of the skies from Ruby the red dragon's back. They'd come to the capital as well.

Hal and his men, the dratroopers, were keeping an eye on how the forces of the Great Tiger Kingdom responded.

I'd thought that if I showed how confident I was, Fuuga's wild instincts would pick up on the danger and he wouldn't attack, but it looked like it was the northern knights and nobles of the Empire who'd made a move. Or maybe he'd let them in order to see what we'd do.

"Then we'll simply meet their attack as planned. Madam Maria."

"Yes."

"I know I sent you the instructions through Piltory, but were you able to prepare the things I'd asked for?"

"Of course..." Maria replied with a sniffle. She wiped the tears from her eyes and looked straight at me. "When the earthquake and eruption happened in the north, I had 'the things you sent with the relief supplies' placed where you told me to. They're ready to use anytime."

"Okay."

I nodded, then addressed everyone present.

"Now then, let's show Fuuga and his people what we've got. The fruit of two years of research."

Lumiere sent forces to the north, south, east, and west gates of the city in order to assault Valois. Because the Kingdom of Friedonia had only sent a small number of reinforcements and Fuuga's forces still vastly outnumbered the defenders, she believed an attack from four directions would easily take the city.

With the four armies in position and their attack imminent, the sound of a cannon firing was heard from within Valois.

Boom! Boom! Boom!

Lumiere and her men braced for incoming fire, but the sounds were too sporadic for it to be that. No smoke could be seen rising from any of the four directions either.

"What...was that all about?"

As Lumiere was wondering, a messenger rushed over.

"I have a report! Something is slowly falling from the direction of Valois!" the messenger relayed.

Lumiere looked through a telescope and saw something fly from the capital, before a parachute opened above it in midair and it began fluttering to the ground.

She recognized it as similar to the equipment the Kingdom of Friedonia had used to bring soldiers into the capital. This time, however, the parachute wasn't carrying a person but some crystalline object with metal objects around it.

"What is that...? Well, it matters little. Tell them to shoot down whatever it is at once!"

"Yes, ma'am!"

On Lumiere's orders, the mages would attack...or so she thought. However, contrary to her expectations, no attack touched the mystery object.

What are the mages doing?! she thought.

As Lumiere watched with increasing irritation, the same messenger as before hurriedly ran up to her.

"L-Lady Lumiere!"

"What is it?! Why haven't they started the attack?!"

"I have a report! They can't use magic! Not just the mages, but all of our soldiers!"

"What?! How could something so absurd happen?!"

In utter disbelief, Lumiere tried to use her own wind magic. However, while she felt like the power was being sucked away from her, she couldn't produce so much as a slight breeze.

"No...this can't be!"

As Lumiere was recovering from her shock, Krahe came over. "Madam Lumiere. Things have gotten a little bad."

"What is it, Sir Krahe?! Return to your post!"

"The griffons have been restless since that object appeared. Like they want to take off, but can't. We can't use our air force like this."

"No...! Could it have something to do with magic no longer working?"

Was this some unidentified attack from the Kingdom of Friedonia? The moment that thought occurred to her, Lumiere recalled what Fuuga had said to her.

"Being a little cautious is just right. Against an opponent like Souma, at least. He's not so easy that I want to be taking him on at the same time as Maria."

Was this what Sir Fuuga was talking about...? Finally understanding what he meant, Lumiere ground her teeth in frustration. She hadn't anticipated going onto a battlefield where all magic was completely sealed off.

Her common sense told her it was impossible. However, what she was witnessing defied common sense. That was what Lumiere, who had a sharper mind than most people, considered.

"It's likely that the object is obstructing our use of magic. But they shouldn't be able to block our magic while still being able to use their own. So we should assume that thing renders all magic unusable. It's disrupted us, but the conditions are equal for both sides."

Lumiere gave up on using magic and decided to give the order to lay siege to the castle using only conventional attacks. If the enemy couldn't use magic either, it was going to be a slog, but they would be able to take the city with overwhelming numbers and conventional siege engines. However...

Pop! Pop! Pop! Pop! Pop! Pop!

Before she could even give the order, there were countless popping sounds from the castle, each of them like a smaller version of the cannon from before. The sounds then overlapped to the point where you would think there had to be thousands of them. Lumiere got a bad feeling as a new messenger rushed over to her.

"I have a report! Our forces took heavy losses when they fired small iron balls at us from on top of the city walls as we attacked!"

"No! Can they use magic?! Wait, those pops... Don't tell me...!" As she realized the possibility, Lumiere shuddered. *Gunpowder weaponry.*

Gunpowder had already been discovered in this world but had limited usage. Because magic was greatly weakened at sea, the cannon had been developed as a replacement. With it becoming the standard for naval combat, small arms development ultimately fell to the wayside.

If King Souma was anticipating a battle under conditions where magic was unusable to begin with, of course he would come armed with equipment similar to what's used in naval battles. We never had the chance to fight properly from the outset! Damn!

Lumiere thrust her sword into the earth in frustration.

Boom! Boom! Boom! Boom!

I could hear our artillery firing from the walls of the Imperial capital. Around now, Fuuga's forces would be attacking the walls without magic and finding themselves stymied by 2,000 lion-dog cannons. I'd put in a massive order with Shabon, anticipating a battle like this one. I was glad I'd sent them to the Empire along with the relief supplies.

In this world without rifles, the lion-dog cannon was the most maneuverable kind of gunpowder weapon. They looked silly but had proven exceptionally reliable in battles at sea, which were similar to the conditions we faced now. And it'd taken a significant amount of capital to purchase them from the Nine-Headed Dragon Archipelago Kingdom.

Fuuga's forces were thrown into disarray as they found themselves suddenly without magic and exposed to a hail of fist-sized projectiles. They'd come with countermeasures next time. This strategy was the type that was only guaranteed to work on someone who hadn't seen it, but it was enough to break their will to fight for now.

"Ugh, this feels weird."

I looked over at Naden, who was acting like she had a hangover. Naden and Ruby started to feel ill whenever they were present during cannon fire. That was probably because they used magicium in order to assume their dragon or human forms.

"Sorry, Naden. Can you hang in there a little longer?"

"Ngh..."

As I patted her on the head, Naden gave me a look that said, "Fine, if I have to."

"Sir Souma. What is it that you had us fire from the cannon? We prepared it for you because you said it would make magic unusable..." Maria asked, pointing outside the walls.

Yeah, she would want to know that, wouldn't she? I thought, then said, "It's made using curse ore, the energy source we use for the drill, only compressed to concentrate its effect. When it's activated, it will nullify or weaken all magic. The machine sucks up all the energy used to manifest magic effects. I guess you could call it a magic canceler."

"Sucks it up... So it doesn't nullify it like our magic armor soldiers' armor, then?"

"Right. You've got the idea," I said, nodding.

If magic were water, their magic armor would be like a dry suit, while our magic canceler was like a lump of diatomaceous earth, sucking it all up in an instant. But what that thing was sucking up wasn't harmless water—it was energy.

"So if you keep trying to use magic near it, eventually you'll go beyond its capacity and—"

Ka-boom!!!

Before I could even finish, there was a loud explosion, followed by a ground-shaking impact. Looking over, I saw a massive plume of black smoke rising from one corner of Fuuga's forces.

"It'll blow up like that..."

I was treated to the rare sight of the Saint of the Empire staring at me in blank confusion. It was likely destroyed from an attack by those among Fuuga's forces who'd figured out the magic canceler was rendering magic unusable. Given that soldiers in this world enhanced their attacks with magic, with magic nullified, it might have only looked like they were whaling on a hunk of metal with ordinary swords—but without knowing it, they had been pouring magical energy into the canceler. Then it hit capacity and exploded.

"The reason curse ore is so hated isn't just because finding it while mining means you can no longer use magic, but because if you keep trying to use magic, it explodes and causes cave-ins. We designed the magic canceler with that negative aspect of curse ore fully in mind."

With my idea that magicium were nanomachines and curse ore was made up of nonfunctional nanomachines, Genia, Merula, and Trill had spent the last two years researching curse ore. The magic canceler was a by-product of that research.

When I heard that curse ore nullified magic and exploded, my first thought was that it could be scattered as a weapon. But I gave up on the idea because it would linger in the soil, causing harm to people long afterwards like cluster munitions or depleted uranium. However, with the development of the magic canceler, which denied the use of magic over a wide area without scattering it, I was able to force my enemies to fight without magic.

Incidentally, the one that just went off had *deliberately had its capacity lowered.* That was Hakuya's idea.

"When we use the magic canceler, we should deliberately include a number of them with lowered capacity. If we show them early on that it will explode, we can reduce the enemy's attacks on the canceler. They're also unlikely to carry it back after the war that way. No one wants to take something dangerous into their own camp, after all."

I thought that was what he said. My prime minister was reliable and nasty. *But, well, it's not purely advantageous to us...it's like an EMP attack.* If we used the magic canceler, the enemy couldn't use magic, but neither could we. Near a magic canceler, Naden and the wyverns couldn't fly, and our options for ranged attacks were limited to simple bows and cannons. Also, while the magic canceler was in use, there was no way to cast healing magic on the wounded. We needed to fight a defensive battle without magic. This time, we had a large number of gunpowder weapons ready, but preparing them and using them cost an incredible amount.

In all likelihood, we had spent an incomparably greater sum on this battle than Fuuga's forces had. There was also the simple fact that we couldn't mass-produce magic cancelers. It just wasn't a method we could use every time. However, in its big debut, it proved extremely effective.

When Fuuga's forces saw the massive explosion, they lost all will to keep on fighting and pulled back from the walls of Valois like a receding tide. It was safe to say the crisis in the capital was at an end for the moment.

Once the main body of Friedonia's National Defense Force arrived from the west, it would be impossible for Fuuga's forces to completely annihilate the Empire, so I expected Fuuga was going to have to take the win I was offering him.

"Once Fuuga's forces retreat, I want you to retrieve and shut down the magic cancelers. Don't let your guards down," I ordered my subordinates.

Soon after that, the messenger came bearing word that Fuuga had accepted our ceasefire.

Meanwhile, around that same time, Jeanne was crying at Jamona Fortress.

Jeanne had seen it all for herself over the broadcast, the way Souma had saved her sister. She'd heard it for herself, the state of the war all across the continent. And that the one who'd devised the plan was Hakuya, the Black-robed Prime Minister. Despite refusing his help, and despite the difficult situation it put the Kingdom of Friedonia in, he had still extended a helping hand to her.

"*I won't let you die.*"

Jeanne could have sworn she heard his voice.

Thank you... Sir Hakuya...

Jeanne gripped her chest as she silently shed tears. In order to give her a moment to compose herself, her second-in-command, Gunther, silently watched Fuuga's forces outside the fortress.

CHAPTER 10
Shedding Tears

THAT NIGHT, in Valois...

I had taken off my uniform and changed into a shirt before taking a broadcast call with someone.

"Fuuga has sent an envoy accepting the ceasefire," said Liscia on the other end, looking relieved.

"I see. We can relax for now, then."

She was currently with Excel, leading the main body of the Friedonian National Defense Force that had landed on the west coast. If we'd used our shipping capacity and the Empire's transport network to their fullest, they would have arrived here sooner. However, though we'd announced over the broadcast that the Friedonians were the Empire's allies, we were still a force of more than 10,000 foreign soldiers appearing out of nowhere. The towns and villages along their route were no doubt trembling in fear. We had to be considerate of that, which slowed them down a little.

If Imperial citizens decided we were an enemy they had to resist, it would lead to unnecessary casualties. In order to prevent that, we had to send people ahead to explain the situation, calming the citizenry as we advanced. That limited our march to a cautious speed.

"Still, I expect we'll be there sometime around tomorrow. But don't let your guards down until then."

"Yeah. I want to see your face soon too, Liscia."

"Hee hee, thanks... Wait, now's not the time to think about me." Liscia leveled a finger at me from the other side of the broadcast. "Souma, you need to be with Madam Maria now... I'm sure she must feel crushed—like you were that day."

"Yeah..."

Although we'd made it through the current crisis, Maria was staying shut up inside her room. Her fate, and that of the Empire, rested on negotiations between Fuuga and me. While the Empire wouldn't be destroyed outright, they were the defeated party in a war. I couldn't even imagine what a defeated empress like Maria must be feeling right now. Liscia was likely worried she might try to take her own life again...

"I told her off for it, so I don't think she'll throw herself from the balcony again..." I said.

"It's still more than one person can bear on their own. The only one who can be with Madam Maria right now...the only one who understands the burdens she was bearing...is you, right? You're the one who can protect her heart."

Of course I would, I thought. I had every intention of trying to help Maria. "But what can I do...?"

"Go and spoil her."

"Spoil...her?"

"Do whatever she wants you to. Madam Maria's been shouldering a nation all by herself this whole time. As a fellow woman, and as a fellow royal, I respect her. So, just...set her free. Accept her wishes, her loss, her desire, her regrets, and her pain. As your first primary queen, I give you my permission to do whatever you have to do."

"Ha ha ha..." Liscia sure was amazing. I needed to prepare myself. "Okay. I'm going to spoil Maria absolutely rotten."

I headed straight to Maria's room as soon as I wrapped up my talk with Liscia. Outside Maria's door, there was one dratrooper whom I'd left to guard her, plus one Imperial guard. I greeted them quickly, then stood in front of the door, steadying my breathing before I knocked.

"Madam Maria, it's Souma. May I come in?"

"Sir Souma...? Please do," came Maria's voice from inside the room.

I opened the door and entered. My first impression: it was dark. The candles were unlit, and there was only pale moonlight shining in through the window. I was glad it wasn't cloudy tonight. If not for the moonlight, it would probably have been too dark for us to have a proper conversation.

Closing the door behind me, I glanced around at the expensive-looking furniture and other decorations. Overall, the tone of the room was light and feminine.

Maria was standing by the window. When I walked close enough that we could see one another's expressions, she smiled faintly at me.

"...This reminds me of the time we met in Zem."

"Now that you mention it...the moon was bright that night too."

Maria chuckled. "Yes. And we made a promise under the moonlight. That's why you're here with me now."

"I'm still not sure...it's something to be happy about, though," I said with a shrug.

That day, when we first met in Zem, in exchange for the Empire's help with the (then) Nine-Headed Dragon Archipelago Union, Maria proposed that I promise her something in exchange. At the time, it had been something that seemed unthinkable.

Here is what Maria said...

"If at some point in the future...the Empire looks like it may break apart, I intend to split it without hesitation."

I was taken aback. I doubted my ears and could say nothing in response.

Not letting my reaction stop her, Maria continued. "Our country has grown too large. The population is too great for us to handle. I've accepted my position as the head of the Mankind Declaration up until today because I understood the necessity of a powerful nation as an emotional support in the confrontation against the Demon Lord's Domain... But now, the Kingdom of Friedonia is firmly established as a powerful nation in the east, and Sir Fuuga's faction has been rising as well. The era in which people relied on the Mankind Declaration to keep them going is drawing to an end."

She shook her head.

"No, that's not it," Maria corrected herself. "It's an old, ossified system that needs to be done away with. If all that remains in the hearts of my Empire's people is their pride in being the head of the Mankind Declaration, that's not a healthy place for us to be. I can't allow blood to be shed over pride. To that end, I think I am going to begin making preparations."

Maria's eyes were filled with conviction as she spoke.

"In order to cut off the hard-liners who obsess over how the Empire was once the greatest of all nations and want to get proactively involved in dealing with the Demon Lord's Domain, I will slowly gather them in the north by moving their domains there. That will make it easy for them to separate from the Empire when they give up on me."

"You're going to make them exercise the right of self-determination?!"

"Yes. The hole in the Mankind Declaration that you taught me about, Sir Souma. Because the declaration respects the right of cultural and racial groups to self-determination, we have no way of stopping them from leaving. The rules say we're not allowed to. I will have them 'take advantage' of that."

I held my head in my hands because I realized Maria was serious about dismantling the Empire. The breakup of a great power and the shifting power balance among countries in the vicinity—that was sure to cause great waves that would swallow up the nearby countries. It was guaranteed to have an effect on our country too.

I've gotta prepare, I thought urgently.

Then, in a quiet voice, Maria said, "I have a request for you... when that time comes."

"A request?"

"Yes. When that happens, the Mankind Declaration will be no more. The Empire will cease to be the strongest nation, and I believe it will be difficult for us to sustain the state on our own. Even once it comes to that...I still want to protect those who believe in me. I want to dismantle the country, not destroy it. So, when the time comes..."

Looking resolute, she stated her request.

"I want to form a non-secret alliance with the Kingdom."

Overcome with various thoughts, I managed to muster, "You shouldn't say ominous things like that..."

"It's important to prepare," Maria said with a laugh.

I was surprised that there was a leader who could prepare for that sort of thing. It gave me a new appreciation for her as the person who had supported the dignity of that great nation all by her lonesome.

At the same time, I realized she had reached her limits and was reaching out to me in search of salvation.

"Okay..." I said, taking her hand.

I felt both the rational desire as a king to prevent the collapse of the Empire and its effects on my country, as well as a personal wish to save the woman I saw in front of me. They both had the same answer, so I felt no hesitation.

"If that time ever comes, the Kingdom will do as you wish."

"I have faith in you, Sir Souma."

That was the promise we made.

"The Empire broke..." Maria said.

Hearing her, I came back to my senses.

She spoke of the breakup of the Empire like someone who was disappointed their favorite mug got broken. But...I knew better than to assume that the way she was talking was the same as how she felt inside. She'd been wearing masks all this time. The mask of the empress of the greatest nation in the world. The mask of the leader of the Mankind Declaration and all mankind. And the mask of a saint who was kind to everyone, yet her heart was always breaking.

No matter how she wished to be a single, ordinary person, those masks had stalked her everywhere. At times she used them, and at times they used her. To the point she'd forgotten what her original self was truly like.

Maria smiled softly as she continued. "I've spent a long time preparing so this day could come. I took those who wanted me to be a saint, those who wanted to take proactive steps towards the Demon Lord's Domain, and those who blindly worshiped me, and I concentrated them in the northern regions. I did it slowly, so they wouldn't notice. It even included Sir Krahe, who would have given his life for me, and Jeanne's former friend Lumiere."

I listened intently to her words.

"I made it easy to cut them loose. So that when my powers were no longer enough, I could let go of those lands and reorganize the Empire into something easier to rule... No, it can't be called an empire anymore. I can finally let go of the title of empress."

With a smile that could have been read either as wryly amused or as self-mocking, Maria put a hand over her chest.

"Still, now that it's come to this, my emotions are swelling up. Despite wanting to cast it aside all this time, sometimes I even desired to just break it outright. Now that it's broken, though, I feel pathetic. I'm overcome by a sense of regret I didn't expect to feel. Heh heh... I'm such a hopeless ruler."

"Madam Maria..." I walked closer, saying her name. But she continued talking.

"Heh... The truth is, I feel terrible for getting you, the Kingdom of Friedonia, and even the rest of the Maritime Alliance caught up in this. I'm sorry, but I have to count on you to look after things from here. I know you can be a healthier ruler than I was—one who the people won't turn into an idol. So..."

"Maria!"

I grabbed her by the shoulders and looked directly into her eyes, as if to say, "Look at me." Although she had been smiling as she spoke, she hadn't been looking at me at all. It seemed she'd killed her heart to the point where she couldn't see the face of the person she was talking to.

"Ow…! That hurts."

The smile that had been plastered on her face twisted with pain. I'd finally torn that mask off her.

I squeezed harder. Her arms were so slender that even my grip—which, despite all the training Owen had given me, was little better than a common grunt's—was painful to her. Yet still, these slender shoulders had been supporting the weight of a massive nation. How much of a toll must that have taken on her heart?

"That's enough, Maria…"

Something flowed from my eyes, down my cheek. The next thing I knew…I was crying before she had.

Maria stared at me, taken aback. Of course she would be. She was the one who really wanted to cry, but I'd beaten her to it.

"Sir…Souma?"

"That's enough, Maria. You don't…have to hold it in anymore."

The next moment, a large tear rolled down Maria's face. She touched it, overcome with surprise, and then looked down at her own hand.

"Ah…"

Her face, so composed before, scrunched up.

"Ah… Ahhhhhhhhhhhhh!!!"

She cried out loud.

Once I released my grip on her shoulders, she tried repeatedly to wipe the tears away. But that was impossible. She gave up and instead buried her tearstained face in my chest.

I gently embraced her delicate body.

The day my father died, I, Maria Euphoria, became empress.

During my father's reign, the distortions in the nation caused by past emperors' policy of expansionism had fueled unrest, leading the Gran Chaos Empire to enter an era of decline. Father was a temperate man, so he likely didn't mind that. However, with the emergence of the Demon Lord's Domain, people looked to our declining Empire to become the flag-bearer of mankind, and our authority began to recover. This led to the combined forces of mankind launching an incursion into the Demon Lord's Domain...and their utter defeat.

Father was grief-stricken at the thought of all those who died, and it ruined his heart, ravaged his body, and ultimately took his life. Even so, I inherited a massive empire. Those were dark days.

The towns were full of voices of uncertainty... Refugees driven from their homes with nowhere to go. Those living on the border worried they would be next. Rulers suspicious of one another. Friction with the refugees, and my own people struggling with the poor economy.

"What'll happen now...?"

"There ain't nothing we can do. The attack on the Demon Lord's Domain was a bust..."

"It's only gonna get worse from here on."

They all hung their heads, none of them able to see a bright future.

Those with some degree of affluence, fearing it would be taken away, were unable to show compassion to others. That left the refugees, the poor, and the other downtrodden of society to suffer. It was an era without hope. I wanted to do what little I could to change that.

First, I set up the Mankind Declaration, serving as the chief signatory to the pact, and showed the world that things were not going to get any worse than they were. At the same time, I used my position as the empress of a superpower to keep other countries in line, preventing wars between all the other nations of mankind. I wanted to be the hope that would allow people to raise their heads.

As I did all of this, the expansion of the Demon Lord's Domain led to the pressure from monster attacks to be distributed more widely. That created a stalemate, and the Empire and other countries began to calm down. Then, as calm returned, they came to call me the Saint of the Empire.

While I was pleased to have become a source of hope for people, I was hated by the Lunarian Orthodox Church as a result. Still, I had accepted that.

Donning the mask of a peaceful ruler, I smiled at them harmoniously. The rulers who, despite their wariness of my country, requested our assistance and looked for any opportunity to take advantage. The impoverished people, longing to be saved from their miserable standard of living. My own retainers, ossified by their pride in belonging to the greatest country and calling for revenge against the Demon Lord's Domain... I had to act so that all of these people would see me as a good ruler.

The only one I could show my true self to was my sister, Jeanne. I would go to her room, sit by her bedside, and chat with her about silly nonsense as she looked at me in exasperation.

"Jeanne...I'm tired. Can I borrow your lap as a pillow?"

"Oh, for goodness' sake. And you act so dignified in front of everyone else..."

Despite her sighs, she would always relent and let me rest my head in her lap. Thinking back to it now...I may have been wearing a mask even then. The mask of Jeanne's undisciplined big sister.

I acted that way to keep Jeanne from worrying, letting her see me slack off so she would think I still had some flexibility. The truth was, I had actually hit my limits long ago and was only acting the way people demanded of me. I could even play at being a lorelei. But...I had one small sliver of hope: Sir Souma Kazuya, the hero summoned by what was then the Kingdom of Elfrieden.

I had offered performing the hero summoning ritual to the Kingdom as an alternative because I knew they couldn't pay us war subsidies. I never thought it would actually work... And I never in my wildest dreams imagined Sir Souma would rebuild the declining Kingdom, annex the Principality of Amidonia—albeit with Princess Roroa's help—and become the greatest power in the east.

I had finally found someone who could shoulder the burdens of the world with me. Souma, unlike myself, would not become anyone's ideal. He would keep his eyes firmly set on reality and would steadily carry out his political vision, even if he had to be cruel to do it.

From the time he appeared, little by little, I was able to show more and more of my true self: the Maria Euphoria who was not an empress or a saint but an ordinary human being.

"You and him are like oil and water... It feels like you two are facing entirely different directions..."

Come to think of it, that's how Jeanne saw Sir Souma at first. How did I respond? Hmmm... Oh, yes!

"But if we're both facing different directions, don't you think we could eliminate our blind spots if we cooperate?"

That's what I said. Right, Jeanne? What I said then. What I felt at that moment. Maybe you understand it now?

Having a king in a faraway land, one with a different perspective, who was willing to be my trusty ally. One who'd extend his hand to me as my country fell into ruin and I was on the verge of death. And who, even now, was lending me his chest to lean on as my heart felt ready to tear itself in two.

Do you see how wonderful it is to have someone like that?

"Wahhhhhhhhhh!!!"

I was now shamelessly bawling my eyes out on Sir Souma's chest. When was the last time I could show my true feelings like this?

Souma gently embraced me as I was, stroking my back.

"I...! I—"

"Yeah..."

"I-I didn't want to just be nice to everyone!" I stammered as I sniffled. "The truth is, I just wanted to protect those I care about—the people who care about me! I wanted to play favorites!"

"Yeah..."

"The ones I really wanted to protect were the normal people in town... The people struggling in their ordinary lives... The refugees driven from their homelands... I wanted to be their hope! But if I was only kind to those people, I was sure to meet resistance! For the people who wanted me to liberate the Demon Lord's Domain, to show that the Empire was the greatest nation in the world...I needed to act like I was a good ruler."

"Yeah..."

"In my heart...I didn't care about that... If people could live in peace, that was enough for me... But I was forced to wear the mask of the serene and powerful ruler. I...I don't want to do that anymore..."

"Yeah...I know."

Sir Souma's arms tightened around me. I was close enough now that I could feel his heartbeat, and he most likely could feel mine too. It felt like proof I was revealing everything to him.

Sir Souma whispered in my ear. "The world is stronger now because of all your desperate efforts. The Kingdom of Friedonia, the Republic of Turgis, and the Nine-Headed Dragon Archipelago Kingdom have all come into their own. And, while I know it's weird to say this about a person who just tried to destroy the Empire, Fuuga is a great man. The world won't be destroyed easily. This isn't an era for everyone to keep their eyes downcast anymore. And the one who led us out of those times… is you, Maria. Never doubt that."

"Yes…"

Held in Sir Souma's arms, I turned my eyes up at him.

"But I didn't do it on my own. It's because you were out there too."

"Ah ha ha… I'm honored to hear that. Well, I've got allies like Kuu and Shabon, and family and friends who support me. Even a powerful enemy like Fuuga. If any one of those were missing, I don't know that I could have come this far. So…"

Sir Souma pushed away from me before placing his hand softly on my cheek.

"There's no need for you to shoulder everything anymore. We'll carry the burden with you."

"Sir Souma…"

"I'm powerless alone, but I have all the help I'll need: family, people, and allies aplenty. There are lots of us to carry the world on our shoulders, so let's take it on with a human wave attack."

"Hee hee… You're pushing it off on all of them." Hearing the way Sir Souma talked about it finally brought a smile to my face.

"There's nothing wrong with that. In my country, our style is to delegate things to people we can trust to do them. So…" With his hand still on my cheek, Souma smiled softly at me. "You can do what you want from now on too."

Those words smashed all the masks I'd been wearing all this time.

The burden fell from my shoulders, the tension faded, and I even felt like I was floating weightlessly in the air. I must have had a real goofy look on my face when I was set free.

I reached out, touched Sir Souma's cheek...and pinched him.

"Ow..."

"I thought I might be dreaming."

"Don't you have to pinch your own cheek to test that?"

"I can feel pain in my own dreams."

"Yeah, I dunno then."

As we were having such a silly exchange, the tears went away.

"Is it really...okay for me to do what I want?"

"I don't see why not. I'm sure you've been repressing yourself for one hell of a long time."

"I see..." I grinned at Souma and said, "There's something I want to do right this second. Do you mind?"

"Mm. Sure, if it's something I can do. Liscia told me to spoil you, after all."

"Lovely."

I grabbed Sir Souma's face hard with both my hands. As he stared at me in surprise, I stood on my tiptoes, and...the very next moment, my lips locked with his.

Seconds later, when our faces parted, his eyes were wide. I chuckled at his goofy expression.

Then, as he stared at me in a daze, I told him:

"From now on, I think I'll do what I want without holding back. So...accept me for everything that I am."

HOW A REALIST HERO REBUILT THE KINGDOM

CHAPTER 11

Sisters

I HAD LEARNED one thing.

"Purr..."

Maria was basically like a cat when spoiled absolutely rotten.

The Saint of the Empire was purring with her head in my lap. She murmured contentedly each time I ran my fingers through her glossy hair. I rubbed my eyes as the morning sun shone in through the window.

Last night was...tough.

Maria had likely been at her limits emotionally. Her guilt over splitting the country and for having thrown away others for the sake of those she wanted to help, the uncertainty over how the people would view her action, and the relief at being set free from all her burdens... All those thoughts and feelings were whirling about inside of her, keeping her awake. And the few times she did manage to get to sleep, she'd sprung awake again right after.

And every time she did, I held her close.

True to my word, when I said I'd spoil her rotten, I did everything she asked me to. If she couldn't sleep, I'd chat about all sorts of inconsequential things with her, and if she woke from a nightmare, I'd hold her tight and whisper I was by her side. If she cried, I would pet her gently, and if she shivered, I would share the warmth of my body. Basically, I responded to and accepted all of her desires in order to lighten her heart. That all led to now, with her head in my lap.

I was wearing a shirt and pants, while Maria was wearing a negligee, but I didn't remember when we got changed... Actually, I was so tired that all my memories were kind of vague.

I'm gonna need to get a psychiatrist, or a counselor, or...something, I thought with whatever part of my brain still worked.

Even if I knew what kind of work they did, I didn't have any specialized knowledge of the field. That was why I was currently gathering people interested in the mind at Ginger's Vocational School and having them collect medical cases. In this world, where faith was deeply tied to people's lives, many issues of the psyche were brought to the church. Thus, I had Archbishop Souji and the confessional rooms of Kingdom Orthodoxy cooperate with them.

"Sir Soumaaa... Pet me mooore..."

"Fine, fine."

I got back to the job of petting Maria's head. I was a little worried she'd reverted to some childlike state.

"It's morning..."

"*Mew*... I don't wanna go to work."

"Yeah... I think you can rest for a while. The talks will probably be in the afternoon."

The situation was still tense, but Liscia and Excel would arrive with the main force soon, and Hakuya was supposed to pick up Jeanne at Jamona Fortress on his way here. I'd told Fuuga to call Hashim from Jamona Fortress too. It would probably take until midday before everyone arrived.

I wanted to get some shut-eye in preparation for that, but...

"Hee hee, Sir Soumaaa."

Maria held my hand, rubbing her cheek against the back of it. She was looking better now that she'd gotten some sleep, but was she going to let *me* go anytime soon?

Meanwhile, as dawn broke, Hakuya the Black-robed Prime Minister had arrived at Jamona Fortress. While he descended from the wyvern's gondola, Jeanne—who'd been informed in advance and was waiting for him—leapt into his arms.

"Sir Hakuya!"

"Ah! Madam Jeanne..." Hakuya embraced her as she snuggled up to his chest. "I'm...so glad you're all right."

"Urkh... Sorry. I told you we were going to be fine, but look at this sad display... We dragged you and the Kingdom into it."

"No. I am here at His Majesty's command, searching for the optimal outcome for us."

With that, Hakuya let go of Jeanne and wiped away the tears from her eyes.

"If I'd lost you, I wouldn't have been able to come up with the best possible future anymore."

"Sir Hakuya..."

Jeanne had tried to hold them in because of all the soldiers watching, but she was unable to hold back the flood of tears. Gunther and the soldiers of the Empire's eyes widened at the sight of Jeanne bawling. It was the first time she'd shown so much emotion.

She'd always been on edge. As the younger sister of the empress, and as a general of the Empire, Jeanne had been unable to rely on anyone due to her own incomparable talents, forcing her to stand strong and dignified all this time. But she had someone to lean on now. The soldiers who understood this wept with her—even the taciturn general Gunther.

Hakuya waited for Jeanne to settle down before he spoke.

"After this, I will be heading to Valois for armistice talks. Madam Jeanne, I would like you to accompany me."

"*Sniff*... You would?" Jeanne wiped her tears and looked up at Hakuya. "Of course. I'd like to go with you. However...I am not sure I can leave our defenses here..."

"Go, Madam Jeanne," Gunther said, interrupting her objection. He thumped his armored chest. "Leave defending this place to us. Even if the Great Tiger Kingdom's forces attack once you leave, we'll send them packing as many times as we have to. Am I right, men?!"

"Yeahhhhhhh!!!"

The Imperial soldiers cheered loudly in response.

That was to be expected with so many who loved the House of Euphoria gathered here. Gunther gave Jeanne what was definitely a smile, even if it was hard to recognize it as one due to his brusque nature.

"We will hold down the fort here, so you go and support Her Imperial Majesty. I am sure she'll be wanting to see your face."

"Sir Gunther..."

"Black-robed Prime Minister of Friedonia. Please, look after Lady Jeanne for us."

Gunther bowed his head to him, and Hakuya gave the man a firm nod.

"I'll do just that."

And so, the two of them boarded Hakuya's wyvern gondola and soared away into the skies.

In the wyvern gondola, Hakuya looked worriedly at Jeanne, who was sitting across from him. Because her face was turned downwards, Hakuya, who was taller and whose seat was higher, couldn't see her expression.

"What will become of the Empire...and Sister?" Jeanne murmured. Hakuya hesitated, but decided to be frank with her.

"I'm sure it won't be able to remain an empire anymore. Madam Maria won't be an empress either."

"Oh...is that right?"

"Yes. But that was what Madam Maria wished for."

"Huh...?"

Hakuya explained the events leading up to this situation to Jeanne. How Maria wished to shrink the Empire. The little changes she'd made to her vassals' domains. The overtures she'd made to Souma so that she would have the support of the Maritime Alliance when the time came. And lastly...how she'd executed her plan to cut loose some of her territory when Fuuga's forces came to attack.

When Jeanne heard it all, she covered her face with both hands. "I made my sister carry all the burden again...!"

"I must admit, Madam Maria is incredible to have been able to plan out this entire scenario all by herself," Hakuya said, his voice calm. "However, she has needed the help of many people to put her plan into action and to clean up after it. It was not the product of her efforts alone. This may, in fact, be the first time she has reached out to others for help."

"Reached out...for help?"

Hakuya nodded silently.

"And His Majesty took her hand. He turned to many people in order to save Madam Maria. While His Majesty may not be the kind of ruler who stands out, he has the earnestness to seek help from others, and the power to make them want to lend him their strength. That's how he was able to mobilize not just the Kingdom of Friedonia, but the Republic of Turgis and the Nine-Headed Dragon Archipelago Kingdom as well. When I offered my services to him, I told him he has quite some potential as a king."

"Is that supposed to be a compliment...?"

"It's the highest praise I offer."

The way Hakuya said that with a nonchalant expression got a chuckle out of Jeanne.

"Sir Souma must be amazing to be able to support my sister."

"I told you, didn't I? His Majesty has a talent for getting other people to help. Without the others, this wouldn't have been possible. Obviously, that includes you and your people as well."

"Us too?"

"By delaying the Great Tiger Kingdom's forces, you gave us the time we needed to get there. If they had been able to take more than just the northern lands, negotiations would have been far more difficult."

"I see..." Jeanne teared up a little and smiled slightly. "You think I was able to help my sister, even if just a little."

"Yes. And..."

"And?"

"It seems likely...that the time when we will truly need your power is about to come, Madam Jeanne."

"My power?" Jeanne blinked at him.

Hakuya nodded. "Whatever the result...this war will be a defeat for the Empire. Even if everything has gone as Madam Maria wished, it's still an armistice with the northern territories stolen. Madam Maria will have to take responsibility as the leader of the defeated army."

"Ah...!"

"Obviously, her life will be in no danger. As parties to the negotiations, we wouldn't allow that. However, in the new, smaller country, it will be impossible for Madam Maria to stay on as empress. I don't know if it will be a queen or empress who rules, but that title will have to go to someone else. And as for who that someone is..."

Hakuya stared intently at Jeanne. Suddenly, it hit her.

"Huh?! *Me*?!"

"Did you think that your other sister, Princess Trill, could?"

"Oh, no! I'm sure that's impossible... But I'm not fond of politics either! I could never be a ruler like my sister..."

"There's no need for you to shoulder everything the way Madam Maria did. You can take someone well-versed in politics as your royal consort and work with him to rule the country."

"Royal consort...? But..."

Essentially, Hakuya was telling her to take a husband. Jeanne was shocked into silence, hearing those words from him. The feelings she had built up for Hakuya during their broadcast conferences were screaming inside her. However, that was only to last a second.

Hakuya slowly stood up, then dropped to one knee before Jeanne.

"S-Sir Hakuya?"

"I will support you. Not over the broadcast, but at your side from now on," he said, offering his right hand to her.

He was offering—proposing—to be her royal consort.

Jeanne blinked rapidly. "Huh?! You're going to come be my husband?! You, Sir Hakuya?!"

"Yes."

"What about the Kingdom?! You're their prime minister, right?!"

"I've already received permission from His Majesty. It means I will have to serve as the prime minister of both countries for a time, but I intend to live in the Empire. I'm sure my duties in the Kingdom will slowly be assumed by my successor, Sir Ichiha."

Hakuya was predicting the new empire would be in a personal union with the Kingdom of Friedonia. If you looked at the closeness of the relationship between Souma and Maria, it was entirely possible to predict she would marry him now that she was no longer an empress. Then Souma would be entrusted with the imperial title like he had the princely title of Amidonia. But unlike the Principality, which had been their neighbor, the Empire was not connected to them geographically, so it would be difficult to annex. This meant there would be a personal union headed by Souma to strengthen relations between the two countries, while the actual ruling would be done by their new ruler, Jeanne. In that situation, Hakuya could be the prime minister of both countries.

Jeanne looked at him, confused. "Are you sure? It's going to be difficult, you know?"

"I am prepared for that. His Majesty told me to be ready for it too."

"You're really okay with coming to the Empire?"

"I find myself looking forward to it, surprisingly enough..." Hakuya wore a faint smile that you would never have expected from him normally. "I hear that the Great Library of Valois is even more wonderful than the archives we have in the Kingdom."

"Murgh... Your number one reason is books?"

"Heh, certainly not. My number one is you, of course."

"Well, that's fine then." Jeanne took Hakuya's hand. "I suppose...I'll be able to touch you whenever I like from now on."

"For so long as I live."

"I'm starting to feel like I can give it my best. But that means I'll have to get used to ordering you around..."

With that said, Jeanne let go of Hakuya's hand and patted the seat beside her.

"First, I'd like you to sit beside me."

"By your will."

Hakuya sat next to Jeanne as directed. Jeanne kept going.

"Let's see. I think I'll have you put your arm around me next."

"Heh, is that an order?"

When Hakuya pointedly asked that question, Jeanne smiled shyly.

"No. It's a cute request from the woman who's going to be your wife."

Around two o'clock that afternoon, the Friedonian National Defense Force arrived in Valois.

Fuuga seemed uninterested in continuing the war, and the forces of the Great Tiger Kingdom had broken the siege of the Imperial capital, so the National Defense Force deployed across from them. This was done intentionally in case Fuuga's forces desired to keep fighting.

While the National Defense Force led by Excel and Ludwin kept the forces of the Great Tiger Kingdom in check, Liscia came to Valois Castle with Aisha. Naden and I met with them in the castle's governmental affairs office.

"Souma, you okay? You're not hurt anywhere, are you?" were the first words out of Liscia's mouth as she started touching me all over, checking for injuries. I felt like now that she was the mother of two infants and helped the other queens with theirs too, she was even more prone to fussing over me.

I smiled wryly and placed a hand on Liscia's shoulder. "I told you, I'm fine. You saw the broadcast, right? I've been in the castle ever since."

"But you caught Madam Maria as she was falling, right? No one told me there'd be a show like that, so I got the shivers."

"Yeah...so did I," I said. *Thinking back...because Maria opted to pull that stunt herself, I shudder to think what would've happened if I hadn't made it in time.*

Liscia waived to Aisha, who reacted with evident glee. She was wagging her metaphorical tail as she came over to have her turn with me.

"Your Majesty! I've missed you so!"

"Oh, come on, it's only been a few days, right?"

"But you didn't take me with you when you were going to a castle under siege," she complained, her cheeks puffing up. "That made me feel so lonely as your queen and bodyguard. If I were with you, I could have mowed down the onrushing hordes of Great Tiger Kingdom soldiers."

That's an awfully violent thing to be saying with cheeks puffed up so cutely...

I smiled wryly as I patted Aisha on the head. "Sorry. But I had to consider the possibility that, if Fuuga decided not to be reasonable, there might be a fight between our forces. I wanted to have you at Liscia's side if it came to that."

"Hrmm... Well, yes, I do want to protect Liscia too..."

"Hee hee, thanks for always being there, Aisha," Liscia said.

"Yes, ma'am! You're too kind!" Aisha snapped off a salute in response to Liscia's smile.

They got along great thanks to all the burdens they'd shared and the experience of raising children together. Although, you could say that about any two of my wives.

Next, Liscia smiled at Naden. "Thanks for taking care of Souma, Naden."

"Hey, it's my job. I'm not much of a dragon, but he's still my knight," she replied with a smug snort. All the while, Naden's scaly tail flopped back and forth, slapping the ground behind her.

She's so easy to read. It always brought a smile to my face watching my wives interact.

"Hee hee! By the way, Souma?" Liscia looked at me suspiciously.

"Hm?"

"It's been in the corner of my eye all this time, so I've been wondering...what is that?"

Liscia was looking at the curtains covering the windows next to the door that led out onto the balcony. One of them bulged out unnaturally, wrapping around itself.

"Oh, that..." I scratched my cheek. "...would be the empress of this country."

"Come again?" Liscia looked at me sideways. I could practically see the question mark floating over her head.

"Ah...Madam Maria? Would you come out already?"

The lump in the curtains twitched as I called her name. Then, spinning to unwind herself, she emerged bright red, her airy, long hair a little disheveled and her eyes somewhat teary.

Liscia stared, dumbfounded to see the normally calm and self-possessed Maria in this state. "What...on earth happened to her?"

"I spoiled her like you said, and, well...this is the result."

I'd indulged Maria's every whim the night before. Spoken and unspoken. This led to Maria mewling like a kitten until almost dawn. Unlike me, who had been caring for her all night, Maria's complexion had been improved greatly by proper rest. That meant she was more conscious than I was.

Yes, having come back to her senses, Maria remembered all the things we'd done last night. Everything from the moment she kissed me, to the things we got up to after that—most importantly, the time she spent acting like a kitty. So...

"Sir Souma, pet me moooore."

"Mrrow... I don't wanna wooork."

She remembered all the times she'd talked to me in that purring voice.

When she'd woken up in bed, resting on my arm, and found me asleep beside her (I'd obviously hit my limit), a flood of memories from the night before came flooding back. By the time I myself woke up, Maria was too embarrassed to look me in the face. Instead, she thrashed around with her face buried in a pillow. It was kinda cute.

"And that's how we got to where we are now?" Liscia asked after hearing my explanation, and I nodded.

"Yep."

"For Madam Maria to be so embarrassed... Just what did she do?"

"You should have seen the way she purr—"

"Don't tell her!" Maria cried, covering my mouth to shut me up.

Then, trying to cover up the awkwardness, Maria cleared her throat.

"Um...it's been a while, hasn't it, Lady Liscia?"

"Huh? Ohh, yes it has. Since the leaders' meeting in the Dragon Knight Kingdom, I think?"

"That sounds right. About two years, then?"

"At the time, I'd never have guessed our next meeting would be like this." Liscia looked into Maria's eyes. "But you were already preparing for this at that point."

"Yes, I was..." Maria said with a slightly apologetic smile. "The leader of a nation, preparing to break it up. It was cowardly of me, wasn't it?"

"No...I actually respect you for that. You stayed true to yourself, defending those you wanted to defend—even if that meant the country broke up and people blamed you for it. As someone born into a royal family myself, and as a fellow woman, I find that so impressive it makes me jealous."

"Oh...! Thank you, Lady Liscia." Maria smiled, her eyes dewy with tears. She'd found another person who understood her.

Liscia, meanwhile, groaned, a difficult expression on her face.

Maria looked at her quizzically and asked, "Is something the matter?"

"I've heard from Hakuya what happens next. You're probably not going to be empress anymore. And once you're free, you want to come marry Souma, right?"

"Well...yes. If it's possible, I'd like that," Maria said, blushing and glancing in my direction.

Liscia, Aisha, and Naden's eyes all stabbed into me. They weren't blaming me per se, but I still felt guilty. It was like I was sleeping on a bed of needles.

Liscia let out a sigh. "Will I be able to do a good job standing above you as the first primary queen...?"

"I'll make you look better. Unlike me, who cast it all away, you've bravely carried the burden your blood placed on your shoulders, haven't you?" Maria smiled slightly at Liscia. "And I'll do what little I can to support you in that, of course."

"Madam Maria..."

"Hee hee. Though, now that I won't be empress, I've found something I want to do, so I think I'd like to put that before any work in the castle."

"And what might that be?" Liscia asked.

With a mischievous smile, Maria just put a finger to her lips. "It's still a secret for now," she said. "We'll talk when I've gone back to being 'just Maria.'"

Maria looked so beautiful when she said that. *What does she want to do?* She hadn't told me either, but it was clear she had some bright future penned out for herself. That made me happier than anything.

While we were chatting, a messenger rushed in to inform us that Hakuya and Jeanne had arrived. We all hurried to the court-yard of Valois Castle.

Jeanne was just coming out of the gondola as we got there.

"Jeanne!"

"Huh?! Sister!"

Maria ran over and dived into her sister's arms. Jeanne looked surprised at first, but was soon shedding massive tears as she hugged her, verklempt to see her sister was safe.

Seeing the Euphoria sisters reunited, I felt a heat in my chest. *I must protect these two.* It burned hot enough to make me swear that to myself.

"Honestly, Sister! Do you have any idea how much trouble you caused for everyone?!"

"Yes..."

Once they were reunited, Maria and Jeanne asked the others

to give them some time alone, and they retreated to Maria's room. Now Maria was being forced to kneel on the bed while Jeanne gave her an earful.

Maria was shrinking into herself like a little girl despite being a woman in her mid-twenties.

"When I saw you jump…it nearly tore me apart! The soldiers at Jamona Fortress were all screaming too! You've always been like this! You don't value yourself enough! It's just unbearable for everyone else watching!"

"Yes…I'm sorry."

"Yeah… You…better be…" Jeanne said, her voice rising in anger. But gradually it stifled as her eyes filled with tears. "Big Sister…"

"Jeanne…"

"I'm… I'm just so…so glad…you were…all right… Wahhhhhh!" Jeanne squeezed Maria tight as she bawled. Maria wrapped her arms around Jeanne and softly stroked her back.

"Jeanne. You're making it a little hard to breathe."

"Ohhh… Just put up with it for a little while…" Jeanne said, sniffling.

"Hee hee! Okay."

Maria continued gently embracing Jeanne as she cried.

Some time later, once Jeanne had settled down, Maria stopped kneeling and had Jeanne sit next to her. The two sisters sat side by side on the bed. Maria was patting Jeanne on the head when she brought up something they needed to talk about.

"Hey, Jeanne. There's something I wanted to ask you for."

Jeanne sniffled before asking, "What is it…?"

"It's something I can't do well myself, so I wanted to ask you," Maria said with a soft smile.

"A-are you sure about this, Sister?" Jeanne asked hesitantly as she stood behind Maria, who was sitting in a chair.

Maria, however, was completely relaxed. "Yes. Chop away," she said in a chipper tone. That made Jeanne steel herself for what she had to do.

"O-okay... I'll start cutting, then!"

With those words to rouse herself to action, Jeanne squeezed the scissors she was holding.

Snip! The scissors snapped shut, and a lock of Maria's beautiful golden hair fell and scattered across the floor.

"Eek!" Jeanne cried out in surprise, jumping backwards.

Jeanne had fearlessly faced Nata Chima, a man who was like the incarnation of violence. Yet now, she was reacting like a peasant girl who'd suddenly come across a frog.

Maria chuckled at how odd that was. "Hee hee, what are you screaming for?"

"B-but! Your hair!"

"Don't make such a big deal of a little haircut," Maria said, toying with her bangs. "Ever since I heard the story of how Liscia cut her hair as a show of determination, I've wanted to do the same thing. I feel like it will help me get a fresh start."

Jeanne blinked repeatedly. "You're doing this so lightly?! But you've been growing your hair out forever, haven't you?"

"I did it because I thought it would help give off the

impression of a dignified empress, but...it's heavy, you know? And hard to take care of. I'm starting to feel like it's the embodiment of my title as empress."

"Don't say such heavy things so easily."

"That's why I wanted to take the chance to chop it off. But I'm not confident I could cut it as neatly as Liscia did, which is why I wanted you to help me."

"That's fair... It would probably go horribly if you were to attempt it yourself."

Maria was kind of clumsy when it came to anything other than being charismatic or taking care of her administrative work. It was easy to imagine that even if she were just evening out her bangs on her own, she'd cut them strangely and then come crying to Jeanne for help anyways.

When Jeanne imagined her sister looking like such a goof, whatever strong feelings she'd had over cutting her sister's hair rapidly cooled.

Maria beckoned her sister. "Come on, Jeanne. The job's not done yet. If you leave me like this, I'll look weird, missing just part of my hair. I'd be too embarrassed to let Souma and the others see me like this."

"Right, right..." Jeanne sighed and got back to cutting Maria's hair.

Snip, snip. Each time the scissors went into Maria's hair, strands of gold scattered across the floor.

"Isn't it such a shame to do this, though? You have such pretty hair."

"Then once you're done cutting, how about we gather it up and start a business of some sort? We could sell wigs made from the hair of the Saint of the Empire, or maybe string."

"There are certain maniacs who would appreciate it..."

"I'll bet you Krahe would pay a lot, don't you think?"

"None of what this is making me imagine is pleasant, so please, just stop..."

Snip, snip.

"Well, how about I give it to Sir Souma, then? As his first present from his new wife."

"His first present from you is your hair? That's way too heavy!"

"I don't think there's enough of it to get in the way, though?"

"I'm talking about the *emotional* weight!"

"Whaa..." Maria looked dissatisfied. "I thought it was a good idea. That black uniform of his has a lot of gold embroidery, so I don't think he'd notice if I wove some of my hair into it."

"You were going to do it without telling him?! Okay, maybe he wouldn't notice, but that's still heavy! Making him carry your hair with him at all times? That's the kind of thing you do for someone who's deceased! To remember them by!"

"Oh, but wouldn't it be lovely for him to remember me at all times?"

"No... Your lack of romantic experience has given you strange ideas."

Snip, snip.

"Oh, and you said it casually before, but..."

"Yes?"

"His new wife? You're going to be marrying Sir Souma?"

"Yes...that's the hope. We'll have to talk it over still."

"Erm...congratulations. It's okay to say that, right?"

"Hee hee, thank you, Jeanne. But..."

"Hm?"

"You have a partner you want to share the rest of your life with too, don't you?"

"Huh?! Ah, right..."

"Is it Sir Hakuya?"

"Yes. He'll be coming here...um...to this country to marry me."

"Oh, my!"

"Urgh... You're making me feel embarrassed..."

Snip, snip.

"Sorry, Jeanne... I know I'm going to be putting a heavy burden on you from now on."

"No, don't worry about it. You've carried an even greater burden all this time, so I'll manage. I won't be alone, after all."

"Hee hee, because you'll have Sir Hakuya with you?"

"Don't bring that back up!"

"Hopefully Trill can find someone nice too."

"Ah... She's currently going around acting like Sir Ludwin and Madam Genia's nosy sister-in-law... If Sir Ludwin would just marry her... No, that wouldn't be fair to him; she'd give him stress ulcers."

"Hee hee, the drill princess would live up to her reputation by punching a hole right through his stomach, would she?"

"That's not a funny joke if you're Sir Ludwin... Anyway."

Snip...

"We're all done, Sister," Jeanne said as she handed Maria a mirror.

Looking into the mirror, Maria's own face peered back with her short and neat hair. She'd lost the dignity lent to her by her long hair, but in exchange, Maria as an individual woman stood out all the more.

Maria tilted her head, inspecting all around her, then nodded. "Yes, I think I look good with short hair too."

"You're going to say that yourself...?" Jeanne sighed in exasperation.

Seeing her sister's expression, Maria smiled and said, "Thank you, Jeanne. I finally got that load off my shoulders."

Maria showed off her new hair to Souma and the others later. Their eyes went wide with surprise at first, but once they recovered, she received a whole lot of compliments.

Hearing all the positive feedback, Maria flashed Jeanne a triumphant peace sign.

"We did it, Jeanne!"

CHAPTER 12
Resolution

THAT EVENING, I received a report that Hashim had arrived together with the wyvern cavalry Fuuga had dispatched to go pick him up.

We would begin the peace talks between the Kingdom of Friedonia, the Gran Chaos Empire, and the Great Tiger Kingdom immediately. In order to prevent undue confusion, we would set up a camp in between the forces of Friedonia and the Great Tiger Kingdom, keeping the delegations from each side small.

The two sides were both on edge, making it clear they were ready to charge in the moment anything happened to one of their VIPs. In this tense situation, here is who was chosen for each delegation: The Kingdom of Friedonia sent me, Hakuya, and Aisha. The Empire sent Maria and Jeanne. The Great Tiger Kingdom sent Fuuga, Mutsumi, Hashim, and the traitorous Lumiere. Old general Gaifuku came as well, serving as a bodyguard.

Because the Kingdom and the Empire were already viewed as being on one side, the Great Tiger Kingdom's team was the size of both of ours combined. Incidentally, I'd told Fuuga in advance to keep Krahe out of this because he would just complicate things.

"Lumiere..." Jeanne murmured when she saw her old comrade on the other side.

Jeanne had thought of Lumiere as a close friend, so Jeanne didn't know how to feel about the fact she'd sided with Fuuga over her sister. Hakuya put his hand on Jeanne's back, gently supporting her.

Lumiere, on the other hand, didn't so much as bat an eye. In fact, she had such a serious expression on her face that one would suspect she was suppressing her own feelings. She'd done this in order to pridefully insist she hadn't done the wrong thing.

Inside the camp, we were divided into our respective teams, and everyone but Aisha and Gaifuku took a seat. From where I was sitting, Hakuya was across from Hashim, Jeanne was across from Lumiere on my left, and there was a map of the Empire in between them.

"I'd like to get straight to determining borders for after the war," Hashim began, and Hakuya nodded.

"Very well. Madam Jeanne, Madam Lumiere, is that all right?"

"Yes," they replied in tandem.

And so, the four of them began discussing our respective domains. I was trusting Hakuya to negotiate for me, while Fuuga had Hashim negotiate for him. They were both smart, so they'd probably find a decent compromise. They'd be integrating the areas of the Empire that defected into the Great Tiger Kingdom as is. After that, it was a matter of working out the fine details.

While the smartest people in the room were negotiating, Maria, Fuuga, Mutsumi, and I discussed what was going to happen from here on in the larger sense.

"I wasn't counting on you intervening now," Fuuga said, sounding exasperated, but I just shrugged.

"My ally was in peril. I couldn't just leave her out to dry."

"Even though you might have gotten the entire world if you did?"

"Unlike you, I don't want the world."

"Um..." Mutsumi, who had been listening, raised her hand. "You called her your ally, but when did the Kingdom and the Empire form an alliance?"

"The secret alliance wasn't long after I came to this world, so...since 1546, I think?"

"Huh?! It was that long ago...?"

As Mutsumi's eyes widened, Maria chuckled.

"Yes. Souma has been a reliable ally ever since then."

"Ha ha ha, you really pulled one over on me. I underestimated the strength of the bonds between the Kingdom and the Empire." Fuuga scratched his head. It had been a while since I'd seen him without his helmet on.

Then he flashed a combative glance at Maria.

"Hold on... You cut your hair? Looks good."

"Thank you. It was heavy. It feels like a load off my shoulders."

"Did you cut off the guys in the north the same way?"

"Hee hee, I have no idea what you could possibly mean."

Fuuga gave a toothy grin, while Maria's smile was relaxed, yet had a mysterious intensity to it. Mutsumi and I watched, both breaking into a cold sweat as these two massively charismatic figures butted heads. It was like being thrown into a cage with both a lion and a bear.

I've got to mediate between these two...? I felt like I was going to be overwhelmed by the position I was in, but I had to keep myself together.

Suddenly, Fuuga spoke up, breaking my train of thought. "So, how do you plan to settle things?" Fuuga asked, resting his cheek on the palm of one hand. "We can let all of them hash out what the borders will look like, but what's going to happen to the Empire from here on? The Mankind Declaration's pretty much dead at this point. Maria...or should I ask Souma instead? What are your plans for the Empire?"

"Maria should probably be the one to say."

I looked at Maria. She silently nodded.

"First of all, I am disbanding the Mankind Declaration. You will have control of the north of the continent, while the Maritime Union will expand across the south. Our country will be participating in the Maritime Union as well, so the stagnant era that needed the Mankind Declaration is already over. At the same time, my country will completely relinquish our former vassal states the Frakt Federal Republic and Kingdom of Meltonia."

"You're stepping down from representing mankind? Souma, Maria, you both have the strength to take the world. Why are you so passive about seeking glory? I can't understand it," Fuuga said contemptuously, his brow furrowing.

Maria gave a small smile and said, "It is not good to let your reach exceed your grasp. My wishes are smaller, but no less important."

"The wishes you have not as Empress Maria, but as just Maria?"

"Yes."

Maria nodded firmly, and Fuuga let out a hearty laugh.

"You've got unswerving eyes like Mutsumi. I can't disapprove of that."

"Thank you."

"So, what about the Empire itself?"

"The people who submitted to you and the lands they rule will not be returning to us, I'm sure... With the end of the Mankind Declaration, my country is greatly diminished. I don't think it's fitting to call it the Gran Chaos Empire any longer. Henceforth, we will be the Euphoria Kingdom. I will abdicate the throne, and my younger sister Jeanne will replace me as queen."

"What...?"

The dismantling of an empire, the founding of a new kingdom, the abdication of Maria, the coronation of Jeanne... Even Fuuga had to be surprised, getting hit with all this at once.

"The Euphoria Kingdom? Wasn't that the name of the country destroyed by Emperor Manas?" Mutsumi asked.

"Yes," Maria replied with a nod.

The Gran Chaos Empire was founded when Manas Chaos, the King of Chaos, annexed his wife's homeland, the Euphoria Kingdom. I'd heard that he might have felt guilty for doing it because Manas inherited the Euphoria name from the land he destroyed. *Was that why later emperors used the Euphoria name?*

Basically, Maria planned to restore the Euphoria Kingdom. The former kingdom had been situated in the northwestern part of the Empire, so this was a restoration in name only. But it would be enough to hold on to the nobles and knights who followed the traditions of that country.

Hakuya, Jeanne, and I were all surprised when we heard this. Just how thoroughly had Maria prepared for such a conclusion?

"What happens to you after you abdicate? You're stepping down to take responsibility for this war, right?"

"Well..."

"I'll be taking her," I answered Fuuga on Maria's behalf. "While Madam Maria is stepping down to take responsibility, we will be the ones to take custody of her. I won't let anyone lay a hand on her, Fuuga. Not even you."

Fuuga and those who had submitted to him likely wanted to capture Maria and persecute her politically in order to make the lands they had taken easier to rule. If they subjected her to a kangaroo court, loudly crowing about the righteousness of their own actions, it'd make great propaganda. But I wasn't going to let them do that.

"I'm fine with this being a win for you on paper, at least. The Great Tiger Kingdom was able to secure human resources, and minus any deaths during skirmishes, you haven't lost anything. But if you're going to demand custody of Maria, reparations, or anything more, that will change."

"Do you think you could win a fight with me...?" Fuuga glared at me. He was scary, but I held my ground.

"Yeah. Or force a tie that only hurts both of us if I couldn't. You'd lose your 'win' here if that happened. That ought to be a painful blow to you when constant victory is what lets you bring people together."

"Yeah, you've got a point."

Oh, so he gets it himself, then? That was a relief.

Fuuga looked at Maria. "What're you going to the Kingdom for? To marry Souma?"

"I hope so."

"My sister Yuriga's there too, you know?"

"Well, from what I've heard, we'll get along swimmingly. I hear that Miss Yuriga's decided that you can't defeat Sir Souma as you are now. I think we'll get along fine."

Seeing the smile on Maria's face, Fuuga gave an exasperated shrug. "Too many tough women out there these days. They keep defying my expectations."

"I found that out a long time ago..." I murmured.

"I'll bet," Fuuga said with a wry smile.

As Souma, Maria, Fuuga, and Mutsumi were having a surprisingly relaxed discussion of what was to come after the war, Hakuya the Black-robed Prime Minister and Hashim the Wisdom of the Tiger were engaged in an intense war of words.

Hashim slammed his hand down on the map between them. "We currently hold the east of the Empire as far as Jamona Fortress," he said. "That land is an important connection between Zem and the Orthodox Papal State. We'll be keeping it."

Hakuya retorted, "If you return some of the northern lands of the Empire along the coast, I will be willing to accept that."

"These lands have already fallen to us."

"Then you should exchange other lands for them. There are a number of knightly and noble houses in the northern territories that chose loyalty to the House of Euphoria despite finding themselves surrounded by members of the Fuuga faction. We will take custody of them, so you can redistribute their lands."

"But domains that have ports are valuable."

"And we will be conceding territory that is important for overland shipping, so it is an equal trade. Madam Maria has moved most of the Imperial Navy to the south anyway. If we were to force the issue with our fleet, do you suppose that you could defend that territory?"

"Not likely... Very well, then we will take some land north of Jamona Fortress."

"That is inevitable, I suppose... Let's discuss the three cities the Republic has seized from Zem."

"You're not going to give them back even if we ask, right?"

"Right. While they are part of the Maritime Alliance, the Republic is an independent nation, so I'd like to negotiate that matter separately."

"Heh, it's no great pain to us if Zem loses territory, but...this one, near the center, they'll have to give back. If they do that, they can keep the other two."

He wants them to return the city that will be hardest to defend in the event of an attack, does he? Hakuya thought. "I will pass the message to Sir Kuu."

The two of them were both brilliant minds, so they understood what was important to their own countries, what wasn't, where would be easy to defend, and where would be hard to attack. They saw where the points of compromise were in these negotiations, so they didn't waste time holding out to try and maximize the amount of territory they gained. They decided on the apportionment of territory after the war appropriately and in few words.

Next to them sat Jeanne and Lumiere.

Jeanne had a pained expression on her face, while Lumiere looked at her with frustration. They had been good friends, but they often ended up disagreeing over Maria's policies, and Lumiere had chosen Fuuga over Maria.

"Lumiere..."

"Don't say it, Jeanne. I've chosen my path."

Lumiere pushed her away at first, but then she gazed up at the ceiling.

"No...I thought I'd chosen my path, but looking at it now, I may just have been dancing in the palm of your sister's hand. Now that I see the results, I can tell that your sister predicted we would lose faith in her and prepared to cut us loose in advance. It's hard to say who gave up on whom at this point."

Lumiere let out a self-effacing laugh before looking at Jeanne.

"What I don't understand, though, is why you provided support for the reconstruction of the north. If you intended to cut us loose, why provide support at all? If you hadn't, it would have been a financial blow against Fuuga when he acquired the territory."

"I think...Sister was torn over what to do," Jeanne said with a glance over at Maria, who was chatting with Souma and the others nearby. "Up until now, she always tried to be the empress people believed in. But she'd reached her limit. I think that if you'd continued to believe in her, she'd have kept going, but if you gave up on her, then that would be that... That's why she kept working for the benefit of the northern territories until just before the end."

"If she had that kind of resolve, I wish she'd have used it to liberate the Demon Lord's Domain!"

Jeanne pitied Lumiere, seeing the frustration on her face.

Ultimately, they'd just had different goals. Still, Maria and Lumiere each had their own positions to consider, so a large number of people got caught up in the disagreement, and the rift had developed into a conflict there was no coming back from.

Even so, I'm happy it turned out this way. My sister will finally be free now, Jeanne thought.

Soon enough, Hakuya and Hashim's negotiations came to a close.

"Would you say that will do for now?" Hakuya asked.

"I suppose it will..." Hashim agreed.

Hakuya and Hashim exchanged a handshake that was entirely formal.

Here is an overview of what was decided at the talks:

1) No reparations were to be paid by either party.

2) The Great Tiger Kingdom would not hold Maria responsible for the war and would not demand custody of her.

3) The Empire would relinquish the northern territories and the eastern part of the Empire.

4) The lords of the relinquished territories would decide which country they wanted to belong to. (Most of the lords and knights of the north would switch their allegiance to the Great Tiger Kingdom.)

This whole war was to be known as the Armistice of Valois. People would no doubt view this as a victory for the Great Tiger Kingdom. While they were unable to get reparations, they did gain land and human resources and only ended up at a disadvantage in one skirmish against the Kingdom of Friedonia at the very end.

Meanwhile, the Empire, having lost land and people, was viewed as the loser of the conflict. Their land forces were particularly diminished, and the core of their air force left for the Great Tiger Kingdom with General Krahe, so their ability to wage war on the ground was cut roughly in half. However, with their naval forces practically untouched and the decision made to join the Maritime Alliance, they were still a force to be reckoned with.

Maria abstained from taking responsibility for the crisis and announced the dissolution of the Gran Chaos Empire. With the founding of the new Euphoria Kingdom, her younger sister Jeanne would ascend the throne in her place. Jeanne immediately announced the Euphoria Kingdom's intention to join the Maritime Alliance.

Now the continent was divided into two between north and south, Fuuga and Souma.

The era of the three-way confrontation ended, and a new era of north-south contention began. The Great Tiger Kingdom pulled its troops out of the Euphoria Kingdom's territory, and once the Friedonian forces had seen them off, they would return home too.

"Fuuga. What do you plan to do from here on?" I asked as we were preparing to pull out. "The Great Tiger Kingdom's big enough. You've got the personnel to run a great nation now too. What else is left?"

"The Demon Lord's Domain, obviously," Fuuga said, the fire of ambition burning in his eyes. "What people want from me is a world without the threat of the Demon Lord's Domain. The world's neatly divided between you and me now. Once I firm up my support on the home front, I'll finally be able to raise an army for the final liberation of the Demon Lord's Domain. I'm gonna strike the final blow against the heart of what's been causing this era of turmoil."

Fuuga was fired up. This had to be what drew people to him.

"I see... Will it go that well?" I was uneasy.

That was partially because I'd seen that massive cube in the Star Dragon Mountain Range. I suspected there was something up north that this world's knowledge wouldn't be able to handle. Fuuga couldn't just walk into the Demon Lord's castle, slay the Demon Lord, and get a happy ending like this was some old video game. There was a lot to think about between the relationship between monsters and demons; the mysterious cube's message to "Go north"; and the name "Demon Lord Divalroi," which seemed familiar to me somehow...

However, Fuuga seemed unconcerned.

"We've become the greatest country on land. You people rule the sea. We'll head for the north by land and by sea. Let's change the times with our own hands."

"Right..."

I could only give that noncommittal response.

HOW A REALIST HERO REBUILT THE KINGDOM

That Is Her Way of Life

S OME TIME after the signing of the Armistice of Valois...
When Fuuga's forces had fully withdrawn from the newly decided borders of the Euphoria Kingdom and the world was at peace once more, Souma and Maria appeared together on broadcast receivers in fountain plazas around both of their countries.

"Hey! Look at Lady Maria's hair!"

"Yeah. But she looks so peaceful now—like she's been set free from something that was possessing her."

"She's so pretty... I wish I could be like her."

Many in the crowd were surprised by Maria's short hair. However, there was no shadow over her expression now. Seeing the peaceful look on her face, they were relieved to see that she hadn't been forced to cut it or anything like that. For the citizens of the former Empire who had watched her throw herself from the balcony in despair, it was a relief to see her alive and smiling so peacefully.

"We have something to tell everyone in the Kingdom of Friedonia and the Euphoria Kingdom today," Souma began, and then Maria stepped forward.

"It involves what has happened so far, and the futures of our countries."

Then, the two of them went on to explain the Armistice of Valois to the people of both kingdoms. The northern territories of the former Empire would become part of the Great Tiger Kingdom, while Maria would abdicate the throne to take responsibility for their loss in the war, and her sister Jeanne would reign as the new Queen of Euphoria. They also explained the Euphoria Kingdom would join the Maritime Alliance.

Souma had prepared a new map of the continent, showing that the Maritime Alliance rivaled the Great Tiger Kingdom in size. Because he showed them a physical map rather than just telling them, it put the people of both kingdoms at ease. For the people of the Euphoria Kingdom, who had narrowly escaped destruction at the hands of Fuuga, having their security guaranteed for the immediate future made them welcome this alliance.

"Now then... Jeanne."

"Yes."

When Maria called her sister's name, Jeanne appeared on the broadcast and knelt in front of her. She placed the tiara that had marked her as queen on Jeanne's head, saying, "From now on, I entrust you with this country's future."

"Yes, ma'am! I will work with all due diligence so that I don't bring shame upon your name, Sister."

With the formal transfer of power completed, Maria announced that, to strengthen their country's bonds with the Kingdom of Friedonia and also ensure that her influence in the Euphoria Kingdom would not be a hindrance to Jeanne, she would be marrying King Souma, the head of the Maritime Alliance. At the same time, they announced that Hakuya the Black-robed Prime Minister would be marrying the new Queen Jeanne as her royal consort.

Because Souma had saved Maria during the war and rescued the Empire from its plight, people in both countries supported the marriage.

Although the Kingdom of Friedonia and the Euphoria Kingdom were two separate nations, they would move as one. The people would informally call the combination of these two countries the Gran Friedonia Empire. And Souma, who was to become Souma Euphoria Friedonia, would be called Emperor Friedonia.

With the curtain falling on the conflict, we left Hakuya, who was now prime minister of the two nations, with Piltory and his family in the Euphoria Kingdom and took Maria back to the Kingdom of Friedonia with us.

There was a mountain of work waiting for me when I got back to Parnam Castle. Now that we were working with two countries under one system, the amount of work that came my way had increased.

Liscia and I both looked at the high piles of paperwork with dismay.

"You know, this sight brings back memories," Liscia said, and I agreed entirely.

"Yeah...and we don't have Hakuya with us this time. Though, we do have more people than we did back then."

"R-right! I'll do my best to help!"

I glanced sideways at Ichiha, who was clenching his hand with enthusiasm.

The moment I got back, I'd appointed him, Hakuya's protégé, to be acting prime minister in his teacher's absence. He had Hakuya's seal of approval, and he'd be taking over Hakuya's role in the Kingdom going forward.

"Huh?" Liscia tilted her head to the side. "Come to think of it, where's Madam Maria? She'd be a lot of help..."

It was true, considering Maria had supported a great nation all by herself, that having her administrative abilities would be a great help. Not to mention her charisma. She could more than fill the hole left by Hakuya.

"Ah...I wouldn't count on Maria to help," I warned Liscia. "I mean, if we really can't manage, she might lend a hand occasionally."

"Hm? Why not?"

"As soon as we got here, she ran off, saying she had things she wanted to do."

"Things she wants to do, huh? Well, we can't force her if she doesn't want to do it, then." Liscia sighed and shrugged.

Maria had worked herself to the bone for her people and country before now. We all felt that, since she was finally free, she should do as she pleased for a while.

I clapped my hands and tried to change gears. "Well then, how about we get to work? Liscia, call Roroa and Colbert... He's going to need to put up with this for a while before assisting Mio."

"Got it. I'll send a messenger to the Carmine domain."

"Ichiha, send any documents that need royal assent to me."

"Will do, sire."

Some time after that, Roroa and Finance Minister Colbert were in the governmental affairs office to discuss the budget.

Bang! The doors of the office flew open.

"Wh-what's goin' on?!" Roroa exclaimed as this unannounced guest came in without so much as a knock at the door.

Colbert and I were both surprised. We looked towards the door to see a "casually dressed" Maria wearing overalls and a shirt. The white hat she was wearing was just barely fashionable, but everything below that wouldn't have looked out of place on a farmer.

Behind her was Naden, looking exhausted.

"Souma!"

Maria strode on over, walking past Roroa and Colbert to stand in front of my desk. Then, she laid a map of the country with a bunch of marks on it down in front of me.

"There's been repeated crop failures in the village of Osahl, halfway between Red Dragon City and Lagoon City. It looks like harmful insects and lack of sunlight are responsible. It could lead to a famine there if we don't do something." We all looked at the map as she talked. "I'm requesting you send agricultural gelins to eradicate the pests and food aid to support the people for the time being."

"R-right. Got it. I'll get on that right away."

"Also, Roroa."

"Whuh?!"

"The village of Ryan in the northwest is a center of trade and has a large population. I want to set up a school there. Do we have the budget for it?"

"Uh, listen, if you just ask me that all of a sudden, I'm not gonna be able to tell ya anythin'..." Roroa said, dodging the question, but Colbert sighed and stepped in.

"We have the profits from the recent lorelei event, don't we? Couldn't you use those?"

"No, no, I was plannin' on puttin' those towards the next event..."

"I do believe I helped you with that lorelei event, didn't I?" Maria said, rounding on Roroa with a pleasant smile.

Her beautiful and intense smile is intimidating Roroa... I could relate.

"You used my publicity to make that money, yes? Calling it a dream collaboration between the Prima Lorelei and the Singing and Dancing Former Empress? You're going to tell *me* I can't use that money?"

"Augh, fine! Take the money, ya darn thief!"

"Oh, goodness, a thief? That's not a very nice thing to call someone." Maria chuckled.

She had Roroa right where she wanted her. Well, it wasn't easy outmaneuvering the woman who once ran the Empire in these sorts of negotiations. I sure as hell couldn't...

This is what she wants to do, huh? I thought, looking at the smile on Maria's face.

The night I'd arrived in Valois during the war, she'd told me with tears in her eyes...

"I didn't want to just be nice to everybody!"

"I wanted to play favorites!"

And Maria had chosen to do just that. She began helping the people she really wanted to, those left behind by society without support. Shortly after arriving in the Kingdom, she had hounded Naden into flying her all over the place so she could investigate the situation in this country. Now that she'd found all these potential seeds of future discontent, she was going around remedying them one by one. Basically, she wanted to do philanthropy.

It was also the reason she'd cut her long hair. Because going into the hinterlands usually meant getting dirty, the long hair was likely to get in her way. Without the pressure she'd been under before, Maria had now become incredibly aggressive about getting things done.

Having attained the result she wanted, Maria rolled up the map again and smiled. "Okay, I'll be taking off for a while. Oh! And I'm borrowing Naden again too."

"Hold on! You've been riding me however you please, but the only one who's normally supposed to ride me is my partner!"

"The partner of your partner is your partner. Come on now, let's go."

Maria talked Naden into it, then led her out of the office by the hand. Jeanne had said before that Maria was like a tempest, and, well...that was exactly what she was like.

Then, as she was almost out the door, Maria stopped and turned to face me. "Oh! I'll be back for our wedding. Love you, Souma."

As she said that, Maria blew a kiss in my direction.

After that, Maria refused to become a primary queen because she didn't want the restrictions, and went on to do great things as our third secondary queen, a lorelei, a medical practitioner, a philanthropist, and in a variety of other roles.

She built fountain plazas in areas where the broadcast could only be listened to before, and she rolled out equipment so it could be listened to in areas where even that hadn't been an option. She built schools where there were none nearby, and she supported industry in areas that suffered from poverty. Maria even made the case for improving our system of medicine, and she got the motion to increase taxes to improve medical coverage to finally pass the national assembly where it had been defeated before.

"That was faster than I thought..."

"Sure was."

Roroa and I were both flabbergasted when we heard this.

And with the funds she procured, we would go on to build hospitals and clinics all over the Kingdom. Sometimes she would hold charity concerts with Juna and the other loreleis, directing the money they raised to further help the needy.

Thus, she came to be called the Angel of Friedonia.

"Wait, that's a rank up from being a saint!"

"Hee hee, I wonder why."

AFTERWORD

T HANK YOU for purchasing the sixteenth volume of *Realist Hero*. This is Dojyomaru.

I only have one page this time, so I'll skip the silliness.

This volume depicts the collapse and rebirth of the Empire. At the same time, it's also the story of Maria being set free. Maria has been appearing since near the beginning, but the story needed to come this far before she could be freed from the heavy burdens she was carrying.

Ironically, it was only with the combination of an ally like Souma and an enemy like Fuuga that she was able to dismantle her country. She's a year older than Juna, which puts her in her mid-twenties, but I'm sure she's going to go all-out trying to make up for some of those youthful days she missed out on.

On top of that, Jeanne and Hakuya's long-distance romance was able to find its resolution. It was a long one too... How many years has it been since readers following the web serialization started telling me they wanted to see the two of them happy together? I never expected it to take until volume sixteen. But that's just how heavy of a burden the Euphoria sisters were carrying, I suppose.

Oh, there was no room for Trill, so she has to wait until next volume.

Until then, thank you to everyone who was involved with this book and all of you who purchased it.

Maria Visits the Senior Queens (Liscia Version)

HELLO, EVERYONE. I'm the Maria who people used to say was married to her country. Now that I was going to get married to Souma, I wanted to chat with my senior wives more so that we could live together happily. This afternoon, I was visiting the daycare to learn about child care from First Primary Queen Liscia.

Liscia was pulling along a pair of twins with the same color of hair as her.

"This is Cian, and this is Kazuha. My kids with Souma. They're four now."

"Wow, what cute twins."

I bent down to look at them. Kazuha looked at me with interest, while Cian hid behind Liscia. They were both adorable.

Kazuha pointed at me before cocking her head to the side.

"Mommy. Is she my mommy too?" she asked.

"Huh? I'm your mommy?"

While I was still surprised at suddenly being called a mommy, Liscia slapped her own forehead in dismay and let out a sigh.

"I gave birth before the other queens, so we all doted on these two. Roroa got carried away and started saying, 'Mommy's here,' and the twins started thinking all of us were their mommies."

"O-oh, is that right?"

"Yes. Once even my own mother started saying 'Mommy's here' to them, I did everything I could to stop it though."

"I...can see why you'd feel that way."

Cian, who had been hiding up until this point, said, "Mommy?" quietly and toddled towards me with a smile.

Oh, wow, this kid is just too cute, I thought. "Lady Liscia... Can I have him?"

"No! What are you saying crazy things out of nowhere for?!"

"I mean, he was scared of me just a moment ago, but the moment he thinks I'm his mommy, he smiles at me with no wariness whatsoever! I want to mother him!"

"Settle down," Liscia said, punctuating it with a light karate chop to my head.

"Ow ow ow... Ah! What was I saying?"

"I see you've come back to your senses. Cian, Kazuha, go play with everyone."

The twins responded with an energetic, "'Kay!" and took off, hand in hand.

Aww, I wanted to talk to them more... As I was thinking that, a blue-haired girl who was around three years old came over with a chestnut-haired boy who was maybe two or three. *Oh! They're cute too!*

"This blue-haired girl is Souma and Juna's daughter Enju, while the chestnut-haired boy is Souma and Roroa's son Leon. They're both around two years old."

"Hello, Enju, Leon."

I got down to their eye level to greet them, as I'd done with Cian and Kazuha.

"Hewwo," said Enju in a slightly drawn-out way, giving me the smile of a future pretty girl. Meanwhile, Leon fidgeted shyly.

"Oh... They're cute too."

"Hee hee, they really are. Enju is fearless, as you'd expect from Juna's daughter, while Leon is introverted, unlike Roroa. He must get that from Souma."

Enju and Leon both hugged Liscia.

"Mommy Cia!"

"Mommy Ciaaa."

They wanted attention. I stared at Liscia.

"You're making them call you mommy too."

"I-I don't see the problem," Liscia stammered, beginning to turn red. "They make my kids do it."

I chuckled at how flustered she got. Lady Liscia then handed Enju and Leon off to a lady with wolf ears (I later learned she was Tomoe's real mother) and brought a baby who was less than a year old to me in their place. This baby with faintly blue hair was sucking their index finger, looking at me as Liscia held them in her arms.

"This is Souma and Juna's second child, Kaito. Would you like to hold him?"

"Yes. Very much so."

I felt the weight of the child I accepted from Liscia, along with a warmth in the air around him. Kaito looked at me and smiled.

Overcome with emotion, I looked at Liscia. "You all raise the children together and have a community of women who provide mutual support in child-rearing. It's the sort of thing that could serve as a guiding principle for a nation-state."

"That's some complicated stuff you're thinking about there. I can tell you used to be an empress," Liscia remarked, sounding impressed.

I chuckled. "I want my own children now too."

"Once you do...I'll adore them with all my might. Just like the others."

We looked at one another and smiled.

Maria Visits the Senior Queens (Aisha Version)

HELLO, EVERYONE. I'm the Maria who's a little worried about gaining weight now that she's been released from her intense workload as empress. Now that I was going to get married to Souma, I wanted to chat with my senior wives more so that we could live together happily. Today, I was watching the Second Primary Queen Aisha train.

"Hngh! Hah! Yah!"

With each cry of exertion, Aisha swung her greatsword downwards, causing silver hair to stream behind the beautiful and powerful dark elf warrior. My own little sister, Jeanne, was a capable warrior in her own right, but Aisha's martial arts had a visible power to them that Jeanne's didn't. She had a natural intensity and techniques refined by daily training. No warrior in the Empire could have matched her.

"You really are strong, Aisha," I said from where I sat in a corner of the indoor training area.

Aisha let out an embarrassed laugh, continuing to swing all the while.

"With my abilities so concentrated in the martial arts, this is the only way that I can be of service to His Majesty."

The brown skin of her cheeks flushed red. *Oh, my. She's so cute it's hard to believe she's swinging a massive sword around like that.*

"You keep up the effort even now that you're a queen, I see."

"Yes...! That's true. I initially pushed myself on His Majesty as a bodyguard, so I wouldn't want to neglect that duty now that I've become a queen."

"But you're the second primary queen, right? Hasn't he asked you to stop doing dangerous things?"

"In this country, we use the people we have, even if they happen to be royalty. It's not just me—Lady Liscia and the other queens are all still doing the work they did before marriage. Well, aside from Liscia, who carries the blood of the royal house of Elfrieden, and Roroa, who carries the blood of the princely house of Amidonia, the rest of us don't need to be so stiff about things."

I think that's strange for a royal family, though... The queens all raised their children together, and each had her own work. Souma tried to look after the kids as much as he could too, and I'd witnessed Liscia kicking him in the butt and saying, "That's enough; go to work already," several times now.

The king and queens each had valuable jobs, and because they were so busy with them, they divided the labor of raising children. It didn't result in a situation where, after getting married, all that was left to do was struggle for power inside the family. It was so unusual...yet, at the same time, so comforting for me.

It lets me do what I've always wanted to, after all. I looked at Aisha as I was thinking that. Just as I had things I wanted to do, Aisha had her desire to protect Souma.

"Souma is a lucky guy, having a woman like you to defend him."

"I wonder..."

Aisha stopped swinging. *Is something the matter?*

"Did I say something to offend you?" I asked.

"No, not at all. It's true that I defend His Majesty in situations where my martial abilities allow me to do so. If Fuuga Haan were to attack His Majesty, I would make the battle last at least ten strokes. And yet...in any other situation, more often than not, he's the one protecting me. As the king, His Majesty has a great number of people at his disposal, and he makes such tasty food too."

Yes... I supposed that was true. There were times when you needed martial prowess in order to protect others, but the world wasn't so simple that you could solve everything by strength of arms alone.

Aisha let out a short sigh. "I feel so pitiful at times like that. I don't know how I should react when the person I hope to protect has to protect me..."

Aisha had the look of a young maiden in love on her face. Despite her incredible strength, she had a delicate side to her too. That had to be part of her appeal.

"I think it's simple, really."

"Madam Maria?"

I smiled as she cocked her head to the side in confusion.

"You should just say 'thank you' when he protects you. It makes you happy when Souma thanks you after you protect him, right?"

"Thanks for always being there, Aisha."

"Sorry for the trouble. You really saved me there, Aisha."

Aisha nodded as if remembering the times he'd thanked her.

"You're right. It makes it feel like it was all worth it."

"Yes. It's the same for me. Jeanne was always helping, so when she thanked me for something, it just made all the exhaustion from my hard work go away. I'm sure Souma's the same."

"Thank you, Madam Maria," Aisha said, smiling, then picked up a wooden sword that was lying on the floor. "It must be boring for you, just watching. Come sweat with me."

"Uh... About that... Er..."

I tried to object, since I was not very athletic, but if I was going to be traveling around the kingdom, it might be wise to learn to defend myself. This was as good a time as any.

"Could you go easy on me, please?"

Maria Visits the Senior Queens (Roroa Version)

HELLO, EVERYONE. I'm the Maria who can only be described as "unemployed" right now. Now that I was going to get married to Souma, I wanted to chat with my senior wives more so that we could live together happily. This afternoon, I was called on by Third Primary Queen Roroa, who had a request for me.

When I arrived in a workroom for bureaucrats in the finance ministry, Roroa noticed me and started speaking in a coaxing voice.

"Hey, hey, Big Sis Mari. I've gotta li'l favor to ask ya."

"Big Sis Mari?!" I'd never been called that before.

Roroa put her hands together in a pleading gesture, resting them against her right cheek and tilting her head to the side. It was a calculatingly cute pose.

"Settin' our positions aside, I like havin' older people to think of me as their honorary li'l sister. I'm already callin' the others Big Sis Cia, Big Sis Ai, and Big Sis Juna, so that makes you Big Sis Mari."

"Oh, I see... Huh? What about Naden?"

As a member of a long-lived race, Naden was likely older than her, as well as all the other queens.

"Nya ha ha..." Roroa let out a wry laugh. "Y'see, with the way she looks, it'd be strange for me to go callin' her my big sis. Even Tomoe and Ichiha are lookin' older than her at this point."

Sorry, Naden... I can't refute what she's saying.

"Well, that aside, your cute little sis has got a favor to ask ya."

"The little sister thing's already a done deal, I see."

"Our country's gonna be comin' together with your old country in some kinda two countries, one nation deal, right? So, there's been talk of unitin' our broadcast programmin' too, while we're at it."

"Ohh, that would be convenient, yes."

Each country had a limited number of broadcast jewels, which meant a limited amount of broadcasts. With our two countries working together, we would be able to afford larger budgets. There were only benefits to it, but...

"There's close to a half-day difference in time zones between our countries."

"Well, there's nothin' we can do about that. We could each make half the content and show the same things twice—in the morning and noon in each country. We'll find workarounds."

"So for music programs, it'd be like having multiple performances. That sounds reasonable."

Roroa was always quick with ideas like this. As a large nation, we could make most things work in the Empire, and there wasn't much call for creativity. That led to a lot of the bureaucrats becoming inflexible. They couldn't have come up with ideas like hers.

"So, now on to the main ask. You were a lorelei in the Empire, right, Big Sis Mari?"

"Hm? Yes. I tried it out once, and a lot of people asked me to continue."

"Mm-hmm, I hear you were pretty popular. So, as our first program in the new unified lineup, I was hopin' to do a Parnam Music Festival headed by a dream team of Big Sis Juna, our Prima Lorelei—the pride of the Kingdom of Friedonia—and you, the Empire's Singin' and Dancin' Empress."

A music program? And one where I'd be collaborating with Juna? I thought. "I'm no longer the empress, you realize?"

"Ya don't have to be an empress anymore, but that's no reason to give up bein' a lorelei, is it? Big Sis Juna's still out there workin' hard despite bein' married and havin' two children. If the people hear that you and Big Sis Juna—who they all love—are puttin' on a music show together, people'll talk. I'm sure those with a nose for profit like Lucy's folks at the Evans Company'll be eager to put up the funds as a way of advertisin' their businesses."

"We'd be doing this for the money, would we?"

I knew Roroa had a strong sense for finance. But I had to question her fixation on making money; especially when she'd be using family members like me or Juna in order to do it...

"You want to help the weak, don't ya, Big Sis Mari?"

Perhaps picking up on my hesitance, Roroa dropped her

goofy smile and put on a serious face. It was undoubtedly the face of a queen.

"The important thing with money's where ya make it and who ya use it for. If you're just makin' money for money's sake, that's exploitative. If ya give cash to people without them earnin' it, you'll make 'em decadent. Ya've gotta earn it, use it, spread it around, and keep that virtuous cycle goin' as long as you can. Don't ya think?"

"You have a point..."

My ears burned a little with embarrassment. Still, being the idealist that I was, it made me grateful for someone who would shove reality in my face. That was true of both Souma and Roroa.

"Okay...I'll do it."

"Ya will? Whew, you're a lifesaver."

The friendly smile returned to Roroa's lips. She really made use of a lot of different expressions. But I wouldn't lose to her on that front. I had the smile I'd cultivated in my time as empress.

"But you'll be diverting the profits to my charity work, won't you?"

"Huh? Uh, I was hopin' to use some of 'em to fund the next event..."

Roroa averted her eyes. I wasn't going to let that fly.

"You'll be making money off of *me*. You'll let me decide how it's used, won't you?"

I smiled at her. Roroa finally caved.

"Aw, fine! I get it! This time it'll be a charity event!"

"Hee hee, thank you."

I might have found myself a good backer.

Maria Visits the Senior Queens (Juna Version)

GOOD EVENING, EVERYONE. I'm the Maria who's decided to live for the people and her beloved family. Now that I was going to get married to Souma, I wanted to chat with my senior wives more so that we could live together happily. Tonight, I was appearing as a guest on a music program with First Secondary Queen Juna.

It was Roroa's idea to hold a music festival where Juna Doma, the Prima Lorelei—pride of the Kingdom of Friedonia—and I, the Empire's Singing and Dancing Empress, would appear on stage together. *Clever, isn't she?* I was wearing my lorelei dress—which Jeanne had kindly sent from Valois Castle—for the first time in a long while.

The broadcast jewel always projected images from the present, so we only got one chance to get things right.

"Maria?" Juna called out to me as I was waiting in the wings, feeling the pressure.

The blue-haired beauty was wearing an outfit with a thin veil that managed to balance both elegance and sexiness. It was graceful, yet at the same time sensual. Even though we were both women, I found myself a bit short of breath when I saw how beautiful she was.

Juna smiled at me. "Are you feeling tense?"

"Yes. It's been a while since I've sung in front of people."

"I understand. I've heard your schedule was always incredibly packed."

Her eyes were sympathetic, her words compassionate. There was probably no one who rivaled her ability to read people's hearts. Souma had told me that Juna had been there to comfort and support him when he was struggling more times than he could count.

Juna gave me a soft smile. "Do you like singing, Maria?"

"Huh? Uh...yes. I do like it. I used to sing for Father and Jeanne when I was little."

It was a distant memory, from before I had the weight of being an empress thrust on me. Back then, I just loved singing and wanted people to hear me.

"I think...that's why I had so much fun with being a lorelei."

"Hee hee, you'll be fine, then." Juna pressed both hands down on her chest over where her heart was. "Songs are one with the heart. First, they come from the heart of the singer, and then they come to rest in the hearts of the listeners. And they're passed down and spread."

With her left hand still over her heart, Juna reached out and touched my chest with her right hand.

"Just have to do as your heart commands, singing the way you enjoy. Maybe it won't be a song that everyone will love, but a song you enjoy will move more hearts than a song you don't. That's what I believe."

"You're right," I hesitantly agreed, putting my hand over Juna's on my chest. "You're the Prima Lorelei, after all. I'll remember your advice and sing my hardest."

"Hee hee! It's embarrassing when you make it sound like such a big deal."

What a mature smile. It's hard to believe she's a year younger than me. I was starting to feel a little competitive.

"Sorry if I steal the spot of Prima Lorelei from you."

"I've already withdrawn that battle. I'm not concerned with how people rank us."

"Oh, and what if I stole your popularity with Sir Souma?"

"That, I'd get upset about."

Juna puffed up her cheeks angrily. I was satisfied to have gotten an expression out of her that was more fitting for her age. Soon enough, her face morphed into an intense smile.

"I understand. I'll take you on with everything I have."

"Yes. Let's fight fair and square. As loreleis, and as queens."

We exchanged harmonious smiles.

"Um, I'm the one feeling the most worried here, you know?" said a timid voice from behind us.

I turned to see a cute girl in a lorelei costume.

"Juna? Who is this?"

"This is Miss Komari Corda. She's currently the top lorelei in both popularity and ability."

When Juna said that, Komari looked at her with tears in her eyes.

"Ohh... When you say that, Juna, being number one among the active loreleis really weighs me down. You're still incredibly popular with the people after stepping back from the spotlight, and I'm going to be standing next to this lady who used to be an empress too. Try to imagine what it's like, standing next to you two and being introduced as the current number one lorelei."

Yeah. I could see where she was coming from.

"Is that really true?" I asked.

"Maria?"

Sure, Komari felt less like a finished product than Juna. But I felt as though that incompleteness might draw people in too.

"It's not possible to empathize with someone you worship because you've positioned them in a different place from yourself. Juna and I can move people's hearts, but the listeners can't insert themselves emotionally into our performances. If anyone here can let them do that, it's you, who's on the same level as them."

"Yes. I think that's part of your charm, Komari," Juna said with a nod, taking Komari's hand. "Your incompleteness makes people excited to see what you'll show them in the future. That's something that we, having reached some level of completion, can't do."

"Lady Juna, Lady Maria..."

As Komari teared up again, Juna and I reached out to her.

"Come on, let's go, Komari."

"Everyone is waiting for us."

With a sniffle, she said, "Okay!"

Now, let the music festival begin.

HOW A REALIST HERO REBUILT THE KINGDOM

Maria Visits the Senior Queens (Naden Version)

GOOD MORNING, EVERYONE. I'm the Maria who just lost the job she held for many years. Now that I was going to get married to Souma, I wanted to chat with my senior wives more so that we could live together happily.

Early in the day, Second Secondary Queen Naden said she'd be going down to the castle town, so I joined her.

"Souma tells me you do the weather forecast and also act as a sort of jack-of-all-trades in the castle town?"

"Well, that's how it's worked out, yeah," Naden said, awkwardly scratching her cheek as we walked down a cobbled road in Parnam. "When I was killing time in town, I helped out an old lady who was in trouble. Then I did a bunch of other stuff, like delivering some things a customer left behind or moving a damaged cart out of the road. It kept happening to the point that people just casually ask me for favors now."

Naden was a black ryuu from the Star Dragon Mountain Range. She had strength and mobility, which probably made her a big help to the townspeople.

"You lend an ear to the common people. That's lovely."

"It's not that big a deal."

I was serious, but Naden waved it off.

"Ah! Naden. Thanks for that delivery earlier."

"Hey, Lady Naden! I've got good vegetables in stock—would you like some to take home? Your husband loves cooking, so he'll be grateful for them!"

"Lady Nadeeen, let's play hide and seeeek."

The baker's wife, the greengrocer, and a child walking down the road all called out to Naden like close friends. Naden turned and responded to each of them.

"Your kids are still little, right? If you need anything else, just let me know."

"I'll drop by on the way home, so hold on to them for me!"

"I'm showing someone around today, so no can do! We'll play next time!"

So she played hide and seek too, huh? The number of people calling out to her never let up. My eyes widened with surprise.

"You really are popular, Naden."

"They've all forgotten I'm a queen." When things settled down a bit, Naden said, "They respect Souma, Liscia, and the others like they're supposed to. I'm the only one they treat so casually. Your people loved and respected you too, right?"

"They did, yes, but...that's not always a good thing, you know?"

"Hm? It's not?"

"No. People respect kings or queens because they don't see them. Obviously, they see our faces over the broadcast, but they aren't closely involved with us. That's why the common people fear and respect royalty."

"That...could be right."

Naden looked somewhat but not entirely convinced. I was telling her what I really felt, though.

Thinking back to when I was an empress, I said I was doing things "for the people," but never had the chance to actually come into contact with those people. I never spoke to them directly, so could I really hold my head high and say I was a good ruler?

"I think their relationship with you is healthy, Naden. If anything, I see it as close to ideal, the way you're able to hear the voices of the townsfolk directly."

"It's not that big a deal. But I don't mind hearing you say that," Naden said with a smile. That was when I had an idea.

"I know!" I exclaimed, clapping my hands together.

"Huh?! Wh-what was that about?" Naden gave me a dubious look.

I didn't let it bother me. I grabbed one of her hands with both of mine. "You have a lot of free time, right? Let's use that time to travel the country together! Then we can meet people all over the kingdom!"

"Travel?! What's this out of nowhere?!"

"If you let me ride you, I'll be able to hear from people all over the kingdom. From the weak and downtrodden, whose voices rarely make it to those at the top too. With you there, we won't need bodyguards. Naden! Let's go hear from lots of people, and make this country better together!"

"H-hold on!" Naden hurriedly shook free of my hands. "I respect the idea, but the only one who's supposed to ride me is my partner, Souma, you know?! I can't just let you ride alone and take me all over the place..."

"The partner of your partner is your partner. So it's fine!"

"It's fine? On what basis...?"

"Now, with that decided, let's go and get Souma's permission!"

I took Naden's hand and started walking along.

Naden started protesting, "Listen to meeee!"

But...that was fine! We were going to get along great!